LEFT OF FOREVER

LEFT OF FOREVER

—

A Novel

TARAH DeWITT

ST. MARTIN'S GRIFFIN
NEW YORK

First published in the United States by St. Martin's Griffin, an imprint of St. Martin's Publishing Group

LEFT OF FOREVER. Copyright © 2025 by Tarah DeWitt. All rights reserved. For information, address St. Martin's Publishing Group, 120 Broadway, New York, NY 10271.

www.stmartins.com

Designed by Gabriel Guma

The Library of Congress Cataloging-in-Publication Data is available upon request.

ISBN 978-1-250-32944-8 (trade paperback)
ISBN 978-1-250-32945-5 (ebook)

Our books may be purchased in bulk for promotional, educational, or business use. Please contact your local bookseller or the Macmillan Corporate and Premium Sales Department at 1-800-221-7945, extension 5442, or by email at MacmillanSpecialMarkets@macmillan.com.

First Edition: 2025

10 9 8 7 6 5 4 3 2 1

For the ones who hold on to their indomitable hope.
Me, too, friends. I bet we make it.

Dear Stranger,

Welcome back to Spunes. And if this is your first time, thank you for deciding to pay this little world a visit. I confess we won't be spending the bulk of our time actually *in* Spunes for Wren and Ellis's story, but the people who make up the heart of that small town are never far away.

Left of Forever is an interconnected standalone featuring side characters from *Savor It*, but you certainly do not need to read Sage and Fisher's story in order to enjoy this one.

Actually, very early into writing *Savor It*, Wren and Ellis jumped out at me so viscerally that it was hard not to veer off course and write them straight away. Never before have I had characters be that demanding, that quickly. Prior to this experience, I was notoriously set against writing a series because I felt I wouldn't want to be tied down. The Byrds, however, had plans of their own, and I'm thrilled they continue to let me tag along.

Left of Forever is the book of my heart for many personal reasons. I met my husband when I was seventeen. We went to two proms together, went to college together, got married too young, and had babies before we had fully developed frontal lobes. Staying together and staying happy together does not come without its share of struggles. And you know what? So often the villain is simply Life. Life doles out circumstances that make relationships hard. Healthy communication and conflict resolution are so much more difficult than anyone talks about. I can so easily see how two people like Wren and Ellis, who have always been the leaders and caretakers of their own world, could fail to seek help with their own struggles.

But, for as much as it deals in hardship, Life hands out those occasional chances, too. Sometimes second chances. And lasting love ultimately comes down to Choice.

I hope you enjoy watching Wren and Ellis as they choose to be vulnerable and own their mistakes, facing all the ways they went wrong before, and taking the chance that is handed to them.

I hope you love watching them choose each other again. I know I did.

Love,
Tarah

CONTENT WARNINGS

- Ectopic pregnancy—occurs off page
- Conversations referencing infertility in the past
- Explicit language
- Explicit sexual content
- Death of an unknown character that occurs off page, caused by a fire

PLAYLIST

- "exile" by Taylor Swift, featuring Bon Iver
- "How Did It End?" by Taylor Swift
- "Francesca" by Hozier
- "King of Wishful Thinking" by COTTA
- "Halloween" by Noah Kahan
- "Unknown / Nth" by Hozier
- "happiness" by Taylor Swift
- "Supercut" by Lorde
- "The Night We Met" by Lord Huron
- "I Need My Girl" by The National
- "Ghost (Acoustic)" by Ben Woodward
- "Anti-Hero (Country Version)" by Josiah and the Bonnevilles
- "loml" by Taylor Swift
- "evermore" by Taylor Swift, featuring Bon Iver
- "It's All Coming Back to Me Now" by Celine Dion
- "Silver Springs" by Fleetwood Mac
- "State Lines" by Novo Amor
- "Don't Delete the Kisses" by Wolf Alice
- "Roadtripsong" by Abby Cates
- "Heartbeats" by José González
- "Eucalyptus" by The National

- "What Part of Forever" by CeeLo Green
- "Far Away" by Nickelback
- "Take Care" by Beach House
- "Everywhere, Everything" by Noah Kahan, with Gracie Abrams
- "Birds of a Feather" by Billie Eilish
- "This Love" by Taylor Swift
- "This Year's Love" by David Gray
- "Still into You (First Dance Cover)" by Isabella Kensington
- "These Arms of Mine" by Otis Redding
- "How to Love You Today" by Son of Cloud

LEFT OF FOREVER

This time, they'll get it right.

PROLOGUE

WREN

When I met Ellis Byrd at age five, I thought he might be the most serious little boy that ever lived.

Later in life, I'd go on to learn that Ellis felt he had to be serious about everything, especially school, since he was starting a full year later than everyone else his age. I'd eventually learn how to make him laugh, though, and would experience the joy of seeing him be carefree.

Actually, I would go on to learn all sorts of things when it came to Ellis Byrd, and most of them would have something to do with love.

I'd learn how love could change; how it could grow from friendship into more, into something that felt infinite. Love could be loud and supernova hot, and something soothing and quiet, too.

Love could be miraculous and fulfilling. It could make you believe things would always work out for the best, because love really could conquer all.

Love could burrow into the loneliest places in your heart, but its absence would leave bigger, misshapen holes that are impossible to fill.

I'd learn how love could give you things you never dreamed of having, then trick you into wanting more.

"Shit." I spot the time on the microwave and toss my pen aside with a growl, then haul ass back to my room to finish getting ready. Guess that's as far as I'm going to get for the time being.

Beginning this little project right now was probably not my best idea, not when I'm already running behind for a date—regardless of how apathetic I feel about the date itself. Alas, I woke up this lovely spring morning with an otherwise free day ahead of me, and naturally proceeded to start (emphasis on start) about twenty-nine things that were in no way dire or pressing until I continued my lollygagging and landed myself here, direly pressed for time. I succumbed to Waiting Syndrome. I had the day to dick around, and I overdicked it. Insert another colloquialism for poor time-management skills.

It all began with one of my earlier footles of the day: my trip to Athena's Bookshop. I was greeted by the smells of new books mixed in with secondhand, the sight of a big bouquet on the register counter—chamomile flowers mixed with tulips and tiny strawberries still on their vines. I smiled and let a finger tickle one of the blooms as I passed. My best-friend-slash-ex-sister-in-law, Sage, has been running a floral business on the side here in our small town of Spunes, Oregon (not to be confused with Forks, Washington), for the last few months, and that bouquet is just one of her many whimsical creations adorning our local stores.

I said my hellos to Athena and went on to meander among the shelves, where I quickly slipped into Bad Feelings over my dawdling and guilted myself into the self-help department. Ironically enough, I found that most of the books in that particular section were used—something I'd never noticed before, despite visiting this place multiple times a week and co-owning the bakery three doors down. A testament to how often I go anywhere near self-help, I guess.

But I got hung up on the "used" aspect of the books. Did this mean that these people got the help they needed? That's why they'd turned in the books, right? Because they'd been successful? They must all be Untamed Badass Highly Effective People who've Mastered the Power of Now, presumably after they Washed Their Face?! Was that it? Did they wash their fucking face??!

"What is it you're looking for, Wren?" Athena had asked when she found me sitting cross-legged on the ground a while later (seven open books and a general air of despondence around me). I looked up to answer, and my gaze caught on a poster behind her.

"Perhaps if I make myself write I shall find out what is wrong with me."—Dodie Smith, *I Capture the Castle*

The words practically glowed—a marquee sign lit up in a darkened room. The combination of the self-help books, that poster message, and plain old firsthand experience framed up an epiphany in my mind.

"Closure," I said to Athena. I was—am—looking for closure. I want to figure out how to close the door on my divorce. On my ex-husband, the father of my son, and the man I loved in one

way or another from age five to twenty-eight when we split . . . and maybe even a little beyond that. We grew up together, then kicked that growing up into warp speed when I got pregnant at seventeen.

I know that our story isn't terribly unique. It leans more into a cliché, I'm sure. Had a kid too young, got married too young. Let life chip and file away at us until our edges were too dull to catch on each other and keep hold. And I suppose closure isn't easily achieved in a town like Spunes, somewhere so small it can hardly contain the lifetime of memories between you. But it's been half a decade since it ended and I still can't seem to shake him.

We're perfectly respectful and supportive for Sam's sake, at least. That's effortless enough when our kid is the definition of a Good Egg. Even at our worst, Ellis and I have always agreed that Sam is the sum of all our best traits. He's got my loose curls and easy laugh, with Ellis's height and protective spirit. Neither of us knows how he got as smart as he is, though.

The problem—well, *my* problem . . . My problem is that I've never been able to stop measuring every prospective romance I might have against what I once had with Ellis. That, and I'm worried the true issue is Me. Like, maybe only the unsettling, strange men with an affinity for puka shell necklaces, and the ones who take me to their ex's place of work because I'm "blond and thick in all the best places, the exact opposite of her, and it'll definitely make her jealous" are the only ones who show an interest because these are the ones who can sniff out a sliver of brokenness in me, too.

Don't forget the one that made you feel something again without ever meeting, I think. Another point for the Maybe It's Me column.

I wince in the mirror as I try to pile up my hair, then give it up with a sigh and brace my hands on the bathroom counter.

Shit. I'm about to talk myself out of yet another date if I keep replaying the blooper reel that is my love life of the last few years. Especially if I think about my more concentrated efforts since last fall. That's when this journey for closure truly began.

My eyes snag on my vanity drawer, where the handwritten evidence of that misadventure still lies. I should probably find those letters embarrassing now, given how they abruptly ended. But, in the same vein as so many of the journaling suggestions I found in those self-help books this morning, writing had been an excavation of my feelings. A portal through which I'd been able to examine and understand them better. I was painfully honest in them, unabashedly myself because there was something safe in writing to an unknown.

I have this tiny ember of hope that sparked while I was in Athena's today that writing out mine and Ellis's story might help me unearth everything still buried in me. I might figure out where things began to go wrong, too. So much of it toward the end is a blur, like I'd been doing my best not to feel anything while I'd been living it. Looking back, it's still hard to make out the shape of things.

I've been trying to start over, to tuck the past away and open myself up to something new, but it's like I've got a heel stuck in the door and can't close it all the way.

Although, if recent experience is any indication, the market is also just plain-fucking-bleak.

Actually—come to think of it, fuck this date. The last time I met this guy, I drove an hour outside of town (I know better than to date within a sixty-mile radius of Spunes) only for him to show up either drunk or eminently hungover, carrying an entire baguette that he unceremoniously plopped onto the table before proceeding to devour it throughout the meal. It speaks to the veritable cesspool that is dating in your thirties that this seemed like no biggie compared to some of the other maladaptive male behavior I've been subjected to.

I grab my phone, but before I can call the bread-busting buffoon, it starts to ring. I smile when I see Sam's contact photo.

"Hey, bub," I say. I'll greet him with a pet name until the day he complains.

"'Ey, Mom, where you at?"

I can tell he's in the middle of chewing something. I can't think of the last time I saw the kid not eating, and yet he stays as lanky as a beanpole. "At home. What's up?"

"All right, good," he says. "I'm on my way."

My doorbell rings just before he adds, "I told Dad to come over, too." My stomach dives. "Just wanna show you something— together," he continues. "Don't worry. It's a good thing." I hear the smile in his voice, so I take a deep breath and do my best to gin up one of my own as I walk back down my narrow hallway and open the front door for Ellis.

I avoid direct eye contact as I let him in, pretending to study something on my phone instead. His presence feels too big in this tiny house. His shoulders alone take up all the room in the entryway.

"Uh, I gotta make a call," I say, flashing him a tight smile. "Sam's on his way, though."

He only nods, and I scuttle back down the hall, shutting myself in my room before I dial to cancel my date.

"He-llo?" Lyle says, and in a way that suggests it's the wildest thing in the world that his phone actually rings.

"Hey, Lyle. I'm so sorry to do this, but I'm not gonna make our date. Sorry if I wasted your time." I try to be as concise as possible, at least, because my mama always taught me that politeness is a grace that costs very little.

"I'm at Chili's" is Lyle's slurred reply.

"I'm—okay? Well . . . I'm sorry?" Especially since we were supposed to be meeting at a sushi restaurant.

"I got queso dip." He says it like an offer.

My head tilts with a considerate frown. "Tempting as that may be, I'm gonna have to pass, still." And then another thought occurs to me. "Hey, Lyle, are you at the bar?"

"I'm at the Chili's."

"Yes, got that. But are you sitting at the bar, at the Chili's?" I ask patiently.

"Oh." He pauses to let out an impressive belch. "Yeah. I ran out of chips, but I found a spoon."

"Right. We've all been there, Lyle. But hey, do me a favor? Can you pass the phone to the bartender?"

He slurps. Coughs. Burps once more. "Mmsure," he says.

"Thank you."

I hear my front door open again and try to make out the muffled sounds of Sam and Ellis talking before the bartender picks up the phone on the other end. I make sure she knows to put Lyle into an Uber or some other designated ride, then promptly block his number when we hang up. Another one bites the dust.

And yet, I feel lighter. Relieved, like I do every time one of these things meets an abrupt end.

I take a few breaths and head out to my living room.

When I round the corner, Ellis's eyes find me first, because of course they do. They always have and probably always will. Even if it wasn't him finding me first, I think I'm helpless when it comes to his gravity, like all the life between us created some fundamental reflex. It's not until those eyes trace the length of me and his casual expression dips into a hard frown that I remember I'm in date attire. My cheeks heat, and I tug on the hem of my short, black sundress—suddenly self-conscious, like I'm maybe too old to be wearing it. Becoming a mom too young throws off your perspective on these things, I think. On the one hand, I feel ancient. I have a nearly grown son. On the other hand, I'm only thirty-three, a woman with a great deal of life ahead of me. I lost all sense of "appropriate" fashion when I was nineteen and in the throes of potty training a little boy. I hastily kick off my heels.

"Plans get cut short?" Ellis lightly asks.

"Not at all," I say, using my polite "in front of the kid" voice just like he has, one octave too high to be natural.

His chin dips in a perfunctory nod, and we shift our focus to Sam. Another familiar step in our choreography.

Sam pulls out the chair across from Ellis, motioning for me to take the open one beside him. I comply, my hands clutching each other beneath the little round table that Ellis made for our fifth anniversary—back when we tried to stick to a traditional gift theme; the wood year. Ellis's sharp inhale pulls my attention up, his nostrils flaring as he leans away. He once loved this perfume, but I guess I shouldn't be surprised that his feelings for that have changed, too. I spot something at the base of his neck in the movement, though. There on the back of it, the tip of something on his skin. A tattoo?! It had to be a shadow or a trick of the light.

Whatever. I can't afford to go on a mental bender over his potential midlife crisis right now. Or any woman that might've inspired it.

By the time Sam settles into his spot across from us with a grin, we've both recovered. I note the bashful splotches on his cheeks, and my heart hiccups in my chest, my brain rapidly slotting the pieces together.

He pulls out a large envelope from somewhere behind his back, turns it, and slides it our way.

"I got in," he says. "I got into Davis."

My greedy hands pull the papers closer, the words *Pleased* and *Congratulations* and *Accepted* blurring beneath quick-sprung tears. And then Ellis and I are shoving out of our chairs in tandem, rounding the table with celebratory sounds before we crush our son in a hug, a tangle of limbs and laughter.

"You did it," I say to Sam with a happy sniffle. His dream school, for their viticulture and enology program. He always loved gardening with his aunt Sage when he was little, and since learning about all the ways science could get involved, he's been set.

"*We* did it" comes Sam's reply. He peels his trapped arms out of our embrace and scoops me and Ellis into a hug of his own, forever pulling us together. When he spins back to look at his packet again, Ellis and I lock eyes.

"We did it," he says quietly to me. And suddenly, it's my eighteenth birthday again, a sleeping baby in the middle of our bed, he and I watching raptly as Sam's chest rises and falls. Equal parts fear and adoration emanating between us.

"*He's so perfect,*" Ellis had said, gaze blown wide while he'd studied one of Sam's hands. "*I have to get this right, Wren. There are no mess-ups when it comes to a kid. Think of how much all parents fuck up their kids.*"

"*We won't,*" I'd said, determined. I'd braided my fingers with his, our thumbs each holding one of Sam's chubby feet at the same time. "*We can do this.*" We had to.

A few more hot tears spill down my cheeks. I bat them away and turn to lean over Sam, palm landing on his shoulder. In the corner of my eye, Ellis hesitates before he does the same.

Now, when our hands accidentally brush across the surface of Sam's back, I immediately pull away.

"I want to move down there in June," says Sam.

My face snaps into a frown. "June?! The semester doesn't start until August," I say.

"Yeah, but I need to get a job and get settled and all that. I can sign up to sublet something until I can get into the dorms. I already saw a bunch of forums for housing."

My hand goes to my chest like it might steady the gathering rhythm beneath. June feels too soon. I hazard looking at Ellis for help, only to find him contemplating the grain on the table, solid as a statue.

"We'll have to follow you down with the truck," Ellis says, patently avoiding my stare and going rogue instead.

Shock squeezes tight around my lungs. "*We?*" I ask incredulously. I see Sam tense and immediately regret it.

Ellis shrugs stiffly. "He can't fit all his stuff in the Jeep, and he'll have to keep that down there with him, anyway. And you'll want to see his place, too, yeah?" he asks. "See him get settled?"

I suppress a snort. He knows I'll want that. "Of course."

"We'll make a trip out of it," he adds, deceptively casual.

I give him a sidelong glance. Bare my teeth in a smile. "You mean take Sam on a trip together? Like a grad trip."

Sam's shoulders inch up. "Ehh, no offense—I'd just rather get down there. A grad trip with your parents sounds . . ." He makes a face in lieu of an explanation. "No offense," he repeats.

It's Ellis's turn to shrug again, but his is jumpier. "That's fine," he says, still studying me. "You and I can celebrate on our way back with our own trip."

I feel my eyes round. He's gone preternaturally still, gray-and-brown-flecked irises leveled on me with an intensity that has my heart racing.

We keep things no less than perfectly pleasant with each other in front of Sam. It's a point of pride for us both, I think.

I'm trying to find a way to dial back this conversation in a subtle, friendly manner. My smile weighs a ton.

After a stilted pause, I come up with, "Oh, I'll probably have to just catch a flight back. Not sure I can take the time off, you know?"

"It'll be after Walter and Martha's wedding," Ellis parries. "Since Sam will be expected to go to that"—he nods at Sam in confirmation now—"and before tourist season. Don't you still take your vacation around then, anyway?"

My jaw falls open softly, and I try to find a reply. How dare he push this in front of Sam! Sam, who keeps smiling innocently between us now. And yes, that is when I take my only true vacation of the year, a week over my birthday, but like hell am I going to spend it torturing myself with him. Holidays and family occasions are hard enough, but I can't bear to give up the rest of the Byrds altogether.

I'm not going to ruin this night for Sam by arguing with Ellis, though. We've made it this long successfully shielding him from our mess.

"Yeah! Yeah, that'll be great!" I concede temporarily. I'll have to find an alternative solution later. For now, I want to pull out the honey cake I've got stored in the fridge and redirect the attention onto celebrating our son.

———

After we manage to do just that and they've both left for the evening, I let out a few more happy tears and uncork a bottle of wine.

But when I take a sip, I spot the paper again—my paper. My fledgling project from earlier, folded neatly onto itself in even, crisp thirds, tucked next to my whiteboard calendar.

For the life of me, I cannot remember folding it.

PART 1

———

Last Fall

CHAPTER 1

———

ELLIS

It's when my stomach growls as I watch a buzzard peck at a charred animal carcass that I realize I haven't eaten in over twenty-four hours. "Shit," I mutter under my breath.

I peel off my helmet and wipe at the salt on my brow, wondering how long I'd been standing there before I turn and start to make my way up the scorched hill, boots crunching across the blackened earth. Everything is black, as far as any of us can see. I search the sky, begging for signs of rain, but only find more endless hazy gray. I hear the whir of a distant helicopter, the buzz of a few chainsaws, and the crack and rip of a snag before it thunks to the ground.

"Break time," I call out to one of the rookie firefighters nearby. I can't recall her name. Hardly remember any names, in fact, but this isn't my regular crew. I'm not sure how I ended up in charge of this particular group, but then again, I'm never sure how I end up leading anyone. It's definitely not through any pursuit on my part.

A resounding chorus of relief goes out around me as the message gets passed across the hillside, and everyone starts the trek for the top.

"I love package day," the rookie eagerly says as she catches up to my side. Her bouncy excitement reminds me of my brother Silas. The thought fills my dry mouth with ash.

I lengthen my stride, feet hitting the ground like I might stomp out the memory of Silas's silhouette being engulfed in flames as he skidded down a mountainside a few months ago. An intubation, an induced coma, and multiple weeks in the ICU later; he thankfully made it out with some gnarly scars and his uninhibited (vexing) nature well intact. It left those of us who love him with invisible scars of our own, though, which is why the rest of my regular crew is back home in Spunes, taking some time off.

I, however, needed out. Sitting around Spunes would only continuously remind me of everything I can't control and all that I'm helpless to fix. Like my heartbroken sister with her sad smiles as she tries to push through. We all watched Sage fall in the kind of love that alters you this past summer, and I can't take watching as she grieves it now. Fisher and his niece moved back to New York, and I know in my goddamn marrow that they belong back in Spunes with Sage, but . . . but I guess I rarely know as much as I think I do. Then there's Silas, who made it clear he was tired of my hovering over his rehab progress. Micah, my other brother, is off in California still giving baseball his best shot, far out of my reach. And then, of course . . . there's Wren. My ex-wife.

"What's on the menu today?" says the rookie breathlessly.

"What?" I can't hide the annoyance in my tone.

"What'd you pack for lunch, I mean?" she asks, unfazed. The name tag on her uniform says *Kirby*.

I let out a curse. I meant to grab a few things from the

continental breakfast at the hotel and am only now realizing that I forgot to pack any food altogether.

Kirby chuckles. "No lunch?"

I shake my head and grind my jaw, my stomach voicing its complaints again.

"Married, then, huh?"

I stop in my tracks and glare down at her. "What the hell brought you to that conclusion?" Is it that obvious that I'm only half of something still?

Kirby puts her palms up in surrender. "In my experience, it's the married people who forget to eat and pack food. That's all. Used to either having someone to remind you or someone to take care of you, I guess."

I grunt and continue on toward the truck. I imagine there has to be something in there I can scrounge up to eat.

"Wait," Kirby continues. "Hold up, boss! Care package day, remember?"

That's right. I pivot and barely refrain from running, the hunger gnawing at me viciously. The care packages we get don't all come with edible goods, but local schools, churches, and various organizations like to send whatever small aid they can to keep up morale on these long fires. I'll either have to get to the pile early to find one that looks promising for food, or I'll have to be a dick and pull rank. I spot a few firefighters already gathered around the collection, opening up handmade cards and bags of chips with sooty smiles. My eyes catch on a pink box a few yards away, and my target is determined, feet kicking up in a jog. I swipe the box just as a fellow captain reaches for it. He snaps his hand back with a shocked laugh.

He says something about pink being my color, but I'm already surging away, yanking out my pocketknife with shaky hands before I tear into it. I barely register the sight of something that looks like a biscuit before I find a tree to lean up against and shove the whole thing in my mouth like a rabid animal. A moan escapes me before I'm aware of it. I haven't even swallowed the first before I'm reaching for a second, which is when multiple things come into focus.

The first is the series of flavors that invade my senses. Marion-berry. Lemon. A hint of Earl Grey. My body is sliding down the tree trunk as each one washes over me, until I hit the ground with a thud.

The second is the label on the side of the insulated pink box. I know this logo, the silhouettes of two wrens woven into the de-sign. I know these damned boxes well, too. Spent many an August-tourist-season night at a bakery putting them together each year.

The third is a letter poking out of the hastily opened box. I drop the scone in my hand, but pick it up and dust it off de-spite myself. I haven't had one of these in . . . in, well, over four years now. I stare at the thing—this innocuous fucking scone. It shouldn't elicit this strong of a reaction in me. *God*, I know it shouldn't. It's a goddamned pastry.

But it's also sleepless nights in a rocking chair, the witching hours when we couldn't go back to bed, and drifted into a kitchen instead. Our toddler son dancing on the kitchen island to Right Said Fred until we had tears leaking from our eyes. It's my wife in an apron, wild blond and bronze curls escaping their tie. It's play-ful food fights that lead to stripping her out of her clothes, tracing the marks where her body had stretched for our family with flour dusted fingers.

This scone is everything good, before it wasn't anymore.

I set the box down beside me and pull out the envelope. I slide a trembling finger beneath the edge to pry it apart, pulling out the paper inside. My eyes immediately go to the bottom where it's been signed: *Salem Meridian*—Wren's middle and maiden name.

A possessive urge tears through me. It's the same spike of emotion that had me embarrassing us both at one of our town meetings last summer, when someone referred to her by her maiden name and I couldn't stop myself from reminding them (and by extension the whole town) that *she's still a Byrd*. We've been divorced for over four years, but her last name is still Byrd, so . . . she is still a Byrd.

In any case, the package is clearly from Wren herself. Not something thrown together by her mom or any of the other bakery employees at Savvy's.

The handwriting is familiar, but nothing I could have picked out of a lineup if I hadn't recognized the name combination at the bottom. *Should* I recognize her handwriting? This is a person I learned to write alongside, someone I shared a whole life with. Did we really become that distant? I can't pinpoint why this makes me feel like I swallowed something jagged.

I guess I could blame modern technology. It's not as if we hand-wrote anything much to one another when we'd been married.

So . . . *distant* is probably a mild word for what we became toward the end. And no matter that we co-parent well enough, we're beyond distant now. Proven by the fact that she even sent this care package here, I think. If she'd had any indication I was working this Colorado border fire, I doubt she'd have sent something here. I get a fast, nasty lick of hope that maybe she was aware, somehow, but I smother it just as quickly. As far as I know, we've gone out of our way to avoid as much information as we can about each other since the split.

I really only slipped up once. It had been six months into the divorce when I broke down and made the mistake of asking Sage if Wren had started dating, and after seeing her get pale and visibly uncomfortable, I couldn't stand the idea of putting any of our friends or family in that awkward position again.

No . . . I'm certain Wren hasn't cared to stay updated on my whereabouts, and even if she had, she would've had to find out through Silas, by proxy. Per his wishes, I've been giving him space, so he has no idea, anyway. None of my family know I'm here.

I realize I'm clutching the paper so hard it's creasing, and immediately loosen my hold. I take a deep breath and another bite of a scone before I read.

Dear Stranger—

I have no idea how long I agonized over how to address this letter, but To Whom It May Concern felt too stiff, and Dear Firefighter felt too silly. I'll admit that Dear Stranger felt corny to open with somehow, but for all I know, you could be a complete piece of shit (which will be decided based on your reply or lack thereof to this letter, by the way), so beginning this with Dear Friend felt phony. Maybe you're not very dear at all, and Friend? I have some truly great friends, so that's a title I hold in too high regard to assign willy-nilly.

First off, I hope you enjoyed the scones! Who are we kidding, of course you did if you have any taste at all. If not, please lie. I've taken all the care I could in packaging them so that they arrive in perfect condition. If they're stale, I'm sorry, but please do your best not to hold that against me. I can assure you they were flawless when I sent them.

Now to the reason I'm writing this letter (and if I'm honest, why I've sneaked it off to you under the bribery of scones)... You see, I desperately need someone to get me some information.

Last week, I saw news coverage of the fire, specifically an interview of an older couple at one of the evacuation centers who spoke tearfully about a pair of their horses getting loose in the chaos of them fleeing. A beautiful dapple-gray Clydesdale and an equally beautiful palomino quarter horse. The woman talked about how these horses shared a special bond, and all they'd been through together. I won't risk boring you with all the details—I'm already worried enough that you won't read this thing in its entirety, so I'll keep it as concise as possible. When one of the horses panicked and bolted, the other followed.

I'm writing to you, dear stranger (see? Not as weird now ((god, I hope I get exponentially lucky and you're a woman. Lord knows every fire department needs more of them (((Yes, you'll have to trust and believe me that I KNOW this to be the case. I've got family and friends in the field.))). But I am writing to you, dear stranger, in the hopes that you might be able to tell me what ended up becoming of the pair.

Please do your best not to be annoyed that some crazy woman is bothering you to track down this information while you're busy saving homes and lives. It's just that (not to pile on the pressure or anything), but YOU are my last hope, whoever you are. I've contacted the news station to try to find out the names of the owners, since they weren't disclosed in the story. I've tirelessly searched online every day. Even as I scribble that word, "tireless" seems like it must be incorrect because I am EXHAUSTED. I'm not sleeping, instead lying awake and wondering what happened to them. I've even joined as many of the local neighborhood Facebook groups as possible that will let me in without verification. Dear stranger, I cannot tell you how little time I have to get invested in all of the suburban soap operas playing out in these groups! Did you know that someone on their morning runs has been dropping trou and pooping on people's lawns?! I won't detract from my message here to get too far into it, but just know these people have their cameras ready to catch the poo-poo perpetrator.

Back to _my_ problem, though. I simply need closure. I need to know if those two beautiful creatures made it out of that cataclysmic thing, and . . . and I need to know if they didn't, too. Please don't be afraid to tell me if they didn't make it, I simply ~~want~~ need to know. You can write me back and mail to the bakery address on the box, or you can call the number that is printed there, too. Whichever you're most comfortable with. I'm not giving you my personal number because who knows if you're a complete pervert or not.

Sincerely (hopeful),
Salem Meridian

P.S. If they were caught in the blaze . . . at least tell me . . . were they together in the end?

CHAPTER 2

———

ELLIS

I'm not sure how many times I read the letter over the meal break. Enough times to absentmindedly eat the entire box of scones, at least. When it's time to get back to work, I stand up with an over-filled gut and an even heavier feeling everywhere else.

I go through the lines enough to memorize parts of it, I guess, because pieces of it play in a mental loop the rest of the day. So much of it was her. That unapologetic humor, the rapid-fire stream of consciousness unraveling across the page. The way I could hear the anxiety in her words, even the demanding ones. So much was glaringly unfamiliar, too, between not recognizing the handwriting, down to the *Dear Stranger*.

I guess that must be what we really are to each other now.

Throughout the day, I swear the letter gets warmer against my chest. I take it out time and time again until all the edges feel soft. I start asking everyone if they've heard anything about this story. Some have but don't know any more information or if the horses were found or not.

At the end of the day, after I've just asked another captain the same set of questions, Kirby slides into the pickup truck alongside me and asks, "Does this have anything to do with that letter you keep looking at?"

I blow out a heavy breath. Must not have been sly taking it out so much earlier. "Mind your business, Kirby."

"My cousin was working the other side of the fire when that all went down. I remember seeing the news clip, too. I'll call him for you."

Well, now I feel like a prick. "Oh. Uh . . . thanks. Appreciate it." I turn toward the kid and find her sporting something smug.

"My first name is Lennon, by the way," she says. "And don't wait on my cousin before you write the lady back. Just tell her you're working on her answers."

I snort, but I'm curious. "Why would I waste her time? I'll just wait until I have the info to share." And I don't intend to *write* her back, either way. I'll get her the answer she needs, though. And then I'll text her or call her and let her know. Maybe we can have an awkward laugh over her letter ending up in my hands.

"So it *is* a lady, then?" Kirby asks.

"I—yeah, so?"

"*Oh*, I love this!" she squeals. "I mean, I knew it had to be for a variety of reasons. The way you were holding it, mainly. The yearning stares. That slightly desperate way you were asking everyone for answers. There's something so intimate about words on paper, inked by someone's hand, isn't there? And I assume you're straight just by your generally emotionally constipated vibe?"

"What? Yeah, but—"

"Knew it!" She belts a laugh. "God, I'm good. Oh, please,

please, *please* start a pen pal situation! I had a Canadian boyfriend-slash-pen-pal when I was younger. It was the best." She pouts at the windshield. "Come to think of it, maybe that's why none of my real-life relationships have panned out. They fail to reach the level of intimacy some thirteen-year-old Quebecois and I achieved despite never meeting."

After several perplexed beats, I let out a strangled sigh. "Whatever. I'm not writing her back without an answer." I turn on the truck and start the drive.

Kirby tsks me and shakes her head in the corner of my eye. "Forgive me, sir. But when's the last time you were waiting on an important text?" she says.

I frown. I cannot remember a single time, actually.

She sees the answer in my expression and adds, "That's what I thought. Even waiting on a text back makes a microwave minute seem short. If this woman went out of her way to write a letter, she's already been waiting for a reply for *minimum* two days. And just like good text etiquette, you should at least respond and let that person know you're busy or you'll get back to them ASAP, et cetera. It takes the edge off."

I change my mind about her reminding me of Silas. Lennon now reminds me of Sage. The overly observant and gregarious younger sister.

"So you're telling me it's the polite thing to do? Writing back?" And not just an excuse for me to communicate with her, under false pretenses.

She nods jovially. "Yep. I'm saying it's the polite thing to do."

Well, then. I have to consider that, right?

The longer I consider it on the drive, though, the more I know I can't do it. I'll just have to text her when I get back to my room.

I trudge over to the elevator at the hotel, too tired to hit up the vending machine or the restaurant with the rest of the crew, then drag myself into my room. I take out the letter when I sit at the desk, turning on the light so I can read it again . . . then jolt when my phone promptly rings. Another pulse of anxiety hits me when I see that it's Sage. I answer quickly before my brain starts catastrophizing.

"Sage?" Not sure why I sound guilty to my own ears.

"Ellis, hi," she says cheerfully.

I feel my shoulders ease. "Everything all right?" I ask nonetheless.

She lets out a small laugh. "Yes. Yeah. More than all right, actually. Fisher and Indy are back."

The joy is so sudden and alien that I turn to scowl at myself in the mirror across from me. I tamp it back down with wariness. "For . . . another visit?" I ask.

"For *good*, Ell," she says in a laugh, and I let out a sigh. A force of habit; the parental-branded questions that flit through my head next. *Where are they going to live? Where is he going to work? Are you staying protective of that too-generous heart of yours?* I know they're both adults, but I'm not so sure that him moving in with Sage too quickly would be wise.

What do I know, though? I'm no success story. I decide not to ruin the moment with the third degree.

"I'm glad, Sage. Happy for you," I tell her instead.

"Thank you, Ell," she softly replies. "Umm, so . . . that's also why I wanted to call and ask if you might, like, just give me a heads-up call before you come by? I know Bud's due for new shoes soon, and I know you don't normally have to call—of course you don't—you know I love having you swing by any-time, but . . ."

I rarely call before I come over to take care of my and Wren's horse, but it's not like I expect her to entertain me when I go over there. Sage took Bud in after the divorce so he could be on neutral ground for Wren and me, but he's still our responsibility. It takes a minute for my brain to make sense of the request.

I groan when it eventually does. "*Jesus*, Sage. You worried I'll catch you . . . *with* your boyfriend?"

"We were separated for more than two months. Let me live. I'm only thinking of you."

We both laugh, even if mine is a little pained. We've been through too much together to get too embarrassed of these things. In the background, I hear Fisher's muffled voice say something like, "*Here, try this.*"

"No problem, kid," I tell her. "Have fun."

"Fisher made cioppino," she says in her smiling voice again. "And thanks, Elly. Love you."

"Love you, too."

The moment I hang up the phone, loneliness overwhelms me. I am so happy and relieved, and so fucking miserable.

I've tried to stop missing Wren. I've tried so hard to respect her space, to make it so we could get through raising our son without hurting each other anymore. But I've been fracturing for months. Like time has been a flimsy dam while everything has only seemed to build, and it's all starting to give. All the people who once needed me don't anymore. Or won't soon. And I almost *lost* Silas. Almost failed. Fuck, I wince when I remember seeing Wren come around the corner at the hospital. I don't know how long I'd been awake at that point, I just knew I had to wait for Sage to get there so I could be strong for her, to hold on tight to all the edges of myself for my sister and brother. But then I saw Wren's face soon after, those wild blond curls and warm chocolate eyes, and it was like—like seeing home after decades away.

Like falling into bed after sleeping on hard ground for years, and I . . . I fucking lost it. I miss her. I miss her. I—

Shit.

No. I can't. I have no right to miss her. We've established safe, liminal spaces that allow us to stay separate and contained. No messes, no added hurt. We've had to maintain that for our son.

I physically feel myself start to compartmentalize and zip everything back into place.

I'll write her back, I decide. I know her and know she won't be able to let this go, not with the soft spot she has where horses are concerned. I'll do the polite thing that Kirby suggested, and I'll simply get her the information she needs in the meantime. Actually, this is safest, anyway. She doesn't even need to know it's me. As far as she'll be concerned, we'll still be separate and contained.

I reach for the pad of paper on the desk and dig a pencil out of my pack, too. I don't know how most people write in pen. I rarely get shit right the first time and would love to use an eraser on more than words.

And then I start my reply.

Dear Stranger, I say. I'll only respond in kind to everything she's put in her letter, but I draw the line at calling her by the wrong name.

First, thank you for the scones. I'm happy to report that I apparently have excellent taste, since they were delicious. As far as your inquiry, I'm sorry I don't have an answer readily available, but I will get you one as soon as I can. (Especially since you didn't put any pressure on it or anything.)

For the record, you'd be surprised at how many miracles I see out here, even amid all the devastation.

Oftentimes, there's no explaining the things we come across. I've found an unscathed chicken coop in a scorched field before. A perfectly preserved garden in the middle of some charred earth. A pair of newborn fawns huddled together, totally healthy and untouched under a pile of burnt wood. I think it's okay to hold out hope that they're still alive. Hope doesn't have the power to cancel out worry, anyway.

Sincerely,

I debate how to sign it. I want to use something covert like she has, but also lends some sort of clue, too, for whatever reason I can't fathom. I eventually whittle it down to

—L

My stomach lurches with a growl as soon as I'm finished, and in a fit of desperation, I add,

P.S. I conduct my best research under the influence of chocolate.

For the return address, I put the name of the hotel and the room number under "Guest L," since it's the extended stay that I've reserved for the next month through the mutual aid group. It's not as if they'd give her my name if she called into the hotel, anyway.

I should probably stop and take an assessment of everything I feel again, contemplate how a box of scones and memories have me hungrier and lonelier than ever.

Instead, I collect a stamp from the front desk and ask them to have it sent, hands trembling and heart galloping when I walk away.

CHAPTER 3

ELLIS

It takes four days for her reply. Four days in which I barely sleep and struggle to eat and throw myself into work like a madman. I'm convinced I've done the wrong thing and am about to call Wren and fess up when the hotel room phone rings, and the front desk lets me know that I've got a package.

I catch sight of my reflection on the way out of my room and grimace. I'm filthy, the lines marring my face and hands caked in dirt and soot. The winds have picked up, spreading the fire with it, and we're scrambling to get on top of the thing. Probably why Lennon's cousin hasn't been able to get us any more information on the missing horses, too.

Anticipation bounces violently in my stomach when I spot a pink box on the back counter downstairs, and I shift restlessly in line behind a group checking in until I finally get it. I don't have the patience to take it back up to my room once it's finally in my hands, and I carry it over to a table in the lobby instead.

My grimy fingers tear into the box, and my brain stutters over what to grab first—the letter inside or the black forest whoopie pies that I recognize.

"Did you just *moan*, Cap?" comes Lennon's voice from over my shoulder. Fuck. "It was somehow both a moan and a growl," she adds, chuckling. I see her hover in the corner of my eye now. "You sure you don't need to open that in private?"

"If you shut up, I'll give you one," I say with a pointed glare.

She mimes zipping her lips together, and I hand her one of the little cookie sandwiches. She primly takes it and a seat across from me, and I open the envelope, ignoring her groaned (and predictable) "'Oly fuck" when she takes a bite. I already know they're holy fucking good.

Dear (brazen) Stranger, the letter begins.

What a ride your letter put me on. Here I started out thinking, "Wow, what a polite guy," (assuming you're a guy since you didn't respond to my comment regarding you being a woman), but then you hit me with that shocking little blackmail twist at the end, and it really confirmed it. Now you've dangled more hope in front of me while also fishing for more treats. What's to stop this from becoming a toxic cycle now?! What if I'm some sweet grandmother wringing her hands day and night and toiling away over baked goods? You feel good about taking advantage of me? :)

Something about that smiley face makes me laugh-hum, but then I remember that Lennon is watching me. I school my features into something passive.

In all seriousness, I am very happy that you're able to find those small miracles. I know too many horror stories from living out here on the West Coast all my life. I've seen and heard how fire decimates everything in its path. Frankly, I've burned myself too many times on hot things to ever imagine that sort of death. The raw sting of a good burn is enough to give me chills.

A hiccupping feeling contracts in my throat. I know how much she hates getting burned. Tough as nails when it comes to physical pain, she always had a special sort of weak spot for the burns she'd endure in the bakery. I used to buy her every kind of oven mitt whenever I saw one I thought she'd like. Used to know every scar that marred her pretty hands and wrists, too.

I've also seen how the devastation can haunt you all, though. I've known a number of first responders in my life. So as long as you keep looking for those small mercies, I will do my best to continue to hold out hope for the horses. (I'll also hope that it won't cost me a three-tiered cake or a baked Alaska or something, though. I simply don't know how I'd transport it to you safely.)

Thank you in advance for any info you find. In the meantime, I'll still be trolling the local Facebook groups. You'll be delighted to hear that it seems as if the turbo-turder has found greener lawns to crap on! No reports for the last week!

Still Sincerely Hopeful,
Salem Meridian

I let out a small sigh when I reach the end of the letter. It's too nice getting to hear—*read*—her this way again. Her playfulness and that wry, candid wit. It's so far from the clipped politeness we've maintained since we split. It doesn't help that I can still picture the way she'd say all of it, the way her eyes would pinch sympathetically when she knew I'd seen something awful even though I didn't want to share, or when I inevitably couldn't hide my exhaustion.

"You hear anything from your cousin, Kirby?" I ask, eyes still tracing the paper, all the shapes and curves of the words. I look up at the same time she lets out a small snore, the half-eaten treat still on her lap. Christ, the poor kid. She's maybe ten years younger than I am, but I can't remember a time when I didn't feel downright elderly compared to most of my coworkers and crew. By the end of this fire, after she's inevitably seen family homes destroyed and history lost and an unfathomable amount of ruin, she'll feel older, too. Thinking about it sends a pang through my chest.

Maybe this is why, after I jostle her awake and take myself back to my room, I decide to write Wren again. I'd told myself I wouldn't until I knew about the horses, but . . . but maybe I want to reach for that lightness. Staying anchored to something good is good, right? I might just be too tired to think on it too long.

Dear Stranger,

I won't pretend it's easy to find the miracles. Sometimes I have to look really, really hard. Sometimes I get sick of looking for them. Do you ever feel that way? Like you resent that you even have to look so

hard for all the good things? Sorry if I'm not making sense. Today was a long, heavy day, and I'm so, so
tired. It sounds like the official word is that this was
started by arson. It's hard to see an elementary school
reduced to ash and not be angry at how pointlessly
cruel humanity can be. A whole town was wiped
away, and for what?

Getting a letter from you was the bright spot in my
day, stranger. Hey—guess that's my small mercy,
maybe? I was lucky enough to get your package out of
everyone the first time, and now look at us. We've got
our own little crime ring complete with blackmail,
espionage, and of course, most egregiously of all, your
fraudulent membership in the online community of
local suburbia.

I promise you, treats or not, I've got feelers out to
everyone all across this fire for them to let me know
about the horses if they hear or come across anything.
I still promise to share either way, good or bad.

I wanted to ask, though . . . I was hoping that you
might be open to writing to me again while we're
still searching? At over 200k acres and hardly
contained, I think I'll be here for at least another
couple of weeks. But . . . there's something nice about
this. No agenda, just dear strangers finding a little
comfort. I promise I'm only perverted when explicitly
asked to be.

I understand if you don't have time. Life is busy and days rarely feel long enough anymore. My sister—

I have to go back and erase the part about Sage. I was planning to talk about her ability to live in the present and how it makes her one of the most accomplished people I've ever met. I feel a swift pinch of guilt when I erase it. I don't want to be deceitful, precisely, but I want to preserve this tenuous thing, whatever it is.

I wrap up the letter with:

Also Hopeful,

-L

Dear L,

I guess this will be our trial run to see what you're really about, since this letter comes unaccompanied by treats. But I'll admit that I was also hoping you might want to keep writing. I think this is nice, too. No agenda, I agree. Bold move with that remark about being perverted, though! For all you know, I am that ninety-three-year-old granny who's hard up and swooning over her fireman calendar each time I write one of these. Maybe I couldn't figure out Tinder and I'm working up to asking you for a hand-drawn dick pic?! What are you going to do if I call your bluff?!

Wow, I'm actually laughing out loud. It's a bit strange how easy it is to make these jokes and remarks here in the unknown. Should we establish some rules to keep it that way? No major details. No real names? (Oops, guess this is where I admit that mine's been phony the whole time—you can still address it there to avoid confusion.)

We could talk about what's going on around us. I'll keep you posted on the latest gossip and unimportant news, and you can share whatever you're feeling like getting off your chest, too?

Sincerely,
Nosferatu

Dear Heinous Gruffalo Woman,

I'd love nothing more than to hear about garage sale carnage or the bloodletting of the HOAs. I'm well versed in small-town "scandals," so this will feel very home-adjacent to me, I'm sure. But I think we can talk about ourselves a bit, too, as long as we avoid identifiers?

I'd love to hear something (for lack of a better word) hopeful about you. Today felt like a hopeless sort of day—a sentence that I've erased twice now. I have a hard time sharing the shitty stuff, I realize. It's like putting that on paper makes it aggressively clear. To-day, we recovered a body, though. A man (because they almost always are) who was told to evacuate, and instead thought he could maintain his own fire line and keep this raging thing at bay. I don't get why he'd be so fucking stubborn. Why wouldn't he trust the experts? We were doing everything we could, and no, we still would not have saved his house, but dammit, he'd still have his life. I hate whatever circumstances made him think his home was worth risking his life.

I also hate that I saw myself in that idiot man, though. I keep thinking of how I've done that in my own life. How I've taken on things I had no business taking on, neglected to accept help, and what I've lost because of it.

I don't normally look forward to the breaks during these big fires. It feels like I'm always anxious to get back, as if one dumb man is going to be the difference in containing it. I'm looking forward to going home for a week, for once.

Anyway, tell me something hopeful about you? Even if it seems corny. I'd love to know your hopes and dreams.

I did hear about the horses, but I'm sorry to report that it's not definitive news. Only that they have not been found at all.

—L

Dear L,

One dumb man can do a lot. I think if one dumb man can start the thing, one certainly can make a difference in stopping it. I know you hardly know me (other than the fact that I am utterly grotesque!!!), but I also happen to be an excellent judge of character. Based on our exchanges here, I bet yours is strong. It takes so much strength and bravery to examine and be honest about where we're messiest, AND to open up again. I've fucked up in my life too many times, but I'll be truthful with you since it's just us here … I think I've only learned to barricade my heart. Like maybe that'll protect other people from my broken bits. Does that make sense? It's hard to stay too vague in this, but just know that the people I've hurt the most and let down the most are the ones I love the most, too. The bravest thing I ever did was leave something that was fine, but not making either of us happy anymore. Sometimes I think I regret it even still, but … there are different kinds of hurt. There's the kind you inflict sharply and quickly—like emotional blunt force trauma—and then there's the other kind, like a slow-building poison in your veins. I think it starts with withholding love, but maybe it starts with withholding hurt, too.

God, I've turned this into more of a diary entry for myself, haven't I? My best friend is an avid journaler and is always talking about how writing stuff down helps her reveal and understand things. How she manages to surprise herself. Guess she's onto something.

I hope the jalapeño and cheddar biscuits make amends, but I've also got some juicy news to offer. In my tiny town, two of its most prominent characters have fallen in LOVE! I think they may have even been living a secret love story for years, though from the outside looking in, no one would've known. It's your standard fare; she owns the trading goods store, he owns the diner. She nagged him, he needled her, she accidentally (allegedly) hit him with her car and professed her undying love on their way to the ER. Rumor is, my brother caught them doing something unsavory in one of the fitting rooms yesterday!

As far as hopes and dreams go... I'm a little stumped here. I haven't been asked this sort of question in so long. I have my dream career, honestly. I love what I do, and I love where I live. I have the world's coolest kid. I don't care if you have five incredible children, mine's better than yours. Sorry :|

I'd love to travel. I'd love to see new places, knowing I have my home to come back to. I want to drink wine on an Italian villa and dance in an Irish pub. I live near a coast, but it's cold and craggy all the time. I've never been to a warm, golden-sand beach. I've never been anywhere, really.

There are days that I think I would like to love someone again. But honestly? I'm not too sure about that. I don't know if we need romantic love to be happy in life, and I worry that my perspective would always be a little bit skewed when it comes to that anyway. I grew up with my great love, so I think maybe my heart took shape around his.

My dad left when I was too young to know the difference, and my mom hasn't wanted for a full life. She's fiercely independent, tries whatever hobbies she feels

like, whenever she feels like. She has great friendships and plenty of love to give to her community and
whoever she wishes to give it to. I've seen other people
lose that romantic, soul-rending sort of love, whether
through death or betrayal or... whatever life dealt
them that made it impossible to keep the thing. It was
like watching someone try to function with half a
heart when it was taken away. I genuinely don't know
if I want to risk that again—having to survive something like that.

Even the most consuming love doesn't necessarily
mean happiness in the end. I can attest to that. I can
look back on everything now and see the beauty in
my own personal history and the good things it gave
us, and yet I can't quite pinpoint where it ultimately
died, you know? And sorry if this is TMI, but again,
safe space and all that—I think even sex was ruined
by the end. It was great, don't get me wrong, but it also
felt like a crutch for connecting when we weren't
otherwise.

I also think that maybe the pain and the mystery of that is best left in the past, at least for me. Do
you think that makes me a coward? Maybe I'm just a
cynic. Maybe I still think holding on to hope is dangerous.

How about you? What are your hopes and dreams?

Sincerely,
Gollum

CHAPTER 4

———

ELLIS

Her letter came as I was walking through the hotel lobby, duffel bag in hand, headed on my way home for a weeklong break. I'd packed all my things in case the fire miraculously gets contained in the meantime, and signed up with the extended stay to have my mail forwarded in case anything else comes while I'm gone. I almost didn't open her letter right away when I slid into my truck, knowing I couldn't write back immediately. Now that I'm driving and need to keep my eyes on the road, I wish I hadn't.

I feel . . . fuck, I feel devastated. Like I ripped into a freshly healed scar. And electrified, like my whole system endured a shock. This was a terrible idea, stealing this connection this way. I feel a little sick.

She *is* a stranger to me; it's easier to justify this in part because this is like meeting her all over again. But she's also not. When she referred to her brother, I knew she actually meant mine. And

Silas is who I'll call as soon as I calm down so I can get the details on this Martha-and-Walter development she mentioned, too.

Dammit, I have to pull over and read through it again.

Traveling was something we dreamed about when we were younger, but in the same way that you talk about "when I win the lottery, I'll do this or this," in that it still felt unattainable. It kills me to think she might have set that aside for other dreams.

Dreams that ran just as dry, if they were the ones to do with happily ever after and a house filled with kids.

But to say she can't pinpoint where it went wrong? I know exactly when it did, exactly how many months of negative tests there were: thirty-six. I know the very date one came back positive and can remember how happy she looked and the salty taste of one of her joyful tears on my lips. I know the exact day and time she almost died on a hospital table when it turned out to be ectopic, and I can remember the color of the dark circles under her eyes for months after with disturbing clarity. I remember how it felt when I told her I didn't want to try anymore. I thought the vasectomy would eliminate it from our life altogether, but things only got worse, and the weight of her resentment became a living, breathing thing. And then her mom got sick and the distance between us grew, and *fuck*, I couldn't weather it. I thought I could take her anger enough for us both, but she'd barely look at me, she'd barely speak to me. She'd pull my body into hers night after night, and I'd try to find her and find *us* time and time again, but it was like we were both ghosts. I could feel us both walking on emotional eggshells every day, and by the time she said she wanted out, I was so goddamn tired that I did, too.

My phone rings through the truck speakers, and I jump in my seat, then clear my throat before I hit Answer for Silas.

"Hello?"

"I'm impressed," he says. "You realize it's been, like, over two weeks and you haven't called me once?"

I hope he can hear my eye roll. "You told me to stop hovering, Si."

"And you *listened*," he says. It's almost as if he's miffed about it.

"How's it going?" I ask. "You doing all the scar therapy they told you to?" He's supposed to do specific movements so that the places where his skin is mangled won't heal too tight and become restrictive.

"Yeah, yeah. Been taking myself on little errands and wiping my own ass and everything like a big boy, too. What the hell have you been up to? Micah says he hasn't heard from you either, and Sage is too preoccupied right now to notice either way."

Telling him I jetted off to work feels like admitting to my abysmal coping skills. "Just . . . getting caught up on things."

His silence is weighted. "You're definitely lying."

"I'm not." Not technically, anyway.

"You are, but go on and keep your secrets. Wanna get a beer?"

"Sure, Frodo. Tomorrow. Noon?"

"Sounds good." And then he hangs up without a goodbye.

The abrupt conversation has successfully diverted my thought spiral into something less turbulent, so I let myself ease back into it and onto the highway again.

I hate remembering how we fucked such a good thing up, but I think I've spent too much energy on putting up mental and emotional boundaries to avoid it all, and even though it somehow feels fresh and tender again, I find myself wanting to examine it closer. We somehow made it through having a kid at seventeen and eighteen and grew that love into something so real I know nothing else could ever come close, and yet it still fell apart, and I want to know why, and why I still miss her so much.

Maybe she's right and it's better to leave that pain in the past, but . . . I've certainly been doing my best to do just that for the last few years, and that hasn't changed a damn thing.

I also hate what her merely writing the word *sex* on a piece of paper does to me. The way my mind immediately goes to the last time I had my hands full of her. I don't know if it's because we knew each other in that way so early in life, if it's because we discovered that brand of pleasure and honesty together, but sex with Wren was always more. Just *more*. Likely because being with her so long meant that there was naturally more of it, but I think in the long term, some of the sex became functional. Efficient. Emotionally complicated during the infertility years. More complicated after the ectopic and the vasectomy.

Still, I knew what worked for her and she for me, and it was great and passionate and everything it should've been, but then there were *those* times, too. The ones that stand out in between the rest, still haunting me in a way that makes my bones go hot with a crude sort of lust.

It's as if my very few and fleeting romances with women in the last four years may as well have been experienced in black and white—something full of static, where even these distant thoughts of Wren live in color. In every single one of my senses, in sound and in taste, too. I try to blink away the memories that crest, that final time when I think we both knew it was coming to an end. We were rarely touching at that point, and I wonder if it's because we thought we could trick ourselves into forgetting, like maybe that'd make it easier to leave. Part of me thinks that on some base level, we knew it was the last time—which seems like a ridiculous thought, but . . . fuck, the memory overtakes me, and I give myself over to the swell of it.

It was hours after her mom's birthday party, long past when

everyone else had gone home. Sage had taken Sam for the rest of the weekend, with plans for some sort of distraction, leaving Wren and me alone in our house.

I hadn't wanted her to throw anything in the first place. It had been over six months since her emergency surgery, but I didn't think she'd slowed down for six minutes. She'd thrown herself into taking care of her mom. Drove her to appointments and worked extra at the bakery even while she was still supposed to be recovering. And now she was throwing a party with fifty people when it felt like she couldn't stand to be alone with me.

"What if it's her last one, Ellis?" she'd spat when I suggested we do something more low-key. I dropped it after that. Savvy's disease was a mystery at the time, and there was no reply that I could offer that felt right.

The party was a success and her mom had a great day, because Wren is limitless when it comes to her people. And now, alone in our house together, there was nothing else to clean or put away, but she still wouldn't come to bed. I tried to wait quietly for her on the couch, then in the kitchen, where my presence only seemed to aggravate her more, which grated at my nerves right back and had me silently following her every move. It was after 2:00 A.M., but apparently, she wanted to clear out the fridge, so I followed suit. She started reorganizing the Tupperware drawer, so I stood by and threw away anything that was missing a lid. I could feel her annoyance ratcheting up, hear her growling under her breath and could practically taste her angry tears in the air, but I couldn't just leave her alone. I wanted her to go to bed, I wanted to rip down whatever walls we'd erected between us. I wanted to get to her however I could again and I wanted her to let me take care of her and I wanted her mom to be okay and for us to be happy. And I wanted her to stop fucking cleaning.

She jerked a wineglass off the counter that she'd already scrubbed clean and started going at it again, too hard.

"Wren," I tried to warn, but my voice was stuck in my throat, too quiet. A small cry cracked out of her when the glass broke and sliced into her palm.

I reached around her and grabbed her wrist, instinctively bringing it to my face to check for shards. When she tried to wrench it away, something desperate and possessed roared through me, and I—*god,* I feel like some sort of brute looking back. I distantly hear my curse ricochet around the cab of my truck, but I'm still stuck in the memory. I gripped her slender wrist tighter and brought her palm to my mouth and angrily licked the blood from it.

Her eyes went as black as her sundress, and she crushed her lips to mine, biting, tongue slipping against my teeth. I wanted to devour every short, keening gasp she made, needed to steal every tiny sob before it could leave her lips. She pressed her full chest into mine, nipples tight enough to feel through all our clothes. Her hands came up my shirt and she raked her nails down my back so hard I hissed. I could feel where her palm still bled and I hoped she drew some from me, too, some animalistic part of me hoping they'd mix and bind her back to me somehow. I squeezed and molded her ass in my hands, tilting and dragging her against me. I was begging and pleading with my body and I didn't know what for. She ripped open my shirt, and buttons scattered across the tile; I frantically untied her apron at the same time she shoved down my pants, and then I really was begging, I realized. My chanted *please,* over and over again meeting her *yes,* over and over again. Until she spun around and bent herself over our table, panties tangled around one of her ankles, her dress rucked up to her waist.

"Now," she sobbed out, her eyes clenching shut. Her trembling hands made fists against the grain.

It felt primitive, taking her like this, not having her eyes or her hands on me. I wanted her bound to me again. I gathered her wrists against her lower back and tied them together in her apron strings, like maybe I'd tie her to me, too. And fuck, she *moaned.* The sound of it . . . I spot the goose bumps rising on my forearms, I feel that sound heat, then melt, then harden in my core even now. She squeezed her legs together, and when they came back apart, she was so slick it glistened against her thighs in the moonlight. I should have fallen to my knees and tasted her one last time. My mouth waters at the thought of it. I should have told her how perfect she was, how beautiful she was, flushed and wet and swollen pink with need.

Instead, I nudged her thighs farther apart, wet myself against her before I disappeared into her in one long thrust, like I might get to the very heart of her as quickly as I could. Her breaths came in strangled pants. I'm not sure I could breathe at all. She was hot and snug and holding me so fucking tight, and I was literally holding her from the inside and still she felt too far. Everything dissolved into desperation and my need was punching into my spine too quickly, my hips snapping against her. I slowed when I got close, murmuring a string of obscenities at the sight of her, from the fan of her wild hair and her wrists tied and her spine bowing as she started to fuck herself back against me when I stilled. I peeled my hands from her hips and used one to help leverage her from where she was bound, curled the other around to tend to her clit, letting my rough fingers split and slide against the softest petals of her. I wanted to sink my teeth into her shoulder and make it last. I wanted it to never end, my hazy brain trying to invent a thousand ways to do only this forever. Until I felt the first fluttering clench of her, that battering pulse squeezing me in a rhythm I couldn't outpace and I was losing myself in her before I could stop. I wish I'd said her name, I wish I'd told her what she did to me, all my thoughts and everything I wanted to do to her, how sweet and good she'd been. I wish I'd said every good and bad thing in my head. But then my vision went white with bliss, and I was coming and going at the same time and I was being shattered, crushed into dust. I was still hard when I started to slip myself out of her, then growled like some disturbed beast when I canted my hips and could feel my cum inside. I pulled her up to me by her wrists when I slid out all the way, the tops of her thick thighs still pressing against the edge of the table as her head tipped back against my heart. I dove for her neck at the same time I pushed two fingers into her, felt her tight groan crawl up her throat and vibrate on my lips when we heard the indecent sound of it. Her legs were shaking so violently I knew that my body was the only thing anchoring her there and keeping her upright. My cock was painfully hard all over again, trapped between us beside her tied hands. Jesus, she was soaked with us. I slid my fingers out of her and left a trail around her smooth hip before I swiped and circled messily at her from the front, my hand hidden behind her apron. Her knees buckled, and I ground harder into her to keep her standing.

"I can't, I can't!" she cried out, biting off a curse. I buried my nose in her honey-scented hair and swiped faster.

"Yes, you can. You need it. I need it. Take it, Wren."

A horn blares as a car speeds around me, and I look down and realize I'm going 25 mph on the freeway. I'm wheezing and throbbing in my jeans, and I have to pull over again. I barely get myself in hand before I'm coming in rough spurts and gasping, sweat dripping down my temples.

I flip off the heater and quickly start to clean up my mess, awash in something equal parts shame and panic. I let out a mildly hysterical sound when I look at the clock and see that I've only been driving an hour, if that. It took me less than sixty minutes to open up whatever this Pandora's box in my brain is and for memories and longing to come spiraling free.

Unfortunately for me, I've got a seventeen-hour drive.

Miles and miles of serpentine road, one long sunset and a whole damn sunrise, plus a lifetime's worth of memories.

And I spend every second of it coming to accept that I'm still in love with my wife.

CHAPTER 5

——

WREN

Gray. Gray. Gray. Autumn in Spunes is nothing but wet and gray, and I love it. It's like everything is brighter in contrast. I look forward to my days off in fall, since, aside from a few days in June for my birthday, I hardly get any when the summer tourist season rolls around. I dedicate these days to doing as little busywork as possible, and only doing anything at a very mild pace.

I wake up slowly, taking in the misty view out the window into my modest backyard, tendrils of fog stretching across the lawn and coiling around the windswept trees. I'd like to loiter in my blanket cloud, but the smell of coffee and the sound of Sam shuffling around the kitchen both beckon, so I throw on a thick robe and stuff the bottoms of my pajamas into warm socks before I pad out there to assemble us some breakfast. I find him already nose deep in a bowl of cereal and sigh.

"Was going to ask if you wanted an omelet?" I say.

"Yes, please," he says brightly around a mouthful. "But"—he

swallows a bite—"only if it's quick. I told Indy I'd give her a ride."

"You happy she's back?" I ask, aiming for nonchalant.

He cuts me a knowing look. "We're just friends."

I chuckle and start cracking the eggs, dropping it for the time being. "You get your last application in?"

"Sure did." He starts washing his bowl.

"Proud of you," I tell him, trying to temper my earnestness so I don't embarrass either of us this early in the morning.

"I know," he says, bashfully studying his spoon.

"We should celebrate. Bet Auntie Sage could get Fisher to make us something fancy?" I slide an omelet onto a plate and pass it over his way, the table within arm's reach here in my tiny kitchen.

"Yeah, I'd be into that," he says. A *but* hangs silently in the air. "I'm gonna go to Dad's this weekend, though. I haven't seen him in two weeks."

"Really?" I'm a little shocked by this. Our custody arrangement has always been a free-ranging sort of thing with Sam, but even when he stays here more, he and Ellis make a point to see each other all the time, especially since Sam got his license.

"Internet's better here, and I was doing all the apps." He shrugs, polishing off his omelet with an enormous bite. "All right, gotta go. Love you." He pecks my cheek, steals an apple streusel muffin from under the cloche on the counter, and then leaps to the door, my laughing "Love you" chasing at his heels.

I leisurely get myself ready for the rest of the day after he leaves, half my mind on the task at hand and the rest on my strange, developing pen pal situation. Whatever this is, I think it's good for me. The last letter I wrote felt like pressing on a bruise or deeply stretching a muscle—that odd mix of pain and relief. And even though it's quite literally a two-dimensional relationship, I realize that it's the thread of connection that tugs at some long-dormant hope in me.

Yes, I love my bakery and I know my mom will be officially retiring in the next few years and I'll take it over as my own, and my heart's so full for Sam and everything he's bound to go off and do that I'm surprised I don't swell up like that blueberry girl in the Wonka factory, but . . . I guess, for the first time in years, I feel like there's something out there that I might still look forward to, just for myself.

I also have full—if unexplainable—faith that this guy will find out about the pair of horses for me. And thank god for it, too, because no amount of entertaining gossip from the neighborhood Facebook groups could make up for the gut-wrenching sadness to be found in the displaced animals page. Jesus, if Sage ever saw that page, Spunes would end up being overrun by wayward pets.

Thinking of my friend and her affinity for taking in a variety of creatures inspires a plan for my day, so I give up on trying to tame my wild hair, and tug a beanie down over it before I drive out to her quaint slice of Spunes.

Sage's gargantuan Irish wolfhound lopes down from her porch when I pull onto her driveway twenty minutes later. I spot the tip of a gray tail twitching through the meadow to the right, and gather that her three-legged cat is off on the hunt.

I toss a tree branch posing as a stick for the dog, but just before I start toward the barn, a movement in one of the upstairs windows of the house catches my eye. When I look again, I think I can make out the top of a head.

Strange . . . it's a weekday, so Sage is off teaching at the high school. I look across the meadow to the neighboring house that

Fisher rents and see his truck still there, so maybe he's in her house. But why would he try to hide from me? I know he had some reservations about small towns and busybodies and all that, but I figured the guy was cured since he willingly relocated.

Yeah, actually, screw this. He's in love with my best friend. He's obligated to be friendly with me.

I march up her front steps and rap my fist on the door. Immediately, there's a series of thuds and muffled voices—the sounds of scrambling and putting on clothes if I've ever heard them. There's the drumbeat of footsteps and then Sage herself is here, leaning awkwardly in the doorway in a flannel robe, her hair a mussed-up tangle, skin flushed and covered in a dewy sheen. I feel my smile up to my hairline.

"What are *you* up to?" I ask. "Forget it was a school day, Miss Byrd?"

"I'm sick. I had to call in," she cheeps.

She's the worst liar I've ever met. All the Byrds are. They each have the same tell. A line between their brows as if they're trying to look stern, but eyes that widen like they're scared.

I tilt my head and pout sympathetically. "Aw, poor love. Got a case of the streptoCOCKus?"

"What?!"

"You require an injection only he can provide?"

"I have no idea what you're talking about."

"Don't you play coy with me. I know what kind of fever you got. The kind you stay in bed all day for and get precisely no rest." I cackle merrily. "You're playing hooky with your boyfriend."

She darts a resigned glance over her shoulder before she opens the door wider and reveals an equally love-rumpled Fisher, a furious blush on his cheeks and his hoodie on inside out.

"It's the Friday before Thanksgiving break. We weren't doing anything, anyway," Sage admits sheepishly. I press my lips together hard to contain another laugh.

"Hey, Wren," comes Fisher's warm greeting. But his gaze bounces right back to Sage, tracing her profile in a way that makes me feel like I might blush, too. It's like his entire body *sighs*. He looks at her the same way people look at my fresh chocolate croissants, like he's imagining taking her apart and how she would melt on his tongue and . . . and god, I'm lonely. I need to get laid.

It has to be more than that, though. I've done that. I dedicated myself to going out and trying to have my bodily needs met early on after the divorce—*trying* being the operative word. My efforts were met with dismal results.

This ballooning sensation in my chest isn't wanting physical comfort again. It's more of that dangerous hope, as delicate as blown sugar. I want *that*. I want to feel cherished and wanted again, I want to feel that way for someone again. The realization makes me unsteady, like I'm being pulled in two directions.

"Come in and I'll make us some breakfast?" Fisher offers, and it sends a fresh pain through me. They're already such a *couple*, a unit so melded that he's comfortable enough to make offers when it's technically her home. I'm elated for her and heartsick for me. Another disconcerting emotion. Sage studies me carefully, and I work to keep my expression bland.

"No, no." I wave them off. "I'm taking Bud for a ride before the rain rolls in."

Fisher stretches halfway out the door to peer up toward the sky, one of his earrings glinting in the light.

"Guess that means we should get going then, too," he says.

"I gotta pick up the sample chairs and go through the charade of letting Martha approve them." He grins.

"Take my van," I offer. "They'll fit in the back, and that way if it starts up early, they won't get wet."

"You sure?" asks Sage.

"Yeah, I want to muck out Bud's stall and clean him up and everything, anyway, so I'll stay awhile."

They go about getting dressed and take off in my van, so I set myself to brushing Bud's winter coat, murmuring sweet nothings to him in between his satisfied whickers and snorts.

A cacophony of other animal noises rings through the air. Sable barks happily, the geese honk, and the donkeys bray. I step out of the open barn doors, expecting Sage and Fisher have forgotten something and are back to grab whatever it is, and come face-to-face with Ellis.

CHAPTER 6

WREN

The gears in my mind screech to a halt at the sight of him, even from twenty yards away. I can tell his do the same. His hands ball into fists at his side, the outline of his broad shoulders stiffening. He casts a yearning glance back at his truck and lets out a long exhale that curls silver through the cold air.

I don't blame him for wanting to flee. Part of me hopes he'll leave and save us what is sure to be an awkward exchange, especially given our last one.

My chest splinters at the memory of him falling apart in my arms in that hospital hallway a few months ago, knowing how terrified he had to be for Silas and how wrung out he must've been to let himself lose it like that. I grind my teeth and try to forget the way my heart thudded against my bones like it wanted to break out and get at his the moment he was in my arms. His warmth and the feel of his hair sliding through my fingers.

No. I can't let myself think of those things, not when he's pivoted and marching toward me now.

I'm pinned in place under his attention, getting worse the longer he refuses to look away. This obliterates our carefully constructed, unspoken rules. We are never alone together, and we rarely speak unless we have to regarding something with Sam. We definitely do not have prolonged, intense eye contact while he strides determinedly at me through mist and fog. His steps are silent, and yet I feel every one of them in my belly.

The closer he gets, the more I see . . . He looks like absolute shit. Eyes bloodshot, purple crescents underneath. No one would mistake him for gaunt or skinny; the man has never been able to sit still in his life and has the visible strength to show for it. But he's too goddamn thin for my liking. His stubble-mustache combination has morphed into a beard, hiding the cleft in his chin I used to love, and he's in dire need of a haircut. Ellis is never beautiful, per se. His nose is maybe a degree too strong, his jaw and brow are all hard lines. His eyes aren't big and clear like his siblings', but they are the same signature, striking gray, with striations of brown up close. His mouth, though. His mouth is what I have to avoid at all costs. Framed in all his unyielding hardness is a mouth made for smiling. For pressing whispered jokes and leisurely, drugging kisses into skin. His mouth contains a billion secrets, including how funny and charming he's capable of being. It always felt like my secret to keep. Ellis is the kind of handsome that you absorb in pieces before you notice something new and get the thrill of starting all over again. Even looking as rough as he does now, he's devastating.

I hate it. I'm irrationally upset by it.

"Hey," I say. What an idiotic, pathetic word compared to the emotional anarchy in my head.

"Hey," he mutters back. His voice is hoarse, and lines pinch around his eyes.

Silas is careful to not talk much about Ellis—a well-respected condition of our friendship. But he let it slip the other day that Ellis has been giving him space. Seeing him now, it's clear to me that it's costing him to do so.

Sometimes I wish Silas would try to remember that Ellis's fretting is just as much about him as it is his siblings. He had to raise them; straddling the roles of brother and father, all while becoming a young dad to Sam, too. I can't fathom what it did to him to watch Silas go down in flames.

"I, uh," Ellis says, pulling me out of my swirling thoughts. "Bud."

God, I would have died for this man, once. Now we're reduced to single syllables and stilted silences. "Right. He due for new shoes?" I've told him at least ten times that I would happily pay a farrier. "I was actually here to take him for a ride. I'll come back another time."

"Sage didn't tell me you were here, and I didn't see your van," he says.

"What?"

"Your car. It's not out front."

Oh. He's explaining why he would subject himself to being alone with me, as in: he wouldn't. He didn't think I was here. Got it. "Sage and Fisher borrowed it. They have some furniture samples for Starhopper to pick up but didn't want to use the truck since it's supposed to rain."

He nods in understanding, avoiding my eyes and scratching his bearded jaw.

I know better than to ask, but I do, anyway. "You okay?"

A myriad of things pass across his face in a heartbeat, most notably something like terror. Over one simple question from me. I can't do this with him. "I'll come back another time," I say again, and step around him to leave.

"Stay," he rasps. There's a commanding edge to it that makes my shoulders pull back, awareness running down my neck like a fingertip. Ellis doesn't *ask* for what he needs, let alone make demands. "It won't take long. Get a ride in before the rain," he explains.

"All right."

I proceed to putter around awkwardly while he starts heating up the forge and getting Bud set up. I keep my hands occupied in the dog's coat or hauling out any of the tools I see. Bud nods his shaggy head up and down and neighs in excitement before he starts flapping his gums against Ellis's Carhartt vest. His low chuckle is a spear through my ribs.

"Be good," he murmurs, and my body shivers involuntarily. He pulls a sugar cube from his pocket and lets Bud nuzzle it out of his palm.

"You still give him those?" I ask.

He slides a big palm down the horse's neck lovingly. "They're not real sugar. They're healthier treats I got from Serena's office."

I make a noncommittal noise while he slides over the hoof stand.

Serena's the vet in town, who also happened to carry a torch for Ellis when we were young. She was his first girlfriend, back when he and I were *only* friends, and she's the only other girl he took to a dance. She was his first . . . everything, actually. It's strange that I can still recognize the chalk outline where jealousy might have been before, even though things between Serena and me long ago became cool. But I idly wonder if there's any spark between them again, which is when I recognize that jealous twinge trying to flare up, and I force myself to brush it aside. It's like the old me is gone, but the new me hasn't quite shown up yet, either, and I'm distressingly confused by it. All I know is that I at least *want* to get to a place where I could be happy for him moving on, which in itself is a huge step for me, and I feel a fresh wave of gratitude for those letters.

Still, I'm obviously not so well adjusted that I'm interested in chatting it up with him about his dating life.

"So . . . Silas is doing good," I say to fill the silence.

He lifts one of Bud's hooves between his legs and looks up his brow at me. "Yeah?" He removes the nails and starts clipping off the edges of the old shoe. "I worry he wouldn't say anything to anyone even if he weren't."

Where do you think he gets that from? I nearly blurt. "He'd say something to me," I assure him instead.

He grunts and finishes removing the old metal, and I think that's that. There's only Bud's rumbling noises and the soft hiss of the hoof rasp for a few minutes, until he makes a point to look at me again. "I'm glad you've stayed his friend, Wren," he says. "Thank you."

The sound of my name on his lips and the strange finality in his tone scramble my thoughts. I wonder if there's been a shift for him, too. Maybe his breakdown in my arms was some kind of catalyst for us both starting to move beyond this limbo between us. "It's not as if it's some huge undertaking. He's a good friend to me, too." I reach for a light subject. "Did he mention what's going on with Walter and Martha yet?"

He gives Bud a hearty pat on the rump before he grabs the hot shoe with the tongs. His face is inscrutable before he hauls up the hoof between his thighs again. "No, but I'm grabbing a beer with him tomorrow. I'm sure he's rehearsing his dramatic soliloquy in the mirror now." Steam billows up in a cloud when he places the glowing metal against the hoof. He makes quick work of hammering in new nails and finishing, the rounded muscles at the tops of his arms working beneath his shirt. A small grin slides across his face when he's done, and he gives me a conspiratorial look. "Unless you want to ruin it for him and tell me first?"

I roll my eyes and feel the apples of my cheeks pull up. "No. I know how you boys love your gossip." Oh *no*. Did I just flirt with my ex-husband? Time to rein it in. "He's the one who had to suffer finding them in one of the O'Doyle's fitting rooms doing . . . things." I mime something obscene with my hands, and his boot catches on the ground.

His mouth twists. "He'll be unnecessarily detailed about it," he complains.

"Mm-hmm," I confirm. "He will. I'll never look at Walter the same. Didn't know he had it in him."

I wait quietly while he finishes the rest of the shoes. It's hard to ignore how tired he looks. He always overdid it when he had time off, unlike me and my intentionally slow days. With him and his crew all taking time away, he's probably tackling a thousand projects around our old house, over on the other edge of town. There's a small stable where Bud once lived, but only for a short while. Looking back now, it's easy to see that getting a horse was a foolish, last-ditch attempt at filling the gap between us.

Horseback riding was my only extracurricular when I was younger, though, and I think I was searching for the same feeling it once gave me. The trust and partnership, maybe. The feeling of freedom and limitlessness that comes with depending on a creature who cares for you as much as you care for them. The easy, simple communication and the clear understanding.

"Did Sam finish his applications?" Ellis asks me quietly when he helps saddle Bud.

"Yeah, he did." And I'm instantly too close to that edge of space where nothing links us anymore—where even the son between us is off on his own. No more direct connections. Not even the shared college fund account we've been militant about since we were eighteen. Just our mutual friendships and a quiet expanse. Friendships that still belong to him more than they do me, since they're all his family.

I need to get away from this feeling, clamor back to that hopefulness I had this morning when I was trying to look ahead instead of reaching back.

I swallow hard and kick myself up onto the saddle. Ellis passes me the reins. He looks like he wants to say something else, but he reaches over and squeezes my calf instead. I hate that my breath catches over that tiny bit of contact. I hate how I know I'll imagine it later, how I'll replay it in my head and try to re-create the sensation. His palm through my jeans and the strength of his hand.

"See you here on Thanksgiving?" he asks. I nod before I pull Bud around and ride away, holding my breath as long and as far as I can manage, before I let it and one single tear escape.

CHAPTER 7

ELLIS

"You both know this isn't an open restaurant, right? We are literally not open for business yet," Fisher says to Silas and me as we sit at one of the sample tables he picked up the day before. Starhopper's coming together nicely. They've married the older-town feel with some modern designs—brick walls and metal trims. Behind a tall plexiglass wall sits an array of huge metal cylinder things where I gather beer is brewed. There's a nice patio area, plus a deck up top, and a stargazing tower. Silas and I already snooped around the observatory while he brought me up to speed on our town's self-appointed supreme leader (and trading goods store owner), Martha O'Doyle, hard-launching her relationship with local diner owner, Walter.

"We smelled food," Silas says to Fisher, counting on a finger. "I found out last week that you already have beer"—he holds out his second and third finger—"and you're *dating* our sister." He makes *dating* sound like something more explicit.

Fisher gives me a flat look. "What would you like?" he asks.

I try for a smile and shrug. "Surprise us."

"Any allergies?" he asks with a beleaguered sigh.

Silas rests his chin in his hand and beams at him. "Nope! Hey, did you hear about Walter and Martha?"

"Sage put you on speakerphone last night so you could treat us to a very colorful monologue on all of it, Silas, so yes," says Fisher.

"Oh shit, that's right." Silas chuckles. He's pretty proud of his gossip mongering, bouncing in his seat until the movement makes him hiss and wince.

"What hurts? You're doing everything the doctors told you to, right?" I ask.

He stabs a withering glare at me just as Fisher brings us our beers. "He was in so much pain the other night that he sweated through dinner," Fisher says. Silas turns the hard stare on him. "He barely ate any of his soup," Fisher adds.

"Thank you for sharing that detail, Fisher," says Silas.

"Payback for the many, many details you shared last night while I was trying to enjoy some pumpkin gnocchi with your sister," Fisher says. He lifts a brow and waits for Silas's rebuttal, then spins around and stalks toward the kitchen when it never comes.

"He's gotten a little too comfortable too fast, hasn't he?" Silas grumbles.

"Says the guy mooching free beers and lunch off him," I say.

"I was planning on leaving a tip! Including an IOU to rescue him from any rogue mops."

I snort. Early this past summer, a robot vacuum went off in the middle of the night at Fisher's rental, and he called 911, thinking it was an intruder. We weren't exactly gracious about it when we showed up on the scene. Sage eventually marched over from next door and shooed us out.

I study Silas again, just as he gives a mildly disgusted look at one of the burn scars on his hand. He's always been restless, but there's an edginess to him now that doesn't sit right. Like he's wearing a too-small jacket or something itchy.

"You sure you're good?" I ask.

He heaves an exasperated sound. "You caught me, brother. I'm battling with jealousy over how nimble Martha O'Doyle is. When I try to get down on my knees like that, the skin on my right leg feels like Saran Wrap stretched over hot meat."

"Jesus, Si."

"Speaking of old people in love and lust," he says. "You seeing someone? I'm still trying to suss out why you've been so— elusive."

"I'm barely three years older than you, and once again, you *asked* me to back off." I take a hearty gulp of beer.

"Yes, but you look, sound, and act ancient. And I noticed you didn't answer me," the little shit replies.

"I—"

Fisher slides a bowl in front of each of us, cutting me off before I have a chance to lie. I'm not sure what I want to divulge to Silas yet.

"Carrot jalapeño soup," says Fisher. "To start."

"Do you have salt, pepper, and hot sauce on hand?" Silas asks, and if looks could kill, Fisher would be leveling him. "*Damn*, just kidding, Boyardee. I like your earring, by the way. Where's the other one, though?" He swizzles his spoon around the soup. "Not gonna find it in my meal, am I?"

Fisher's face turns smug. "Your sister's wearing it," he says. "She's been wearing it since it fell out once at her house." Silas's lip

curls. "As far as how that happened? I'll let you use your imagination." He pats Silas on the back and turns to me. "Sorry, Ellis."

"It's fine." I laugh, and Silas frowns at Fisher's retreating form.

"Serves you right. You're being annoying," I say.

He finishes his beer. "No, *you're* annoying. Something is up with
you, I know it," he spits. "Sage isn't the only one who gets weird,
witchy feelings, all right? I can *feel* when something is off with you."
He moodily slurps his soup, his eyes narrowing in pain when he
fidgets in his seat again.

His statement, though . . . it makes the beer turn bitter in my
mouth. Like I've failed again if I can't shield him from my pain, too.

"You don't need to worry about me right now, Si. Worry
about you and healing up."

His spoon clatters against the porcelain bowl. "Dammit, Ellis.
You're not my parent anymore. Talk to me like your fucking
brother."

I lean back in my seat and search his stony face. He's right; I
do default to parenting him, and I could use someone to talk to.
The problem is that I know he'd be caught in the middle of his
friendship with Wren and his loyalty to me, so I'd have to be se-
lective about what I told him. I clear my throat, train my gaze on
the hand that's wrapped around my beer glass, my thumb wiping
circles in the condensation.

"I miss Wren," I quietly admit. "I want her back."

He's silent for too long. When I look at him again, it's clear
I've surprised him. "Sorry," he says. "I—that wasn't what I was
expecting."

I shake my head irritably. "Still working out the kinks in
your brotherly premonitions, I take it? What the hell *were* you
expecting?"

Fisher appears again and unceremoniously plops a basket of

bread on the table. "Bread," he declares flatly. "With Calabrian chili butter, basil butter, and hot honey butter." He spins away again.

I haul everything to my side before Silas can reach for it, and give him a pointed look. "Well?"

He sighs through his nose. "Honestly, I thought you were seeing someone, and it was turning serious or something and you were afraid to tell me because you know Wren and I are close."

I let the bread go, pushing it to the middle of the table. "That is why I was hesitant to tell you, but . . . yeah. Wrong conclusion," I say.

He crosses his arms, calculating. "Why now? Why, after four years?"

I can't bring myself to tell him about the letters. How they unlocked something I'd barely kept at bay. It feels shameful, like I've stolen something. "I don't know," is what I say instead. It's still the truth, even if it's only part of it. "I'm still figuring it out."

He grabs a piece of bread from the basket and angrily slathers the hot honey butter across it. "You're unbelievable, you know that?" he says, before he drops the knife and shakes his head. "Sorry. I'm grateful you're opening up to me, all right? I don't want to make you feel like you can't. But your timing is fucking trash, Ellis." He takes an oversized bite and continues to speak around it. "And I don't think you're in touch enough with your feelings to know *what* it is you want."

"The fuck does that mean, Silas?"

"Think about it," he says, swallowing forcefully. "This is just you wanting something—*familiar*, or something. You're unmoored, and she's the one familiar thing on the horizon or some shit."

"Don't talk about her like that," I seethe. "Don't act like she's some abstract *thing* or idea to me. She's my wife."

He tosses his bread down. "She's not, though, Ellis. She hasn't been for more than four years."

The words slice through me faster than a knife through one of those fancy butters. I move my hands to my lap, worried I might crush the glass in my fist.

"I'm not trying to be a dick," he says more softly, blowing out a long breath. "I just . . . I just think you try to *fix* everything. You can't stand something broken, so you take shit on yourself to the point that it's actually fucking selfish sometimes, and I think that too much is out of your control right now, or changing without you, and you can't handle it. I know you, and I know that no matter how asinine it is, you blame yourself for what happened to me."

"It is my fault," I snap, and I'm mortified that a lump forms in my throat. I know how true everything else he's said is, but I can't pretend I don't feel this way. "I just mean I should have been closer. I lost you somewhere, and that never happens. I always know where you're at, no matter how chaotic it gets. But I couldn't find you, and then I did and you—" I turn and close my eyes. Try to shut out the picture of the ground collapsing from under him, the fire billowing up in his place.

His tone is gentler but still stern when he says, "I don't know how to help you realize that it was a freak accident, Ellis. I don't know how to get it through your thick skull that this wasn't your fault."

"I'm not your responsibility, Silas. It happened to you, not me. You shouldn't need to worry about me, too."

"Man, fuck you," he says, laughing in disbelief. I feel my chin rear back like he's punched me. I've never seen Silas this angry, especially quiet like this. "You're doing it again," he says. "You're taking it all on. *I'm* not your responsibility anymore, either, Ellis.

I'm not something you take on while you fight a fire alone. I'm a capable fucking adult, and I am . . . I was competent—*good* at my job." He rips into his bread again. "I know that a lot is changing, and I know it can't be easy. I know that this shook you, and don't fucking tell me not to worry about you again or I swear to god I'll lose it."

He gives me a long, considerate look before he presses on. "I know Sage is settling down and I know you're happy for her like we all are, but I also know it's a *change*. Micah being gone is nothing new, but I know you worry about him, too. And Sam being in his last year of school before he goes off to college is probably not an easy concept to grapple with. That's probably the biggest one of all . . .

"But, brother, Wren finally seems like she's ready to move on. She's—"

I make a noise and hold up my hand, begging him to stop before he says anything I can't unhear.

"No, Ell. I think it's important." His expression turns pained. "She's just now talking to me about trying to date, yes, but it's more than that. She's actually *hopeful* again. She's herself again. And yeah, you knew her differently, but we've all been friends for basically our whole lives, so I know what I'm talking about, too. So if she hasn't given you any indication that she'd like to rekindle things with you . . . I don't think it would be fair. I don't think it's fair for you to suddenly, miraculously come to this realization on your own and charge in to take care of it all on your own like you'd inevitably try to."

"But what if I could?" I croak. "Fix it, I mean. Wouldn't it be worth trying?" My chest is an empty, barren cavern without her. My heart took shape around hers, too, and it will never go back.

He finishes the bite he's working on and calls over to Fisher for another beer before he looks at me again. "All the stretches and exercises"—he adds finger quotes to *exercises*—"they have me do in physical therapy? They're all things I can do myself in the comfort of my own home. But I go to the experts and will continue going because they will catch it if I develop any bad habits and start doing things wrong. They'll correct me. I am reliant on their expertise." Fisher puts fresh beers down in front of us, hard enough that they slosh and spill before he marches off again. "I could technically fix this on my own," Silas goes on, gesturing toward the half of his body that sustained the most burns. "I could get stronger on my own, but I run the risk of messing it up, healing improperly, inviting infection and a world of misery upon myself." He pouts into his beer. "I'll never have a nail on my pinkie toe again."

I take a drink. "I'm sorry, brother. I know that one is your favorite."

"I had nice man feet," he grouses.

"I'm sure they're great still."

He shrugs, and I feel a strange, pulsing ache in my throat. "You're wiser than you look, you know," I tell him.

He squints out the window into the foggy day. "Had a good example," he says, almost too low for me to catch. "And I'm still not as wise as the real experts," he adds, looking at me again, his knee bouncing under the table. "On top of physical therapy, the union is paying for me to talk to a regular therapist, too. I've only been twice, but it helps, Ell. I know Fisher talks to someone, too."

"Pork belly bánh mi sandwiches," says the man in question, setting plates in front of us with a small flourish. "Can I get you boys anything else? I live to serve." He spears us both with an impatient look.

"Oh my god, Ell, know what I just realized?" Silas says. "This guy's cooking Thanksgiving for us." He smiles and takes a bite of his sandwich, beaming up at Fisher as a shredded carrot falls out of his mouth.

Fisher crosses his arms behind his back. "I am. And you should know that green bean casserole will not be tolerated."

"Duhh fuuuhhhg?!" Silas whines in outrage, mouth full. "That's my favorite!"

Fisher's expression twitches like he knew this. "It's disgusting and it's gluttonous on top of an already heavy meal. If you want it, make your own."

Silas's face is indignant. "I'm so *not* leaving a tip."

"I don't have a working cash register," Fisher snaps back. "I'm not even the CDC here. *We're not open!*" He throws his hands up in exasperation.

"What Silas meant to say," I offer, "is, 'Thank you for lunch. And for the beer.' Let us know what we should bring to Thanksgiving." Another thought occurs to me. "But, hey—don't . . . don't do desserts, all right?"

Fisher's head tilts, a mildly surprised furrow in his brow.

"Why?" Silas asks me suspiciously. "You don't eat Wren's desserts anymore, anyway."

Fisher looks between us, and his features go smooth with understanding before they crinkle in pity at me.

"I'm going to this year," I say. It's time.

———

When Silas and I leave Starhopper a little while later and step into the misty fall air, my phone rings. I send it to voicemail when I see that it's Lennon.

"I want to reiterate something," Silas says as we reach the pathway that wraps around the expansive lawn on this chunk of a cliff. "It's not that I don't think you deserve to be happy again, or to be happy with Wren, Ellis. You guys had the thing everyone wants for themselves, I know that. And yeah, I've never seen two people more in love . . . But I've also never seen two people be so—so *gone* when they lost it." He looks up from his feet. "You were haunted. The both of you were. Don't dredge up old ghosts. Not now. Let that shit stay buried and find happiness for yourself somewhere else. Let her, too."

I take in a breath that's too cold, burning my lungs up from the inside. I merely nod. We hug, and I'm careful to avoid his burnt shoulder. "Love you," I manage to say. "And . . . I won't." Not until I get myself to a place where I feel like I might deserve her again. Not unless she wants me again, too.

"Love you, too."

I hang back and watch him walk away, then slip my phone out of my pocket and return Lennon's call.

"Hey! You listen to my voicemail?" she says brightly.

"Not yet, sorry." I sniff. "What's up?"

"Guess you haven't checked the weather, then, either?"

"Kirby, enough with the suspense." I'm suddenly so exhausted I can barely see straight.

"Jeez, cranky. All right, well, the sad news is that you don't get to see me again. I'll pause to let you be adequately devastated." She waits four seconds before she proceeds. "The good news is that the rain finally rolled in over here. Fire's all but contained, so they'll be calling off the extra crews."

It's illuminating how my first feeling in response to this isn't pure relief but a tepid sort of panic instead. Nothing to distract myself with. No reason to continue with the letters. "That's great," I say weakly.

"The best news?" says Kirby. "The horses were found."

CHAPTER 8

WREN

It's early afternoon on the Tuesday before Thanksgiving, and Mom's already gone home for the day after the rush of people picking up their premade pies came through. I'm alone in the shop other than Fisher's niece, Indy, who keeps coming up to the counter and looking into the display case without buying anything. I feel like she's been working up the courage to talk to me about something, and I watch her visibly gather up her strength before her fourth trip to the register. But the moment she says, "Wren, I—" the bell over the door chimes and our mail lady walks in, lips pursed with a look of disapproval for me.

"Another letter from 'Guest L' over in Colorado," she says, holding out the envelope with a flourish.

"Oh, um, thank you," I say. The look on her and Indy's faces indicate that I might not be succeeding at my "totally chill" impression. They both wait expectantly.

"Sorry, but, did we start tipping the postal service or

something?" I ask the same mail lady I've known since I was twelve. Maybe if I lay it on thick enough, she'll be too aggravated to be nosy. "Is that what you're waiting on?"

She rolls her eyes and tosses me a wave over her shoulder. "Happy Thanksgiving," she drawls.

"You, too," I call back. And then I'm left alone with Indy again. I'm sure as hell not opening it in front of anyone, but I also don't want to hustle her out of here in an obvious way.

"You were saying?" I ask as gently as I can manage. Her eyes flick to the letter before I slide it into my apron.

"I—well, it's awkward, but . ." Her arms cross and she looks at her feet, then at a spot over my shoulder. Anywhere but directly at me, it seems. "It's just that, sometimes you sorta remind me of my mom, and I know this is a *wildly* personal question and it's okay if you don't want to answer it, but I just keep wondering lately, you know, and I wish I could just ask her things sometimes. That's what I miss the most, I think, is just talking to her. I thought it might help if I could ask someone else who went through it."

"Babe, whatever it is, it's fine. I'll answer it as best I can," I promise.

Her eyes find mine now, and she heaves a big breath. "I was wondering what—actually, *why*, you decided to keep Sam when you were younger? I know it wasn't, like, a religious thing or something. I don't even know why I want to know this." She looks off to the side and starts chewing her thumbnail, and something plucks sharply in my chest. The holiday season always stirs up grief in strange ways. I also know that Indy's mom had her when she was young, too, and that their small town was not as kind.

I clear my throat. "I'm afraid my answer is specific to me, and I don't know if it'll help. Everyone's answer is always going to be specific to them, sweetie. But, I'll tell you, anyway, if you want me to?"

She nods, so I continue. "I have what's called a *pituitary adenoma*. It's a small, benign tumor that pushes on my pituitary gland and made it so I did not have any sort of normal cycle at all when I was younger. We found it when I was fourteen, and I'd been told that I would never have kids or that I'd have to take extraordinary measures to get pregnant someday." I let out a long breath. "When I did, anyway, despite being careful, I was worried it might be my only chance to, and I decided that I didn't want to take that risk." It turns out I'd been right.

"Is that why no one was . . . Is that why everyone supported you?"

"I don't know that anyone was particularly *thrilled* about it," I say with a wry look. "I was still seventeen. And Ellis had just lost his only remaining parent." I sigh raggedly. "Life can be a bully sometimes. And a bully doesn't care if you're already having a rough time. In my experience, it's not gonna help you if you keep shouting 'Ouch, you're hurting me!' at it, either. I think you gather up your friends and stand up to its ass and rock a bloody smile while you do it."

She smiles with glassy eyes. "Glad Spunes is my friend now, too."

"Damn straight, kid," I say. "An often quirky, sometimes clingy, moody, and weird friend, but one that'll always have your back."

"Thank you," she says quietly.

"Can I hug you?" I ask.

She nods, and I lean over and wrap her into an embrace, the way I hope another mother would if she were mine and I was gone. "You can talk to me any time, all right?" I feel her nod into my shoulder.

When she pulls away, she chuckles and quickly wipes at a tear. "I'm gonna go check on Fisher over at Starhopper," she says, already making her way to the door, and I get it. Too much vulnerability at once can feel embarrassing. "I'll see you on Thursday?"

"Yeah, I'll see you on Thursday."

The bell triggers the memory of the letter in my pocket, so I wait until she's a safe distance away and go flip around the Closed sign, then slip into my little office in the back of the kitchen. I force myself to wait several beats, as if to prove that I have some semblance of self-control before I tear into it.

Dear Stranger,

I frown, inexplicably disappointed at the loss of a heinous nickname. I already had more picked out to sign off with. "That hair-goop thing clogging the shower drain" was vying for my top contender.

Regarding hopes and dreams—I have to admit that even though I asked you first, I still find that I'm unprepared to answer that question for myself. I can't remember the last time I hoped and dreamed for more than just the safety and happiness of those around me. Which probably makes me sound like some saint. I'm not. I need that to be very clear. We've been honest here, even if we've withheld certain things on purpose, and I don't want to change that now.

As far as dreams go? I want to be connected with my wife again. I want to learn about her dreams and make them come true. I want to love without restraint. I want to say the good things without reservation and not be afraid to say the bad or difficult things, too.

But here's the truth I've been discovering. I'm actually just scared all the fucking time. I'm scared to get things wrong. I'm scared to let people down. I am so scared to fail to the point that it prevents me from acting, let alone taking a risk, or it makes me try to control everything that poses a potential risk around me. I've been living and loving in half-measures for years. Living my life in pencil, because I don't think I can get shit right the first time. Maybe because I think it'll save me some pain. So far, I've been wrong.

All I know is that your letters unlocked something in me again, and your hope for a pair of horses inspired my own sort of hope, too.

In the envelope, you'll find a picture of Major and Kelpie. They were found about forty-five miles from home, thin and a little worse for wear, but in decent health considering everything. They were still together. Their owners have been beside themselves with relief.

Thank you, dear stranger, for this handful of hope you gave me on a few pieces of flattened trees. You'll *probably never know what it's meant to me. The fire is over 80 percent contained, so I won't be headed back, which means that this will be my last letter.*

Sincerely Hopeful,

L

Melancholy bleeds through me like an inkblot on fabric, something that starts at a point and seeps wider and wider. I wouldn't call my feelings for this stranger *romantic*, but I've certainly been romanticizing this thing. Him being married feels . . . wrong, even though I know it shouldn't. If there was a flirty tint to these words on paper, no harm was done.

No harm done at all.

Except that the stupid hope they awoke in me has made the ache of loneliness morph into something barbed, and I immediately want it off. I . . . I think I'd like to meet someone, but I think I need to actually *try* to do it. Not just try to find a warm body—I already know that would be easy and leave me feeling empty.

I look at the picture of the two beautiful horses side by side, having made it through a terrible, exhausting time. My heart trips over itself when I immediately think of Ellis, how we didn't make it through our own disaster together in the end.

Maybe we had to separate and go our own ways for our survival. It probably made it more difficult for this pair to stay together all the time. Different endurance levels, different needs. What happened to Ellis and me was just . . . nature. We did what we needed to. We're not horses, either. We're human beings with obligations and a son who deserved people who weren't distracted by their resentment for each other and the mountain of responsibilities on our plates.

It's over and done with.

"You don't put a burnt cake back in the oven," I say aloud, an expression coined by my mom. All you can do is take away what you learned and begin again. Agonizing over it only wastes time and prolongs suffering.

But what if it's not burnt? I think. *What if it just didn't turn out like it was supposed to? Couldn't you walk through the recipe and figure out where you went wrong—*

"Stop," I say out loud again. I fold up the letter and forcibly regain my composure. No more muttering to myself. No more harping. It's time to start over.

———

My touchstone for recalibrating myself has always been my mom, which is probably why I'm compelled to drive over to her place after I close up the bakery. Savannah Meridian is completely indomitable, in spite of her MS diagnosis four years ago. In addition to being a successful business owner (which she started as a single mother to a newborn me) she attends a combination yoga and Pilates class four days a week, paints, voraciously reads, volunteers, and maintains a healthy social calendar.

And for the vast majority of my life, she's been unshakable. Regardless of whether the bakery had a rough couple of months or if a pipe burst in our house, or if her daughter came home pregnant at seventeen, Mom's been steadfast at keeping calm and carrying on. When I went to work with her one early Saturday morning all those years ago and burst into tears over my expectant news, she pulled some cinnamon buns out of the oven (because irony) and coolly asked me what I would like to do and how she could support me. It was a year too early, but I recognized that I was an adult right then in her eyes.

I've never felt like an extension of her and have always known that I am my own person, which is maybe why joining her side at the bakery didn't give me any sort of identity crisis. My home was a little lonely and quiet too often, by no one's fault other than capitalism, really, since Mom had to work, and owning a business meant long hours and limited energy outside of them. But between the Byrds' house and Savvy Bakes, I could get my fill of noise.

Noise and a pseudo-family. Because while I've always adored and looked up to Savannah Meridian, whatever gene it is that makes her perfectly content being alone unfortunately skipped me. I have always needed people more. I've always wanted to be needed by them, too.

I pull into Mom's driveway and let myself in through the front door, surprising a strange "Oh!" out of her, already walking toward me. What starts as a brilliant smile on her face falters into something less convincing.

"Wren, sweets. Hi," she breathes, a hand flattening to her chest. She's looking at me like I'm a potential home invader and not her adoring (only) daughter. "What are you doing here?"

"I wanted to see you?" I chuckle awkwardly. "Are you busy?"

Her entire face, so different from mine with her hazel eyes and ultrafair skin, scrunches apologetically. "Sorry, sweets. I sorta have plans." She flaps her hands around. "Oh, but I have time for a super-quick visit, I suppose. Did you want something to drink?"

I look back at the door and then at her. She's got a full face of makeup on and a gray sweater pulled off one shoulder behind her apron. "Are you expecting someone or something?" I ask.

She pauses in her fidgeting and knits her hands together at her front. "I am."

O-kay? "Do you have book club?"

"I do not."

"Another coven meeting?"

She makes an unflattering sound and rolls her eyes like a gum-popping thirteen-year-old. "That was not a *coven*, Wren Salem. It was a holistic gardening group, and we were brewing herbal remedies."

"You were stirring a cauldron and chanting in unison while passing around an expertly rolled blunt."

"It was a spring simmer pot! And—" Another scoff. "And you had to be there to get it." She shrugs.

I blink patiently. "Are you going to make me keep guessing, Mom?"

Suddenly, she sways a little on her feet, and her arms lift and freeze at her sides. She stares off to the side at a spot on the ground.

"Mom?" I say, choking on a quick rise of panic. Her gaze lifts blankly to mine. "*Mom?*" I say again, reaching for her.

"Ah, *shoot*," she abruptly groans, spinning away and marching for the kitchen. "My alarm went off to put dinner in the oven earlier and I got sidetracked. Now we won't be eating until late."

She flutters off, and I have to stand in place and collect myself, gulping back a few heaving breaths. She's been in remission for more than two years, but her symptoms had started with things similar to that—random freezing, stumbling—things that would often preclude slurred speech. She'd complain about tingling and suddenly would go numb. She'd blink strangely and suddenly she couldn't see or walk straight. She'd have days where she slept more than she was awake. We were referred and redirected in a million directions throughout the health care system, were put off time and time again and had to fight for answers. The time in which her disease was a mystery was the only time I've ever seen her truly rattled, which in turn, rattled the hell out of me. She was *so* scared. And *angry* that no one could figure anything out, which meant I'd open my eyes some days suffocating beneath my anger on her behalf, too. I was enraged that this woman, who had never needed anyone, who had always been alone and overworked, yet willingly spread all her love and energy wide, was being robbed of her own agency before my eyes. It took almost a year to obtain a diagnosis.

But, in her typical way, once Mom knew the problem and knew what she was fighting, she didn't waste any time screaming up at the sky over it. She carried on and fought.

I can't say the same for myself. Not now, and not then, either. My husband had pulled away from me at home. He'd begun needing and wanting so little of me over the last few years. Other than my son, the only person who actually needed me was fighting something I was helpless to fix, and I was fucking mad about all of it.

I manage to compose myself and find Mom in her kitchen now. She slips a whole chicken into the oven, trussed up and garnished with a variety of things.

"You're *roasting*, huh?" I ask. Cooking and baking are more different than you'd think, and her joy for both are far from equal. "Who are you having over?"

Her chin lifts primly. "I have a . . . Well. I have a man friend." She sighs.

This is the last thing I would have guessed, and I'm sure my expression conveys it.

"Oh, don't look so scandalized," she says, flicking a dish towel my way. "And make yourself scarce. He'll be here soon." She starts herding me back toward the door.

"Where did you meet this . . . *suitor* of yours, Mother?"

"At the gym in Gandon. His name is David. We've been seeing each other for a few months now, and I really like him and this will be his first time staying the night," she says in a rush, patting me forward. "I met him when my friend Diane and I crushed him and his friend in pickleball."

"When did you join a pickleball league?!"

"Like three months ago!" she whines. "Honey, I love you, but *please*."

"All right, all right! Don't get your panties in a wad." I cut her a look when she ushers me out the door. "If you're even wearing any, you old hussy."

She whips the dish towel at me and catches me with the corner before she shuts the door in my face.

I laugh all the way to my car and down her driveway as I pull away. It takes about a block for the loneliness to crash over me again.

I'd gone to my mom's hoping I'd be inspired. Empowered, maybe? That I'd be reminded that being alone is different from being lonely. I've always wished for more of her independence, but maybe that's impossible when you find your other half before you've got a fully developed frontal lobe.

Instead, even she has a *man friend*, now, on top of all her own things.

Meanwhile, I've got my piece of the bakery she began herself, and all my friends are my ex-husband's family. My hobbies include riding the horse that I still share with him and avoiding thinking about him.

And I can't even keep a pen pal.

CHAPTER 9

WREN

My whole life, my mom has always preferred doing Thanksgiving with friends. It was her parents' favorite holiday, she'd always told me, and it is the one holiday that made her wish she had someone. One of the rare instances when loneliness would catch up to her. Not Valentine's or Christmas or New Year's. Thanksgiving. She'd say the day felt like a choreographed dance between properly timing all the dishes, spinning through all the sounds of the day, dipping in and out of all the smells and flavors. She claimed that hosting without a partner felt like too much work, and showing up somewhere where everyone belongs to someone else that day felt too sad. Even after I got married, rather than come along with me to the Byrds', she always went over to Martha O'Doyle's and did something more casual. Usually bunco and a potluck of desserts. I've never judged her for it, but this might be the first year that I truly understand it. Ironic that, also this year, I know she's brought her man friend along to her traditional celebration.

At Sage's house, I float from room to room alongside the smells of roasting turkey and can't shake feeling like an outsider. Indy and Sam are sitting on Sage's couch, huddled together over Indy's phone while she shows him the photo shoot she staged with Gary (a goose) in a hollowed-out pumpkin and a variety of other autumn vignettes. The cat and dog are sharing Sable's plaid bed on the ground. Silas is sprawled out on an overstuffed yellow chair that's been moved into the living room so a dining table could be arranged in the sunroom, and football plays quietly on the television. Silas is also preoccupied with his phone, but when he sees me hovering in the kitchen, he gestures for me to come closer.

"If you had to make an educated guess," he asks me, "does this girl look like she's into mutilated monster romance or, like, hot for the Phantom of the Opera?" He shoves his phone in my face with a dating app open on a pretty girl.

"I don't know. Why?" And then I realize. "You are not *mutilated*, Silas Byrd," I say sternly. He's trying to joke away what happened to him, but I see the flash of real vulnerability there. When he registers my unsmiling expression in the face of his phony-smarmy one, he drops the act.

"I know I'm not." He sighs, deep and bone-weary and uncharacteristically old. "Feels like if I talk about it in the least sensitive way, maybe I'll get less sensitive about it. Just think I need to get out and get laid and, like, rip the bandage off. For lack of a better expression," he says. He's always so achingly open when he feels safe to be.

"Silas, you don't have to do anything that makes you uncomfortable at all," I reply. When this makes him get twitchy, I decide to throw him a bone. "And honestly, Si, you're not gonna have any trouble. People love a scarred hero. You didn't hear this from me, but you could probably use it to your advantage." His eyes light up instantaneously. "With great power comes great responsibility, though, dammit. Use it wisely. Be honest." *Please don't lie and tell women you got those scars saving a litter of puppies or kittens. Have more faith in yourself than that. Have more faith in whoever it is you choose, too.*

Sage and Fisher drift in from upstairs, patting down hair and adjusting clothes before they perform some terrible charade about how they'd been "looking for something together," which everyone dutifully ignores. Their love cloud is so thick it's a miracle they can see anyone else through it.

A timer goes off in the kitchen, and I make my way toward it, just as Ellis bursts in through the sunroom door. He scrapes his boots on the mat and peels off his mist-covered jacket, the scents of petrichor and firewood wafting over and mingling with all the smells of the meal. The sight of him brings the usual pang, but when he looks my way and his mouth hooks into a half-formed smile, I find myself smiling back, reflexively. He stares at me and I at him, and whatever shredded and frayed thread is still between us pulls unbearably tight. *You all belong to each other, with or without me,* I think. *But I want someone to belong to me again, too. I wish it were still you. I hate that I wish it were still you.*

Just as I think he's about to say something, his phone rings from the pocket of his jacket, hanging on a hook that looks like a mushroom growing out of the wall. He scoops it free and steps into the kitchen.

"It's Micah on FaceTime," he says before he answers.

I remember the pie from the oven and spin to retrieve it while Micah's floating head is passed around the room.

"Let me see the desserts," I hear Micah say. "I just gotta lay my eyes on them for a minute."

Sam walks the phone to me, and I smile at Micah's face, sitting with his back up against a headboard in what looks like a cheap hotel room, a carton of Chinese takeout balanced precariously on his chest.

"Walk me through them, Wren. Give it to me good and dirty." He licks his lips.

"You sure? You're only torturing yourself, man," I say with a laugh.

"Yeah, just let me see," he replies.

"All right, well. I made chocolate bourbon pecan," I say with a wince.

"Fuuuucccckkkkkkk," he growls ferociously.

"Sorry, bud. I also did a pear frangipane tart. You know I had to bust out the big guns with the fancy chef here this year," I say.

He makes a sobbing sound, and I turn the camera around to show him. When I bring it back to face me, he's nothing but a flesh-colored blur, his phone pressed into his forehead.

"I gotta go cry in private now," says his muffled voice.

"Okay, bud. We miss you."

He hangs up without a goodbye.

"Poor kid," I say to myself.

A text comes through, and I open it on instinct.

It's a picture of a pretty woman I don't recognize, holding a turkey leg. **I know your grumpy ass is thankful for me**, the message says. I see the name *Kirby* at the top.

Ellis's phone. Not mine.

The synapses in my brain won't fire for a moment. I feel like I'm being held down in canned cranberry, like my heart and head and limbs are all stuck in sludge and can't break free. And once everything does kick over again, it's too fast and with too much force, making me lightheaded. I drop the phone on the counter like it's on fire and try to catch my breath, bile in my throat.

Fisher and Sage start working around me then. Fisher bastes the turkey in the bottom oven, and Sage goes back to chopping celery for stuffing. The dulcet tones of football drift in from the living room, where Silas and Ellis are also making conversation, and Sam and Indy are talking about the PE teacher at school and his refusal to wear shorts with anything longer than a three-inch inseam, all while I'm stuck in one place, coping with the gut punch of reality that is Ellis moving on.

That explains why he invited me to stay the other day at the barn. Why it wasn't *agony* for him to reach out and touch me. How fucking wrong was I to think I was going to get to a place where I wanted this? Where I'd be happy for him? I can't breathe again. Something heavy is sitting on my chest and crushing it down. Down. Down. Down. And what a fucking hypocrite am I? I've slept with other men since the divorce. I haven't tried in earnest to *date*, though. I've barely started to *talk* about dating again. I only caved last week and created an online profile that I made Silas look at for me. I certainly haven't connected to anyone else enough that it would warrant a warm holiday text.

Oh god, she was really cute, too.

"Hey, you good?" Fisher says, touching my elbow.

I shake my head, blinking and clearing my throat with an overly animated smile. "Yeah, sorry. Just zoned out for a second." I force a laugh.

I slip away into the hall bathroom and scrounge for some composure. Turn on the sink and listen to the hiss of the water, then watch my reflection breathe so I know I'm doing it.

I have no right to feel like this. We are split. What did I expect? He's handsome and steadfast and immensely kind, and that's all on the surface. He's even more beneath it. He deserves to be happy. We hurt each other too much. We let our love die. I'm the one who said the words *I want a divorce* first. I'm the one who gave up and admitted that they wanted to leave. Someone else deserves him. To be satisfied by him, protected by him, liked by him. Loved by him.

I just never let myself face it before.

I do my level best for the remainder of the evening, try to maintain conversation and laugh at the appropriate times. Keep my awareness of him as muted as humanly possible.

The placid mask nearly falls away entirely when the desserts start to make the rounds, though. By this time post-gorge, we are all in various spots in the house, whatever place and position allows us to spread out. In years prior, this has made it easy for Ellis not to partake of dessert. It's not as if we're all still seated at the table and he has to outright deny a piece of something in front of my face and make it awkward for anyone else. He just doesn't get up to serve himself some.

When I see him walk back into the living room with a piece of pie on a plate, it might as well be my heart. Later, I know I'll see how illogical this is. I'll remember that it's just a baked good and convince myself that there is no deeper meaning. I'll recognize that I also just had those letters come to an abrupt end and am clearly suffering from a sensitive time.

But . . . the Ellis I knew always dealt in absolutes. We didn't belong to each other anymore and it was painful and messy and we've avoided any avoidable crossover in order to stave off more mess and more pain. Part of that for him meant he never ate my food. Tonight, him casually enjoying something I've made again feels like a confirmation that he really has moved on.

He's not affected anymore. Why would he be?

And why the hell am I?

PART 2

———

Present—Spring

CHAPTER 10

ELLIS

Ever since Silas said it six months ago, I've come to realize how right he was.

My timing *is* shit.

In fact, I realize this has regularly been the case for me throughout my life. I got my teen girlfriend pregnant. Hell, even before that, it'd taken me longer to accept that my feelings for her went beyond friendship, making my timing slower than it should've been. I didn't get to Silas in time to prevent his accident last summer.

Even today, my timing is off. I got to Main Street forty-five minutes earlier than I meant to and have been sitting in my truck, watching the sun burn through the marine layer in short, occasional bursts. Every time it does, it shines on the olive-painted brick of Savvy Bakes and makes it glow a brighter green, like some beacon drawing me in.

Still, after getting this particular shit wrong so many times before with Wren, I can be patient and wait a bit longer, now . . .

And I know what I told Silas that same day he brought these issues to my attention, but from the moment I saw Wren on Thanksgiving, I still found myself needing to try. I took a slice of pie with me and tried to sit near her in the living room after dinner, thinking I'd start up a conversation and that seeing me enjoy something she made would help.

It didn't. She avoided me more than usual and seemed totally put off by my nearness that night. And I tried to let it go, I really did.

I took the winter (my slow work season) and committed myself toward everything I knew I needed to do. Fisher got me a recommendation for a therapist from his, and I started meeting with her. I went to work. I used the gym at work. I fixed the things around the house that needed to be fixed. I helped whenever someone asked for help. I kept tabs on my family as best I could. I made sure Sam applied for the scholarships he was eligible to apply for, and I met with the accountant that manages the college fund Wren and I have for him. We've sacrificed and limited enough of our spending to cover four years of tuition. He'll have to get a job and he'll have to buy his textbooks used, but we should be able to help and supplement him when needed.

It was December when I thought I could use that college account as an excuse to try to talk with her again, but I got too far ahead of myself and swung by her place without calling first. Sam was surprised when he greeted me, and he told me she was out on a date. I didn't sleep that night, then later opted to have that conversation over the phone, where I detected nothing beyond her usual cool manners.

My slow season happens to be Wren's second busiest outside of the summer tourist months, so I found myself making excuses to start going to the bakery throughout December, hoping to see any sort of clue that there was something still there that I could grab onto between us. The first two times I went in, she seemed frazzled and confused when I ordered something at the counter, then slipped off into the back before I could try to make conversation. The third time I went in, she looked downright annoyed to see me.

When she didn't come to Christmas, I started to accept that I was too late and that she didn't want anything to do with me in that way again.

I occasionally heard about her going on more dates, when Sam or Silas let something slip. I kept every reaction in check. Told myself it was punishment for not coming clean about the letters.

Seeing it was different. Starhopper had its grand opening party over New Year's, and when I walked out onto the restaurant deck that night, I spotted her laughing with some guy I didn't recognize, wearing what I assume was his jacket. I immediately turned around and left before I could do something stupid. I'd wasted so much time telling myself we were just being good parents, giving each other the world's most careful distance for our son. Really I was just too coward to fight.

When I admitted all of this to my therapist, she helped me try to see it from a new point of view. She told me how lucky I was to still hold the mother of my son in such high esteem, because it's rarely the case between a divorced couple. She encouraged me to try to find closure, to consider dating myself.

When she suggested that I tell Wren about the letters from fall, I still couldn't. It was hard for me to explain, but it's like . . . like seeing that she had no active interest in reopening something between us made it seem both pointless and wrong that I'd been doing it without her knowing. It was a freak chance that I got her package and her letter, because that's just what life is: a bunch of circumstances that make relationships more difficult, with the odd lucky chance thrown in. I thought I had to learn to be happy for the chances we'd already had.

By the time February came and went, I'd accepted it more. I started to feel gratitude for what we had. I even felt grateful for those letters, even though they reminded me of what I lost. I felt like I might be able to get some real closure now that I was choosing to work toward it.

I found myself genuinely hoping that she'd find love like what we had. Find something better, even.

I still didn't feel like I belonged to myself enough to give anything to someone new, though.

I didn't go to the bakery at all in March. All these things I was working on thinking and feeling were easier when I didn't see her too much.

It was the second official day of spring when Sam called and asked me to meet over at Wren's, saying he had something to show both of us. I wandered into her kitchen after she let me in without so much as a glance spared my way and was opening a cabinet to get a glass for some water, when something caught my eye.

My name, handwritten on a piece of paper. In handwriting that I absolutely recognized.

All that perspective I'd been carefully crafting was gone in an instant.

Probably, a better man would have hesitated to read the rest of it, but I sure as fuck didn't.

And right then and there, I knew there was hope. I've never grabbed on to a feeling so fast or so tight.

So, while my timing is indeed shit, while I've done things in the wrong order too many times before and almost missed my chance again, this time, I'm not going to give up without a fight.

I see Wren flip around the Closed sign in the distance, and that's my cue.

CHAPTER 11

———

WREN

The six weeks after Sam's college acceptance news have gone by in a flurry of activity. Between finalizing his housing arrangements (he is subletting a room since he can't get into the dorms until fall), trial runs for the cake and other desserts for Walter and Martha's upcoming nuptials, and the general influx of business we've had this spring, I've managed to stay distracted and have successfully avoided thinking about Ellis's surprise road trip idea.

For the most part.

When I'm alone in the bakery—my secondary home, really, with how often I'm here—it is normally meditative. Today, I've got a music station playing instrumental renditions of pop hits on, and the door propped open to let in the briny spring breeze. There are no decals on the windows since I got Mom to agree to redo our sign a few years back, so my view is unobstructed across the street and over the park along one of our many cliffs. I used to watch Sage push Sam in a stroller around that trail when he was a baby. And today, he's graduating high school. In under a month, he's moving. Probably forever.

I snap myself out of my nostalgia tailspin and growl to break up the knot forming in my throat. My steps clip-clop over black and white hexagon tiles on my way to shut the door, and I flip around the Closed sign before I head back into the kitchen to finish decorating the sheet cake for Sam's class.

Between tonight and all the other upcoming events where I'll have to see Ellis, I can't avoid acknowledging the trip much longer. Or at minimum, I can't avoid talking about it much longer. I have to call on Sage—something I'm reluctant to do when it comes to anything with Ellis.

It's not that I don't think Sage has the emotional bandwidth to stay objective as both a friend to me and as a sister to Ellis. It's that I *know* she does, but I also know it has to be hard, and I hate putting that pressure on her. I've watched her take on things in the name of other people's feelings time and time again, so I imagine it's a cumbersome load when it comes to the happiness of two people you love. I'm unpracticed when it comes to being on this side of our relationship, though. Being the one who needs something. I much prefer being the one with the advice or the perspective to share.

Silas is another resource, but . . . he's a man and lacks the more nuanced, touchy-feely understanding that Sage has in spades.

At any rate, it doesn't change the fact that I'm at a loss and she's got the burden of being my best friend, so hemming and hawing about it too much longer is pointless. I need to purge some of it out of my head before I see Ellis again tonight.

I slip my phone out of my apron and hit Call before I give myself more time to dwell, tucking it between my shoulder and ear so I can keep my hands busy piping.

"Hey!" chirps her sunshine voice after a few rings.

"Hi. I gotta talk about something uncomfortable, so maybe get comfortable."

"Got it. Sitting down." A rustling noise, followed by a goat bleating in the background. "Ready when you are."

I guess it's fine if the goat bears witness. "Ellis wants us to go on a road trip together after we get Sam set up at Davis," I blurt. "Alone."

Silence.

"Sage?"

"Yeah, I'm here," she says. "I just . . . Did he say why?"

"I haven't asked. He pitched the whole thing in front of Sam, so I didn't want to push the conversation at the time."

"Huh," is all she says.

"Please expand on that," I urge.

"Well. I'm just surprised, is all," she says in a way that makes me picture her shrugging innocently.

"No shit. *And* he's been coming around the shop more." I don't explain that his visits have tapered off in the last few months. Mentioning that the very last time he came in was in February seems like an unnecessary detail. Makes me sound like I've been waiting for him to come back. "He ate my scones."

I finish a decorative line of buttercream just as she finishes exhaling a soft gasp.

"That's. I mean . . . Wren, he won't even eat your baked goods at the holidays."

"He did on Thanksgiving," I correct her.

"What?"

"This past Thanksgiving. He ate a piece of the chocolate bourbon pecan. I tried to make meaningful eye contact with you over it multiple times, but you were preoccupied with eye-boning your pirate lover."

"Well, you didn't bring it up after, either!" she says.

"I decided not to make it a thing after that!" I say defensively. "So he ate dessert at Thanksgiving! Big whoop! It sounded stupid to bring up!"

"Yeah, but . . . the *scones* now? Wren, he won't even eat them when you're not around. He's . . . You think he wants to get you back?"

I will myself to turn to granite and don't let those words get their purchase in me. They're flavored biscuits, for god's sake. "No. He's not asking me out. He's not asking to talk. He's not . . . What's changed?" And then, "No. That wouldn't make any sense. My guess is he's just so—*fine*—that he thinks we can go be friends. Unless . . ." My stomach dips. "Unless you think he's, like, serious with someone and feels the need to break it to me in some elaborate way?"

"By taking you on a trip?" she asks disbelievingly.

All right, valid. Breaking the news slowly over the course of a few days *after* we drop off our son (thus freeing him of his biggest connection to me) seems unlikely. "Well, I don't know! What's changed?" I say again.

"I—I don't know. You know he's a vault when he wants to be, but . . ." She trails off.

"But what?"

"I mean, he *has* been going to therapy? Maybe it's made him realize things."

"He's *what*?!" I yell. I can't hold back the accusation in my voice. Conflicting emotions collide in my chest. An unjustified sense of betrayal, as if I have had any claim over his private life for the last five years. Happiness for him. Hurt and regret that *we* weren't enough to go before. Whenever I brought therapy up in the past, he acted like it was too inconvenient then or like he was personally offended that I didn't think we were competent enough to fix everything ourselves. After a while, I simply didn't want to be the one to push it. I got too tired to push it.

"Honestly, Wren, I'm not even sure I'm supposed to know that," Sage says. "All I know is that he got a recommendation from Fisher and it went from there." She pauses while I stare at the giant cake in front of me, the bold frosting letters that spell out CLASS OF 2025 in mustard yellow and maroon. I adjust the phone again and grab a tray so I can collect the pastries from the front case and bring them over to the gymnasium, too. I need something else to do with my hands, and I might as well not let them go to waste.

"I still don't get it, though," Sage goes on. "I'm not sure why *now*. Have you given him the idea that you wanted to explore things again? *Do* you want to explore things again?"

I halt, pressing against the revolving door with my rear, right as it occurs to me. "The paper," I say, voice hollow. My first journal entry, though I had to go back and actually purchase a journal from Athena's after the fact, even though I have yet to be consistent about writing in it. But that paper on the counter had been folded by someone other than me, the night Sam told us about college.

"Paper? What paper?" Sage says, just as I shove back and rotate out the door and am smacked by the sight of my ex-husband looming beyond the counter.

CHAPTER 12

WREN

The shock sends the phone careening down my chest, and with my hands still clutching the tray, I have to pitch my shoulders forward to catch it . . . right in my cleavage.

The moment stretches painfully. Ellis looks at where it sits, snug in my décolletage, then drags his eyes back up to my face.

"Wren?" comes Sage's voice. "What paper? Why is everything muffled?"

I wince. Somewhere along the journey down my chest, the speakerphone button has been pressed.

"You're in my tits," I say dully, still staring at Ellis. He's got a fresh haircut and shave. My eyes go to the indent on his chin, and his mouth quirks. "Your brother is here," I quickly add.

"Oh . . . *OH*. All right. I'll, uh . . . see you at the ceremony." Thank god she's observant enough to infer that it's not one of the other two brothers. She trills her lips loudly and says, "*Nice motorboating you!*" before she hangs up.

Ellis and I blink at each other. Three feet of counter space and three decades between us.

"May I?" he asks, nodding to where I'm still squeezing the phone.

"All right," I squeak.

He deftly plucks it from my chest and places it on the counter, his jaw ticcing.

"I thought I would come see if you needed help getting everything over to the school," he tells me. His voice is like having my back scratched. That perfect combination of grit and slide, deep enough to feel. I remember when it changed from boy to man. The new, confusing thrill I'd experienced when I heard it for the first time. I remember so many other new discoveries over the years, too. When I turned fifteen and saying his name felt different, all of a sudden. Like it left a taste on my mouth. How I realized I wanted to be so much more than his friend.

"Ellis, we have to talk," I say quietly. I set the tray on the counter and start piling in the pastries. Today, Mom and I made raspberry lemonade blondies and strawberry custard tarts in addition to our regular lineup.

"I did find your paper on the counter," he says abruptly. "If that's what you're going to ask." Our gazes catch and hold. "I do want to help, but I also wanted to talk about it. That's why I'm here. And yes, I did read it. I'm . . . sorry."

I feel my eyebrows crash together. "You don't sound sorry at all."

He struggles to suppress a grin, and I have the sudden urge to mash a poppy seed cupcake in his face. "I *am* sorry that I violated your privacy, but I promise it was an accident," he says more genuinely. "At least, at first it was."

I'm . . . Dammit, I'm embarrassed nonetheless. I don't care if this man's been eight inches deep in me in every conceivable way or that he once was etched onto my heart and soul. Him seeing into my mind, seeing himself still living in there after so long apart, is different.

"It's a journaling exercise," I explain, avoiding his eyes and going back to my task. "It's . . . With Sam heading off to school and everything, new stage of life and all that. It's just something I'm going to do for . . . for closure."

I can't bring myself to look at him, but I feel the shift ripple through the space between us, the notch of tension clicking up.

"But you're not," Ellis rasps. "That means you're not already *closed*. Not entirely." My head whips his way, and I mark something restrained in his eyes. I'm suddenly not breathing well at all.

"Is that—is that a question?" I ask. It comes out like a gasp.

He swallows heavily, and a searing look of longing flashes across his face. It's gone, and he's composed just as quickly, but if I closed my eyes, I'd still see it, outlined in neon against my lids like I stared at something too bright. "Yes, it's a question," he states.

I'm immediately flustered. I think of that kids' movie where emotions are all represented by their own characters, and mine are rioting. They're throwing chairs and falling to the ground wailing, and there's one in the background screaming, "WHAT THE HELL ARE YOU GOING TO SAY!" on a loop.

"Ellis, I've been dating," is what I go with. "Not like one person or something serious, but I've been trying to date and go out, and I've been working on opening myself up to something new." I pick up the tray and turn to flee. "That's the only reason I was starting that letter—*journal* thing."

He comes around the counter in a few ground-eating strides

and follows me to the back kitchen. "But are you over us?" he says urgently. "Seems like if you were, you wouldn't care about writing us down."

"We're divorced," I say helplessly. "We already gave up. And, hold on, haven't *you* been seeing people?"

"No," he says, baffled. "What would make you think that?"

I can feel my pulse in my palms. I can't see a way to sidestep the truth. Whatever, he already saw my stupid paper. This isn't any worse than that. "Last Thanksgiving. I had your phone when Micah called and—and a woman texted you a picture of herself."

His eyebrows go up, and his lip juts out like this is news to him, too. "What was her name?"

I make a face. "I don't remember," I lie. Kirby. Young. Blond. Light brown eyes. A little beauty mark above her lip and enthusiastic about her poultry. Seems like your type. Sent me into an emotional spiral that spun me out so badly it took months for me to see straight, until I attempted to move in another direction. It's been like swimming against a current ever since. And how embarrassing is that? That I've had to try so hard at something that was once as easy as breathing, with him. That I only threw myself into dating in the first place because of him.

He shrugs with a worn-out sigh. "Wren, I haven't been on a date in over two years." When I don't formulate a response, he laughs without humor. "Please, Wren. Just answer me."

"Answer you what?" I say hoarsely.

"Does any part of you think about us still?"

My eyes dart around the kitchen like a cornered animal. I don't know what the fuck to do with this. Five years of having to pirouette around emotional land mines while maintaining polite distance, of having to strike a flawless balance between friendly and unbothered so that I could keep my family and friends even though I could barely handle being near him. He wants to blow it all up in my bakery kitchen in one afternoon. And yet, I watch his hands curl and open inside his pockets like he's holding himself back. "Ellis, I've . . . slept with other people. I've done *everything* to try to move on." My voice breaks traitorously. Every time I think I'm making progress, something pulls me back under.

He's silent for so long that I eventually calm down enough to look at him. When I do, I'm shocked to see him studying me with a gentle look. Not a hint of anger. His smile is soft, like an apology.

"Did you hear me?" I hazard. "I said I had sex with other people." I cannot explain what is possessing me to hammer in this point, but I think I need him to acknowledge that we have been living separate lives. Maybe I want to shock him as much as he's shocking me. Whatever it is, I need to know I haven't been imagining this. Trying to be with other people. Trying to be without *him*. "I just mean that there has been a lot of life in the last five years." I sound like I'm trying to convince myself.

He inhales sharply and steps closer to me. "Wren, you remember when you had me read all those baby books when we were younger?" he asks.

My expression folds. "What? Yes?"

"Well, obviously, a lot of shit went out the window the minute he was born and we started running on adrenaline and instinct, but one thing that I thought was particularly amazing was how, no matter what, your anatomy would forever be changed."

My mouth falls open in indignation, and my cheeks go white hot. *What the fuck?!* "*Gee*, Ellis, what a perfectly flattering reminder that my hips will never bounce back!"

His chuckle warms ten degrees in the face of my ire. "I'm

just saying. My DNA mixed with yours, and it altered your very bones, Byrd." He steps closer still and inhales again, closing his eyes like he's absorbing my scent. When he opens them, his pupils are blown, something raw and open there, too. Something that strips me to my core. "I don't give a fuck who you've slept with or how many times. I don't give a fuck if you have a boyfriend right this minute. We belong to each other in ways no one else ever will." I'm certain he feels my gasp land on his throat. His eyes dip to my mouth and go pained before he takes a step back. "I didn't mean to push this today. I know it's Sam's night and we don't need to do this right now. I'm sorry." He blinks at his feet.

"Just tell me plainly," I say, barely more than a whisper. We were together too long for games, and I need to hear the exact words. "This trip. You . . . It'd be to see if we should give us a chance again?"

His head jerks up, and his gray gaze turns platinum. Three inhales later, he says, "Yes," the sound rough-hewn like he needs a drink. "I want to be up front about my intentions. But I also would like to celebrate something that we did together—together. I'd like to go have fun with you, Byrd. Even if you just want to go as friends." He looks down at his hand as he traces a pattern on the counter surface.

My stomach feels like it's floating behind my ribs. "Ellis, I couldn't promise anything. I—" I search the room like I might find the answer. Instead, I get hung up on the industrial mixer, one of our first major purchases together. The butcher block island he spread me wide on once or twice or maybe a hundred times, taking me apart over and over again until I felt like melted chocolate poured across it. I shut my eyes like I can block out the memories.

"I get it," he says. I can't help but notice it's the same tone he'd use on Bud, back when he was easily skittish. "All I know is that I'm not sure we're through." He looks off to the side with a frustrated huff. "Or at least I'm not sure I ever got closure, either. And then, after the fact, I just got so used to whatever this is we've been doing, separately . . . that I think it got too hard to figure out where the road back was. Or if there was one at all. We're too damn *careful* around each other."

I feel the astonishment on my face. He's just echoed what I haven't been able to articulate, and why I started writing that paper in the first place.

"I wanted to protect Sam, too," I admit. It's so hard, worrying about your worthiness over another human being. Especially knowing you were so young yourself. We were so young. We worked so hard at being great parents. After we failed each other, it became easier to put all my focus on being a good mom than spending any of my limited energy regretting or resenting being an ex-wife. Which meant cutting myself off from him as much as possible. "Being careful around each other. Staying . . . distant. It made it easier to protect Sam."

"That's why I'd like to do this now. Why I think it would be a good time, I guess," he says. "And if at any point you change your mind? We cancel and just come straight home. No matter what, we could make it nine hours in a car together."

"Or if *you* change your mind," I say.

He gives me a sardonic look. "Sure. If I change my mind." He studies his boots before bringing his gaze back to me and continuing. "But if we don't, then I'd like to make a couple of stops on the way back together. Just us. We'd be away. No town, no playacting in front of Sam. No pressure from anyone else. Just you and me." He steps closer. "I think you and I are worth seeing about. Even if all that comes from it is a . . . a happier ending.

Closure." He runs a hand across his mouth like he's missing his facial hair.

"You shaved the mustache," I say a bit dazedly.

He blinks, mildly surprised. "I'll grow it back if you want. I'm growing it back right now as we speak." His face fractures into a smile, and I have to white-knuckle the tray to stop myself from reaching up to poke a finger in that dimple on his chin.

I've always been weak against this side of him. When he's intent on something, he's . . . he's overwhelming. Combine that with some concentrated, affable charm? Done for. Once he's decided something, he's relentless about it. It used to be one of the things I admired most in him.

An idea takes shape again, and this time, it's like a recipe— multiple flavors transforming into one multilayered thing. "What if I wanted to work on my project at the same time? What if I made you go through it with me?" I keep a tight leash on the hope in my voice.

His hands hook into his pockets, and his head cocks to the side. "What project? What do you mean?"

"What if I wanted to go through the journaling thing together? What if . . . what if I wanted to go over us, the parts where we went wrong?" He might be in therapy, but *we* aren't. I need to know if he's trying to pretend the past doesn't exist or if he's going to be willing to share the painful stuff, too. Starting over isn't working, but taking a trip through pretty scenery with nice, romantic plans doesn't seem like the right setup to gauge a potential future, either. Not when you know exactly how unromantic it is to see forever reduced into shit you have to divide up between you. "I'd keep writing things—I don't know what exactly, but whatever pieces come to me, I guess."

"You'd let me read them?" he says.

I wince at that. I think maybe the journaling works because it's for myself or for an unknown entity. I'm not entirely sure. "Probably not that. But writing will still bring up stuff for me, and . . . and I'd ask you how you felt about a lot of things. You'd keep me honest about it all, and we could correct each other if we remember things wrong or differently. Either way, we'd have to *talk*. A lot." I infuse this statement with an appropriate amount of familiarity, reminding him that I know it's not exactly his forte.

"I'd like that," he says simply. Eyes a little wild, like maybe he's restraining himself from being vehement again.

I feel my jaw loosen before I snap it shut. "I wouldn't want to plan any of it, either. You'd have to make all the arrangements." The final few years of our marriage, any time it came to any sort of event outside of our typical day-to-day obligations, I was the one who planned it. Weekend trip? Me. Date night? Me. I bore the mental load of making sure we were on track for so long that the moment I couldn't anymore, we drifted off the map.

"Done." He crosses his arms and curls an eyebrow my way in challenge.

"I'd control the playlist," I say, certain this will elicit some kind of flinch.

"Sounds great," he says plainly.

"I'm gonna want to listen to a bunch of sad folksy shit that makes it feel like we're in our own little indie film. So much acoustic guitar. Maybe even a mandolin," I threaten.

"Perfect."

I've got it. The trump card. "I'm going to bring a list of those prescribed questions along with us. The kind with some title like 'Twenty-Six Questions to Make You Fall Back in Love' or something." I smile triumphantly. He *hated* those kinds of things. Anything that put him on the spot for something he didn't have time to think through carefully or consider long. He'd get nervous and agitated and didn't like conversations that had parameters.

"I've been finding that sometimes prompts can be helpful and fun," he says. "We'd better start loading all this up if you need time to set up?" He gestures at the desserts, but I'm still scrambling.

"We couldn't have sex!" I blurt.

Both of his brows go up. He pivots away, grabbing a box from where he remembers they're stashed, then makes quick work of assembling it before sliding the cake inside. "That's not what this would be about for me," he finally replies, his voice a thick scrape.

He lifts the cake from the metal island and starts toward the door to the back alley where I park, so I move ahead of him and open it. "You're telling me you'd have zero expectations as far as that went? You wouldn't push for any of that on a trip with just you and me?"

His gaze narrows. "I didn't push for it when we were married."

"You know what I mean. I didn't mean *push*, per se." I suck my teeth. "You know what I meant," I repeat.

He stops in the middle of the doorway and looks down his shoulder at me. "I'm not gonna promise I won't give in if *you* push for it."

I scoff from my sinuses. "That won't be an issue. For me." It would be far too distracting to partake in that with him. I know better. He continues past me and waits for me to open up the van before he slides the cake into a designated slot.

"I managed to go almost five years without your baking." This statement is shaded in innuendo. "Don't underestimate my self-control, Wren."

CHAPTER 13

WREN

Ellis helps me finish loading the desserts into my van while I consider everything he's put forth.

My heart feels like it's sprouted brand-new wings—naked ones without feathers—and is being pushed toward the edge of the nest. Ironic, given that I am close to being an empty nester. My budding panic must be obvious because as soon as I shut the final door, I find him giving me a wary look.

"You don't have to answer right this second," he says. "We've got a few weeks."

I let myself look at him. *Really* look at him. I used to keep a mental tally of the laugh lines that'd deepened around his eyes, secretly excited each time a new one would appear. I don't think he's gained anything new over the last few years, and it makes me unbearably sad. He still looks good, though. Painfully so. He's put on some weight again, all his sharp lines strengthened rather than chiseled down. A healthy man in his prime, going gray at the temples.

In my peripheral, I spot Athena from the bookshop walking by, accompanied by her sister, Venus—our town's head librarian. I raise my arm in greeting.

"Hi, ladies," I call out.

"Hey, kids," says Athena, no matter that Ellis and I are in our thirties. "You tell Sam congratulations from us tonight."

"Will do," Ellis says.

"Tell him to come by the library for his gift!" says Venus.

"No problem!" I yell. Our smiles fade the farther they get down the sidewalk, watching them whisper back and forth while they throw glances at us over their shoulders. Ellis and I sigh at the same time, catch it, then laugh.

"You can practically hear the rumor mill start to crank," he says.

"I wouldn't want to get their hopes up, Ellis," I say. "I wouldn't want to get *anyone's* hopes up. No one can know anything more than the fact that we're co-parents taking a detour on the way home to celebrate successfully sending our kid off to college."

"Does that mean you're saying yes?" he asks.

"*Ellis.*"

"I'm kidding." He laughs, putting his hands up in surrender. "I wouldn't want to get anyone's hopes up, either." His eyes link with mine again, and time seems to yawn and settle between us.

"I can't believe we're about to watch him graduate high school," I say in awe.

"I'm so fucking proud of him," he says with a disbelieving chuckle. There's something like *How is this feeling even contained?* in his smile.

"I'm proud of us, too," I say truthfully. "In spite of every-thing."

"So am I," he says, voice hoarse.

After a pause, I try to lighten the mood. "Should we high-five or something?"

"Or something," he replies, like it actually were a multiple-choice question. He scoops me into a hug before I register that it's happening, and I melt and press myself into it automatically.

I'm excruciatingly aware of every place his body fits against mine. The way he always smells a bit like smoke and the same soap he's used since we were younger. Rock-solid thighs beneath his jeans, the firm chest under my cheek that I know is dusted in hair. I arch into the hug, maybe only half an inch . . . because it feels so damn good and he's so damn warm and *dammit*, I'm already grappling with myself. I feel his breath hitch, and mine does, too, but for a different reason entirely. I cannot forget why these hugs lost their power over me or how we fell apart.

We're not the kids who loved each other as friends or the teenagers who were overwhelmed by want. And we're not the bright-eyed optimists who thought we were the exception when it came to young love, who thought *our* love and marriage could conquer all. We're the war-torn adults who loved each other fully and still didn't make it together in the end.

I step back out of his embrace and head toward the bakery's back door.

"I need to get this over there and get changed and all that," I say, stabbing a thumb at the van. I haul my eyes up to his. "I'll see you there."

He nods with a tight smile and walks past me.

"Save me a seat?" I ask quietly. It's an inside joke, one of those very old, tiny traditions made into something bigger over the years, and for a moment, I'm terrified he's forgotten it.

He stops, but doesn't turn to look at me. "I'll save you the best seat in the house, Byrd."

I wait until he's gone to head back inside and change. When I finish the rigamarole of closing up the shop, something on the counter catches my eye.

It's an origami bird, made from one of the flyers for the graduation ceremony, and the recognition sends a clutch of emotion down my throat. Ellis used to leave these in places for me all the time, starting around sixth grade. When we got older and the paper got a bit sturdier, I'd save the more colorful birds he made for me. Even hung some from our porch ceiling outside Sam's nursery window, back before we learned how hard-water air could ruin precious things.

—

After I drop off the desserts at the high school gym, I find the Byrds all in the front row of chairs down on the football field, where I also see that Ellis has saved me a seat between him and Sage. I'm happily shocked when I spot Micah in the front row, too, on the other side of Fisher. The youngest Byrd brother and the tallest at a staggering six foot six. Jet-black hair that is currently cut into a real-life mullet. He sits with his elbows braced on his thighs, spitting sunflower seeds into the grass like it's the middle of the ninth inning. He winces when he pushes up to his feet to give me a hug.

"Ugh, Jesus, *Micah*," I say, lip curling. "You smell like a distillery. Did you seriously come to your nephew's graduation drunk?"

"Unfortunately, no. But I will be remedying that as soon as

we conclude here." He tries for a weak smile. "I was drunk yesterday in California. Sobered up in time to drive here in the same clothes."

"He got released from his contract," says Silas with a grimace. "Did you see his nose ring? Wren, please tell him it looks ridiculous."

"You're coming home with me when we're done, not going out drinking again," Ellis grouses at the back of Micah's head.

"But I don't *want* to stay with Papa Bear," Micah whines to me, jutting out a lip. And now I do notice the tiny silver hoop in his nose.

"You won't fit in my little place." I laugh. "Sam's not gone yet."

"I can't stay with Sage," he groans. "She and the boyfriend made me sick over Christmas with all the tongue kissing and hand-feeding each other." I wouldn't know. I stayed away at Christmas last year.

"Well, you sure as hell can't stay with Silas," says Ellis. And he's right. Silas and Micah turn into the bash brothers when they're together and stir up a world of trouble everywhere they go. Best to keep them apart while one of them is in a crisis, let alone both.

"Can't help you there, bud," I tell Micah.

"He's a grumpy fucker without you around, you know," Micah says to me, low enough that no one else can hear. "I feel like I have to listen to him even though I know, as an adult man, I actually don't. And he never has any treats in the house." He's the only other Byrd sibling with freckles aside from Sage. A spray of them across the bridge of his nose that keeps him perpetually boyish—height, build, and jawline notwithstanding.

"Poor baby." I pat his cheek. "I'll send you home with whoopie pies tomorrow if you stop by."

"I want some!" Silas complains.

"What about me?" Sage chimes in.

I laugh at the three of them, then catch Ellis giving them a fond look, too, and a fissure runs straight through my heart. When his gaze tracks back to mine, it's heavy with a million things. Memories of us all sharing what is now Sage's house. Baby Sam passed around a table while we all ate in a rush and tried to get to wherever we needed to go. Silas throwing a dirty diaper under Micah's bed until it stunk up the entire floor. Kids raising kids and juggling a million things we had no business trying to manage. Those were some of the happiest years of my life.

All of us are safe and *here*, in spite of the shit we've endured.

But . . . the balance we've achieved in this family is safe again, too. The idea that we could harm that in any way by opening up old wounds utterly terrifies me. When Ellis and I got divorced, it felt like we were letting them down almost just as much. I don't know if I could let myself get close to him again only to rip myself away, while still maintaining the boundaries that keep us all comfortable. If we couldn't make it before, why would we this time? What would be different? I suddenly feel like I'm sinking into the grass with the weight of my doubts.

"I'll make you a whoopie pie, sweetheart," Fisher says to Sage.

Micah and Silas both gag, groan, and roll their eyes, just as I hear a mic check behind me. I slip into my seat between Ellis and Sage.

When the music starts a moment later and I see Sam and his classmates all gather by the stage in their awful mustard gowns, I feel winded. My throat stings, emotions tangling in knots. Ellis's quick intake of breath beside me only makes it worse. I am dying to reach over and squeeze his hand, to thread my fingers with his so we might celebrate the best thing we ever did together. When my knuckles accidentally brush up against his, I feel it in every other bodily joint.

Our entire row stands to obnoxiously holler and whistle when Sam is called across the stage early on. I don't dare look at Ellis when we sit back down, afraid of what I'll do.

My mom and Indy meet all of us in the gymnasium for the celebration after, where we take an inordinate number of pictures and eat an inordinate amount of cake. I am careful to maintain a safe distance from Ellis as much as possible for the rest of the evening, but when the kids have all left to continue their celebration down at Founder's Point and it's down to a few remaining adults on cleanup duty, I find him by a garbage bin.

Of course he's one of the last here, too. Perpetually steady and reliable to a fault.

Maybe it's the fear of the unknown that makes up my mind, since we faced the reality of Sam leaving the nest today . . . but maybe it's that thread of hope again. Maybe it's both. Whatever it is, my feet carry me his way. I make it to him in a blink, and before I lose my nerve, I quietly tell him, "Okay. Pitch it to me. How many days, what's the exact objective, et cetera?"

Standing before me with a full garbage bag in each of his hands, it feels like he's taking a moment to drink me in before he says, "One week. And I just want to celebrate with you, Wren. It's your birthday, it's a big change in our lives, and I . . ." He shrugs. "I fucking miss you."

I miss you, too sounds glib. *You have been missing from me* is more accurate. *There's a void where you lived in me.*

"And as far as objectives go, I was honest about mine," he goes on. "One week to see if we want to, I don't know, I guess date again?" His mouth turns down like saying that tasted bad. "Be together again," he amends. "But even if you decide you don't—"

"Or if you decide *you* don't," I say again, repeating myself from earlier.

He shifts restlessly. "Even if either of us decides we don't. I still want you in my life . . . more. More than whatever this has been."

Whatever we've been isn't enough for me, either, no matter how much that scares me to admit. I've never gotten entirely over him, and I have to believe there's a reason for that. Maybe it's because we've always had Sam between us. Who knows if we're really even compatible anymore? If we'd even want to be friends without the ties binding us? This trip could be closure for me, too.

"Okay," I say. "Plan it."

His eyes flare with muted triumph before he nods. The surge of excitement I feel in response to that look is unnerving, and I practically speed walk away.

And when I get home to a dark and empty house that night, my head and heart and stomach too full of way too many things, I figure I'll try to relieve a bit of one of them and sit down to write, this time reaching for the journal I bought from Athena's.

The first compliment I ever received from Ellis was in third grade when he told me my eyes reminded him of a cow's. His compliments would not go on to become smoother or more flowery over the years, but that was what I liked about them. Ellis's goodness was raw. Unpracticed and somehow totally exacting. Even when he proposed, he hadn't made an elaborate plan. He'd just gotten home from working on a fire for three days and came into our room, where I was taking an afternoon nap with four-year-old Sam. He sat on the bed and skimmed his thumb along my cheek until I woke up to his soft smile.

"Marry me," he whispered, his eyes bright with unshed tears.

Still, sometimes I wished for a little more romance, and when I tried to coax it out of Ellis, he did his best. He usually found an alternate route of his own. Something unexpected and just as effective in the end.

When it came to us getting married, we knew our families couldn't afford a wedding, but I still wanted us to write our own vows for the courthouse.

"I can't do that," Ellis had said, frustrated. "I'm sorry. I won't get the right words out, and I can't put everything I feel into some paragraphs that way. I don't know what to say." He gave me a broken look. "All I know is that if I found out heaven was real and got there first? I'd hang back in the waiting room and save you a seat."

CHAPTER 14

___

WREN

Time speeds the same way it always does when there's a deadline or an event approaching. The week between graduation and the Martha-Walter wedding gets bogged down by busyness until the day itself is upon us all.

Having Micah in town has been a boon, though. Sage and I have taken turns keeping him occupied with helping us set up for the wedding at Starhopper the last few days. Watching a gargantuan former professional baseball player petulantly cut sprigs of baby's breath and weave it into a garland is almost worth the dent he already put in my dessert table.

Sage comes to stand beside me in the restaurant's dining space, and together, we watch him pick up a rose, give it a long sniff with his eyes closed, then scowl at it before he shoves it into a centerpiece.

"You think he's doing all right?" asks Sage.

Micah came by my house last week with a bag full of his

baseball gear and asked me to lock it away in my safe. *"I can't look at it anymore,"* he'd declared miserably, nodding toward the bag. *"I already know all of Ellis's hiding places, so I can't have him keep it away from me. I'll find it in no time if all of it stays."*

"Yeah, he'll be all right," I tell Sage. "Just needs to find a new thing to love, I imagine. Hard to see a new path when you've only gone the same way for forever, you know. Give him time." Hopefully, he can look at baseball and remember the good it brought him one day. "How are you?" I ask her. The space around us is stunning, largely because of all the floral designs. I smile at the room and then at Sage and her glowing happiness. "You look beautiful, friend."

"Thank you. So do you. Bea was doing Martha's and Silas's hair and offered to spiff up mine, too," she tells me.

"Silas needed his hair done? Seems excessive." I laugh. I heard that he and Ellis would be walking Martha down the aisle, but still.

"Think he just likes having Bea fuss over him," she says. "How are *you*, though? How'd the talk go with you and Ellis?"

I'm momentarily jarred by being on this side of our dynamic again. And by the excited gleam in her eye. I don't want to crush her hopes, but I'd rather subdue them now than let them build, only to make a bigger mess later if things don't go well.

"It was good," I say. "We just want to try to be better friends, I think. We're both in a good place and want to be friends again."

"Oh!" she says, her smile wobbling. "Oh, good." She does a double take in Micah's direction when she spots him wandering too close to the dessert table again.

"All right, back to work!" She claps at him and shoos him off, then heads toward her ladder, scooping up a bouquet on her way.

I finish reassembling the desserts, sticking spare greenery in the places where Micah pilfered treats before I slip off to the observatory tower and find my seat for the ceremony.

Sam sidles in soon after, closely followed by Indy, Fisher, and Sage . . . the remaining guests not far behind. Butts fill in the chairs, and before we know it, the music begins.

When Silas and Ellis walk in with Martha between them, I draw in a breath that burns. The last time I saw Ellis in a suit was at our senior homecoming, and the sight of him in one now makes me feel like I swallowed a sword. The strong and broad angles of him that fill it out perfectly, the soft smile lifting across his rugged face. His eyes find mine immediately, like they always do, and I can't stop myself from staring back this time.

Hope is cruel in its persistence. It's a tease. I know that we chose to let each other go before and how devastating it was. The kind of pain no one would willingly risk twice. And yet knowing he wants to see if we should give it a shot again is continuously sending an electric current of hope right to my heart.

The vows force me to remember, though. Romantic atmospheres are dangerous. These scenarios no doubt have an influence over how we feel. I don't need us to be encased in some hazy romance bubble to see if we could work again, knowing that's not what we'd come back to.

I'm not sure how many glasses of champagne it takes me to work up the nerve, but an hour into the reception, I'm feeling bold and march up to where Venus has dragged Ellis onto the dance floor for a slow song. One dance can't hurt.

"Can I cut in?" I ask. Venus's entire expression breaks wide in shocked delight, while Ellis's mouth parts in surprise. Shit, I looked at his mouth again.

"Oh! Yes! Of course, my dear. Here you are, yes." She places my hand on my ex-husband's shoulder and one of his on my waist like we forgot how to do this. "I need another one of those lemon cupcakes as it were. Magical as always, Wren."

"Thank you, Venus."

When I eventually bring my eyes up to his, I can barely hear the song over the rushing in my ears.

"You look beautiful," he says bluntly. It sounds like it's causing him pain, which is probably me projecting. It's agony to be touching him and not running my palms everywhere else I'd like, and I realize how much one dance *can* actually hurt. I feel his fingers spread wide on my lower back like he's having the same thought. His eyes trace the bows on each of my straps and the one at my waist.

"You always did like me in green," I reply. Good Lord, why did I say that out loud? What's my big mouth spilling next, unpermitted? *I thought of you when I put it on. Remembered how you loved it when I wore things with ties and how it always made me feel like a gift when you'd unwrap me. Put all my hair up and messy because I know that spot on my neck below my jaw you liked, too. Do you still like my perfume?* Fucking champagne.

"Um, I wanted to talk to you about the trip. I have to know what to pack at least. And we need to figure out a budget."

"It was my idea, Byrd. I'll cover the cost," he says.

"No," I say. "We've got to have even stakes in this." I need to know that we are both equally invested and just as free to walk away. I dart my glance off to the side with a frustrated huff when I get tripped up over his dark lashes, a memory flash of them tickling my skin. "It was—not well thought out on my part. Telling you to make all the plans. I don't think we should go do a bunch of romantic shit and use that as our case study for whether or not we move forward."

He curls our hands around to rest lightly on his pec, the puff of his laugh brushing through my hair. "Shit. Guess I gotta re-think all those wax museum tours," he says. He's smiling again, and he's got those damned lines around his eyes.

"Don't be funny," I say, mouth pulling taut despite myself.

"There's nothing funny about tandem bike riding, Wren," he says solemnly. "Or having chocolate casts made of our naked bodies. I had plans to make us into life-sized Easter bunnies."

"It is genuinely disturbing that you were able to invent that just now. Have you thought about this before? *Don't* answer that. And don't say *naked*." It makes me want to out-joke him and make *him* blush and heat, like another old instinct trying to make a comeback.

It also calls his *naked* body to mind. My cheeks are on fire.

His eyes soften. He swipes his thumb down my wrist. "Your son's the one who keeps telling me to take you to a winery."

"Sam's talked to you about this?!" I ask too loud. "Ellis, I—I don't want him to get any ideas. I—"

"I reminded him we were celebrating him and told him we were just getting used to being friends without him around. I think I was convincing," he says, maddeningly calm. It's disturb-ingly close to the fib I told Sage, an echo of the way we once knew each other's minds.

After searching for any signs that he's stretching the truth, and coming up empty—who knows if I'd recognize them any-more, anyway—I let out a sigh. "What's with Sam and vineyards? He can't even legally drink. How does he know he'll even *like* wine enough to make a career out of it?"

"He's a weird kid." Ellis chuckles. "He's like you." I give him a droll look at this, and he presses on. "Think about it. He likes the science behind it. Using the same stuff with slightly varying methods to make a whole bunch of different things. A lot like baking, really . . . He likes how different environmental factors can affect the taste, too." He snorts. "He read me a whole article about how last summer's California fires will affect grapes for years to come."

I barely suppress rolling my eyes. "*Please.* He thinks it'll get him girls."

He barks out a laugh, his chest shaking under my hand. "You're probably not wrong," he says.

The song fades to an end, and I force myself to step out of his embrace.

"I'll email you," he says.

"What?"

"I'll email you a loose outline of an itinerary and you can write back anything you want changed or if something doesn't work. And as far as the rest of the trip details . . . I promise I'll keep it . . . unconventional. We won't go to any of the major, well-known places. No national parks."

I give him a puzzled look. "Have you *ever* emailed me before?"

He frowns, hands bracketing his hips. "I'm sure I've had to before for something?"

"I literally cannot think of a single time you sent me an email. Maybe you forwarded things before when I needed to print them out and stuff, but . . ."

He drops his chin to his chest, then looks up his brow at me. "Guess we've got a few firsts left in us."

———

I let Sam drive me home later, still too bubbly from the drinks to drive myself. My house is less than two miles away, anyway, so I'll walk to grab my car in the morning if I have to. When I get undressed, I see the edge of something poking out of my jacket pocket. I groan, disastrously warm when I pull it out and see an origami bird made from one of the wedding programs. He's approaching full Ellis on me.

And after I've completed a too-long bedtime routine and spoken an incantation over the two ibuprofen I take to ward off tomorrow's hangover (there is no predicting it after age thirty), I decide to give my phone one last look for the day. When I refresh my inbox, I'm fizzy all over again.

From: ellis.byrd@gmail.com
To: wrenbyrdbakes@gmail.com
Subject: (Completely Unromantic)((and very generalized)) Itinerary for the Byrds

Day 1: 9-hour drive down to Davis. Unpacking Sam. (Trying not to think about this one too hard yet. Fuck, I'm already crying??) Drive over to Santa Cruz after (2.5 hours).

{2 Days, 3 nights at the Dream Inn (separate hotel rooms)}

-I have almost no plans for the first day that we're here. I'm sure after being in the car so much the day before we'll just want to relax. We could go to the theme park next door or hang out at the beach. Day 3 of the trip (Day 2 in Santa Cruz), I thought we could go to the Monterey Bay Aquarium. You mentioned it once, like, a decade ago when we talked about doing a road trip down to Disneyland. (I'm sorry we never ended up doing that, by the way.)

Will make sure any dinner reservations are unromantic options only (will search for liver and onions, specifically)

Day 4: Drive up the coast to Montetesta Ranch & Vineyards in Gualala (3.5 hours).

1 night (separate cottages)

-Activities here: Sam's choice. He made the plans here for
your birthday, so you'll have to take it up with him. Have a
hunch it'll involve grapes.

Day 5: Drive up to McArthur-Burney, CA (5.5 hours' drive
time).

2 nights

Day 6: Hike? I'm fine just relaxing and enjoying the campground scenery.

Day 7: Drive home to Spunes.

Activities to ensure unromance: First, all the drive time. I
know you do your best contemplating in a car, so we won't
need to be chatty. You can ride down with Sam if you think
that'd be best. Otherwise, I'm looking forward to your
unromantic playlists. Do you still listen to the *New Moon*
soundtrack once a week??

I also know you don't like hotels because you don't think it's
natural to sleep anywhere without a kitchen close by. Unfortunately, our son had to go and be great and got himself
into college and now that we have to foot that bill, renting
villas throughout our stay is out of budget. Fortunately,

everywhere we stay is lacking a kitchen, so I've already put us in a good romance deficit as far as that's concerned.

And, the most unromantic thing of all: Camping.* With separate tents. Ending the trip with camping seems pretty unromantic! (Emphasis on the no kitchens!)

*Disclaimer: The place in McArthur was recommended by Fisher, so I actually can't adequately speak to the romance of it.

The very first thing I do is smile like an idiot into the glowing light of my phone. This playful side of Ellis is rare and special, and I feel a dizzying thrill over him taking charge of a plan like this. I *missed* this. The seamless way he could manage something while giving me just as much control.

I have got to stop and get a grip. It's the champagne making my stomach flutter . . .

The second thing I do is click on all the links at the bottom of the email. The Santa Cruz hotel is quirky, elegant, and midcentury modern. It's also right on the beach. *Dammit, Ellis.*

The second takes me to the ranch's website, where I see that the term *cottage* has been applied generously. They are more like sheds that have been renovated, with tiny covered porches and corrugated tin roofs. They sit lined up in tidy rows across from swooping hills of grapevines. The rooms themselves are pretty simple, but the grounds are gorgeous. Gardens and terraces and even a quaint pond. The main manor is a giant white stucco façade that looks like it was plucked straight from the Mediterranean countryside. Terra-cotta tiles on the roof, all of it tucked lovingly around a courtyard decorated with string lights.

I'm dubious about the unromance of it all, but I guess ending the trip on camping should keep things grounded . . .

The final camping destination is even worse somehow. It's *glamping* in every sense of the word. The white canvas tents have wood-burning stoves and puffy cloud beds. There's a trail that runs through the forest up to the camp store and the cliffside restaurant, which are—*yep*—both fancy as hell.

I'm stabbing the Call button on his name before I give myself time to lose steam.

"Hello?" comes his sleepy, grit-filled greeting. At the sound of that gruff, hushed tone, a riptide of memory yanks me under. Under *him*, in that very bed he's lying in right now, my hands holding on to the spindles of our old brass frame above me. Him on his knees between my legs, the deep drag and thrust of him inside me and the feel of his grip on my hips.

"You can be loud, baby, it's just you and me."

I hang up the phone. I am never touching champagne again.

He calls me back.

"Hello?" I choke out.

"Uh, yeah? Did you call me?"

I consider lying. Fuck it. "Every single one of these places is romantic as hell, Ellis."

His sigh makes the hair on the back of my neck stand up, like static electricity through the phone. "I can make anywhere feel as unromantic as you want, Wren. I'm not taking you on a helicopter ride through a waterfall or some shit." He laughs softly. "Might see if you wanna hike to one." My growl makes him laugh harder. "It's your birthday. I'm not going to spend it in a pop-up Coleman down on Founder's Point."

My heart lurches. "I *liked* that birthday," I say weakly. I liked that he'd planned it.

He's quiet for a moment too long. "Yeah, well, we couldn't afford anything else back then, I guess. But I meant it when I said I'd cover it now."

"It's not that. It's . . ." God, *what* is it? He's planned something. He's put in an effort. What am I afraid of? How badly I want it to work? "I'm just trying to stay as clearheaded as possible about this." I recognize the irony of making this statement through the buzz still sparkling in my brain.

He's quiet again for a beat. "I know. I want that, too, but . . . I really don't think the background is going to affect the rest of the picture. It's you and me, and we'll make the rules as we go along. I promise not to back down from going through the hard shit."

After a protracted pause filled with nothing but soft breathing, I say, "Okay."

When we get off the phone, I email him back.

Yes, I do. "Rosyln" is the song of my generation.

CHAPTER 15

WREN

I thought I would be okay when this day came. I truly always thought that I'd get a bit misty-eyed but would be able to give my son a brisk hug, a pat on the back, and smile as he went. I'd be happy for him and proud of the job we did.

I was sorely underprepared for the emotions that have only built over the last nine hours.

I've been to our old house only a handful of times over the years, so when I coasted up Ellis's driveway just after sunrise—with its fresh gravel and the same old honeysuckle vines growing across the pergola over the garage—I wasn't fortified enough to stop the longing that tore through me, imagining coming home again. I snuffed it out as quickly as I could and finished loading Sam's things. I could feel Ellis's eyes boring into me, but I was too fraught to give him more than a brief, tight nod-and-smile back.

The room Sam's subletting in California is a glorified dorm, but he couldn't care less, and at least it cut back on everything he needed to bring, which made the loading-up process fairly quick. The misty spray from the summer storm hovering over Spunes helped to keep everyone else on track, I think.

Micah was there already, since he's been staying with Ellis. I caught him trying to slip Sam one of his old driver's licenses to use as a fake ID and swiped it from him. When Silas and Sage showed up together with no one else in their car, Sam's expression fell a fraction.

"Sorry, Sam," Sage had said. "Indy's not great at goodbyes, still."

"It's okay," he said too quickly. He shook his head and sent water droplets scattering. "She sent me a nice message and stuff. I get it."

Silas kept his sunglasses on despite the rain and the limited daylight, jaw working and mouth quivering as he sniffled. "In the words of the great Dolly Parton," he'd said ominously, voice choked with emotion, "treat every day like it's raining, and always wear your rubbers."

The rest of us groaned, but Sam laughed before wrapping him into a hug. "Thanks, Uncle."

Silas then openly sobbed, and we all said our goodbyes. I had the bleak, terrifying thought that it could be a goodbye in more ways than one. Maybe Ellis and I will come back and be worse off. Maybe I won't be able to be near any of these people without feeling him and I won't be strong enough to stand it ever the same.

But maybe we'll be something new and better. Friends? More?

Hope, hope, hope. Hope is my Tell-Tale Heart, thumping away no matter how hard I try to silence her.

As we reached the town border, my first set of tears fell. A small crowd had gathered around our infamous welcome sign—the one that Sage petitioned when she was barely older than Sam to include the "Not to be confused with Forks" phrase. Beneath their ponchos and umbrellas and behind waterlogged posters decorated in various farewells, I recognized Walter and Martha, Venus and Athena, even Bea Marshall, plus some kids from Sam's class. Fisher must've taken a break from Starhopper because I saw him raising a hand, too. Someone at the very back of the crowd didn't wave at all, which was the only reason she caught my eye, despite trying to be discreet. She was suspiciously Indy-shaped, but I couldn't tell who it was for certain through the rain and glaring sun.

Bright and rainy, like Spunes itself was crying happy tears to watch our boy go.

Since then, Sam spent half the drive with me, answering the full battery of questions I could not stop myself from firing at him, before I started repeating myself and his patience began to slip around the four-hour mark, which is when he transferred over to Ellis's truck to "split time evenly" between the two of us.

I couldn't help it, though. It's as if time sped up on us somewhere, and it's all happening too quickly. Time does that, I suppose. When you spend so much of it looking forward to the next thing, it can easily slip out from under you.

I want to ask Sam if he ever felt that from us. Did he start crawling, and did I immediately say something about him walking? Did I wish away all his phases? Does he want to turn around and come back home and wait a few years before starting an entire adult life in another state? I—oh god, when did this happen? I'm tempted to make a fourth pit stop just to stall again.

I recognize all these feelings and, more importantly, the lack of rationality behind them, so I keep them suppressed as much as I can to spare Sam (and myself) the embarrassment. I wish I could look to Ellis and see how he's feeling, but as soon as I spot him emerging from his truck when we both park in the apartment lot, I'm . . . I'm actually so much worse. He's got sunglasses on, and I can see his jaw working from a distance. He's struggling, too.

We've spent more than half our lives being Sam's Mom and Sam's Dad. Who the hell are we meant to be beyond this? Are we going to find out side by side, the way we came into these roles? The only thing I know for sure is that we can't be expected to keep it together and that I'm deeply grateful he's fraying at the seams, too.

We slip into a rhythm, carrying Sam's things back and forth from the truck into his too-small room. All three of us are quiet and pensive as we work, until it's just me clutching a singular desk lamp so tight my nails dig half-moons into my palm. My brain is genuinely looking for an excuse to take Sam right back out of here.

"Sam, do you even fit in that bunk bed?!" I ask. My voice sounds like a slow-leaking balloon.

"Don't have much of a choice, do I?" he says cheerfully. "Who knows if I'll even sleep here most nights."

The balloon fills back up just as Ellis's chin falls to his chest with a sigh. "Not the time for jokes, son."

The first pealing cry breaks free from me, and both men look like they don't know what to do with their hands.

"I'm—sorry!" I sob. There's no reeling it back now, I let the tears flow freely.

Sam wraps his coltish limbs around me and pats me gingerly on the back. Oh god, he's a grown man. What if he never even lives with us again? I wasn't adequately prepared for this at all. I probably missed so much. There are so many things we still need to teach him.

I don't realize I've said this out loud until I'm being passed into Ellis's arms. "He'll learn them. We did good. *You* did so good, baby," he murmurs into my temple. My sobs settle into a sniveling whimper, but no less embarrassing for any of us. "He's got all the right tools to make the right choices. He's got everything he needs. He knows he can ask us for anything. Talk to us about anything. Right?" Ellis asks him over my head.

"Yeah," says Sam. The catch in his voice turns the knot in my throat to cement. I wrestle with my hysterics and step out of Ellis's warm arms, wiping at tears.

I pull out my phone-wallet and try to read cards through watery eyes, slipping a few from their pockets and passing them Sam's way.

"Here," I say, clearing my throat. "Here are your insurance cards. You have four months to find a dentist and get your biannual cleaning done. I—" Oh, *Jesus*, the crying is starting anew. "Don't let your perfect teeth rot!" I wail. "We spent a lot of money on braces, and . . . and . . . dental care is m-more important than anyone realizes. I love you and I'm proud of you." And with that, I give him one more squeeze before I stomp down the hall, tearing myself away.

To my deep disappointment, it is nothing like the first time I dropped him off at preschool, when I had to peel his small body off mine and pass him to his teacher. When I heard him crying out for me all the way to my car, silent tears running in rivulets down my cheeks. It's not like the time Ellis and I dropped him off for his first day of middle school, either, back when Sam had been at his most awkward and Ellis and I had been at our very worst. Sam clearly found our lingering mortifying, but when he tried to shoo us away with an urgent "GO!" his voice had broken like sneakers on a gym floor. Ellis and I couldn't help but laugh when he walked away. It'd been one of the last times we'd laughed together when we were married, I think.

Instead, I clap a palm over my own mouth to cry into when I exit the building and power walk to Ellis's truck. I'm stupidly grateful when I get to it and see that he's had the forethought to leave it unlocked.

I hope Ellis is keeping it together better than I am, hope he's having a refresher conversation with him about staying safe. About drinking and sex and coming home anytime he needs to. How we will love him no matter what and welcome him home with open arms even if he wants to change course. God, what if Sam's actually nervous or scared and I just tore off in a storm of my own feelings and left him stranded? Did I just make this all about me? Shit.

Ellis emerges from the apartment building, pausing outside the glass doors for a moment with his big hands bracketing his hips before he brings them back up, drags both palms down his face, and marches for the truck.

The closer he gets, the more aware I become, too. I realize I haven't been inside this truck . . . ever. He bought it a year and a half ago or so, when Silas told me his old one bit the dust. Still, it smells like him in an overwhelming way. Something that kicks up an old, full-body response. I'm a Heinz 57 bottle of emotion, upside down and shaken, waiting for the inevitable plop.

A fresh wave of his scent hits me tenfold when Ellis opens his door and slides into the driver's side. He gives me a wavering look from behind his sunglasses, and my chin wobbles anew.

"I'm not doing great at all," he says, his voice a husk of itself.

The admission is so plain, so unlike his normal, solid-to-the-point-of-reticence demeanor, that I immediately devolve into a fit of cry-cackling.

His laugh joins mine, and through my tears, I see him wipe at his own.

"Fuck, how is this happening already?" he asks with an airy laugh. "I just watched them cut him out of you. He *just* learned to walk."

"I just taught him to pee in a toilet using Cheerios for target practice," I say.

"I just had a talk with him about long showers and body odor."

"You taught him to drive yesterday!"

His expression turns apologetic. "I just ran into him buying condoms over in Yoos Bay because he was too scared to get caught around Spunes."

I gasp. "You're kidding! When?"

He shakes his head. "Like two years ago."

I groan and wince. I knew it was probably happening, but this revelation only confirms that everything has gone by in a blink without me noticing it.

Ellis and I fall quiet after that. Like we tossed all those memories up in the air, bending and twisting time between us until it's left us dizzy and disoriented.

"You up for another two-and-a-half-hour stretch?" he gently asks. "Unless you want me to find us somewhere here to stay?"

The gravity of what we're about to embark on settles over me. "If you're up for driving, I'm fine. I worry that staying too close will make me want to come snatch him back," I say with a tired laugh. "But . . . can we just drive? I'm not ready to talk. Yet." No matter how long it's been, the foolish chemicals in my body are predisposed to feel safe with this man, and all I'd like to do now is sleep.

He looks relieved. "Yeah. Of course," he says. His smile flickers shyly, and I remind myself that even though this trip was his idea, he's likely nervous, too. "You want to sync your music to the speaker?" he asks.

"Sure."

I put on one of my favorite calm café stations full of acoustic covers and deconstructed beats. The music and the summer sunset shine through my window and work their magic over me quickly. I relax into the leather seat, eyelids heavy.

"Where we headed first, again?" I ask, the words coming out in a slow drawl as I rock closer to sleep.

"I thought we'd go to the beach."

CHAPTER 16

———

WREN

It's past dark when Ellis rouses me in the parking lot of the Dream Inn in Santa Cruz. I'm too groggy to feel much beyond the allure of getting into a bed, so I climb down from the truck on wooden limbs and don't fight Ellis when he slings two of my three bags over his shoulders, leaving me with one rolling suitcase to trawl along at my heels.

We check into our separate, adjacent rooms, then spend the short elevator ride up to the fourth floor in silence.

"Should we call Sam and let him know we made it to our hotel?" I ask when we hit our floor.

"I already texted him," he replies.

"Oh, okay." Of course he did. "Thank you."

A wall of fear shoots up before me again. Without Sam between us, what do we discuss? Where do we start? Maybe Sam really was the link, and now we're doomed to these silent blank spaces. Maybe this trip will be a waste.

Maybe we're just exhausted and drained from a long, emotional day. We're here, and it's too late for me to back out now. I need to put my ass to bed.

I awkwardly work my key into the slot, then shove my suitcase inside even more clumsily before I turn to take my other bags from Ellis. He steps past me into my room instead, carefully placing them on the floor. I hover against the door, not trusting myself to let it shut us in.

The sight of him silhouetted in the moonlight pouring through the window behind him makes my head go empty for a moment. *Him* . . . next to a bed, in a blue-lit room. I could stack a thousand other memories next to it that look so similar from a distance.

"Thanks," I whisper, keeping my eyes glued to the bags.

He hesitates when he reaches me, and I am instantly cognizant of how narrow this opening is. With only inches between us, I can make out the shape of his firm pecs, his nipples beneath his plain navy T-shirt. The smell of sweet mint gum when he blows out a quick breath. My lagging brain makes the mistake of fixating on his mouth. The mustache he grew back with the heavy five-o'clock shadow across his chin. Goose bumps scrub up my arms, and my nipples cinch when I imagine how that stubble would feel against me.

"Good night," he rasps. "See you in the morning."

"Night," I mutter softly, closing myself in.

———

I sleep in restless fits. Probably because of the car nap.

More likely because of the frenetic buzzing in my veins, knowing he's just on the other side of the wall, only a few feet away. It's night one of us alone, and the devil on my shoulder is already chirping about things that should not be anywhere near the forefront of my mind. Like whether or not hooking up with my ex-husband might be an essential part of this journey rather than a diversion, which, in and of itself, is a very diverting line of thought.

By the time morning streaks in through the open blinds, I fully regret that we've avoided being alone together so much over the last few years. I should have desensitized myself to him and the maelstrom of emotion he stirs up in me. Instead, it's as fresh and bright as the neon sunrise sparkling across the waves right outside my window and just as hard to look at directly.

I let out a quiet groan when I see the time on the alarm clock. Only 6:30 A.M. I'm still on bakery hours, I guess.

It's too early to text Ellis and find out what his plan is for the day, so rather than give my mind time to wake up and overcrowd itself again, I decide to write. The first thing that comes to me is another time in our lives that felt like a new, if slightly awkward, beginning.

It wasn't until we were in seventh grade that I fully realized that the kid I'd always known as my buddy Ellis was, in fact, very much a <u>boy</u>. I'd always known we were different, of course, but not in the fundamental way that it hit me that year. With my mom running a bakery, my hours had to adapt, too. This meant she would usually drop me off with the Byrd family on her way into work, where I'd wait until it was time to go to school.

Ellis always came downstairs a little after I got there. He'd turn on some cartoons and pour some cereal for himself or for us both if I hadn't eaten yet. We'd sit together quietly until we were fully awake, until the entire Byrd house was up and alive with noise.

The first day of school that year, I was especially anxious to see him. I'd barely spent any time with him over the summer. That previous year, his mom had passed away, and it seemed like an imposition to go over whenever I felt like it, like I would have during summers before, or to ask him to meet me. Up until then, the Byrd house had always been somewhere it was safe to be loud. There was always someone bickering or laughing or some kind of ruckus. Compared to being an only child in my softly bustling (often lonely) home, the Byrds had felt like a perpetual recess.

But... since Ellis's mom died, their house felt too quiet, like they were all afraid to wake the monsters of their grief. Ellis seemed to take it on more than the rest of the Byrds. He'd always been a little set apart from his siblings, I thought, despite the fact that their age differences weren't huge.

That first day of seventh grade, I walked into the Byrds' home and found Ellis already awake in the kitchen, assembling a small line of lunches on the counter.

I'd been downright gobsmacked by the sight of him. He had to have grown six inches since I'd seen him last. And when he gave me a small smile, nodding at their kitchen table and saying, "I'm gonna make pancakes," that day, I noticed a new layer in the tone of his voice, like a deeper one was caught somewhere beneath it.

My phone suddenly buzzes on the desk with a text from Ellis. **Hey. I'm sure you're awake already, but take your time either way. Thought we could walk to a coffee shop across the street for breakfast and check out the beach today, whenever you're ready. Maybe go to the boardwalk if you're interested?**

His openness continues to be alarming to me, and I don't know what to make of it.

Another text comes through. **I made a reservation for dinner tomorrow, but I figured it'd be ok if I only made loose plans for the rest of today.**

Like he's nervous about not having a more defined itinerary all of a sudden?

That sounds good, I reply back, after I delete and retype *that* five times, debating if it sounds too eager. **How about we go at 8?**

He hearts the message and then changes it to a thumbs-up, which makes a laugh burst out of me. At least we're both being clumsy about all this.

8 is good. I'll save you a seat in the lobby, comes his reply.

I hop in the shower and get ready for the day, butterflies and anxiety at war in my stomach. I can't think of a nonawkward way to incorporate my journaling journey into a productive conversation, no matter how I mentally rehearse it. Putting thoughts into written text is different, like the distance from my brain to my hand allows time for it to come out the way I want it. The distance between my mind and my mouth is too short.

Either way, it's a twisted joke that I find the idea of going through the past with the man I shared it with more daunting than a first date.

The weather app claims it'll be an idyllic June day here on

the California coast: seventy-eight degrees and sunny. I flip-flop back and forth over whether or not I should text Ellis again to ask if I should wear a swimsuit under my clothes. I make the executive decision to go for it, but it is rapidly becoming clear to me that the continued awkwardness over the logistics of this shit could be the thing that wears on my patience the quickest.

I don't bother trying to do anything with my hair, since the salted ocean breeze will only coil it all back up, anyway. I do slip into my two-piece and study my reflection in the full-length mirror, however. Let myself run my hands over curves. After going through periods when I've felt betrayed by what my body couldn't or wouldn't do, or feeling trapped in it for a while, I make a point to be proud of how I'm shaped. The generous slopes of my hips, and thighs that are equal parts strong and soft. Full chest and flared waist. I can recall the flash of anger I used to feel at this reflection for a time. Felt like these same hips and breasts were mocking me, somehow—an abundance that was going to waste. This body made me a mother at seventeen before I was ready, and I worked hard to catch up. But then when I *was* ready and even desperate to do it again, it wouldn't cooperate. I couldn't understand how I could be living in this body, *present* inside of it, and still not be fully in control. I could ask it to be on its feet all day, and it would. Could tell it to squat down a thousand times and to lift and carry a thousand trays of things, and it would. I could feed it and indulge it and strengthen it, and yet it wouldn't do the thing I wanted it to do the most, when I wanted it to.

Time has made it easier to love my body in earnest, though, and I relish that. I've never been dainty a day in my life, and I feel lucky that I can hardly remember those tender years when I probably wanted to be. It's a privilege to feel good in my own skin and to be grateful for what my body is capable of, as well as what it's already carried me through. It serves me and no one else. I proudly own the space I take up, and maybe that's because of the perspective I've gained.

Earned.

The love I have for myself physically and the scars I bear have all been earned.

Maybe that's how I have to start thinking of this trip with Ellis, too. We earned the scars and those tender spots in our stories. They're not things we have to hide or feel embarrassed or awkward about. We deserve to talk about them, no matter how we do that or how we get there. Now we've got the perspective of time on our side, and I bet we can figure it out together.

We've got a week to search for what we lost in ourselves, and for the first time since this whole thing came about, I feel excited to see what we might find.

CHAPTER 17

WREN

Ellis is already in the lobby when I head down there at 7:45, seated in a big armchair with his back to me. I recognize him by the leg he's got splayed out to the side, the masculine kneecap and calf dusted in dark hair.

"Silas," I hear him say in a clipped tone. "It doesn't matter. It has nothing to do with you."

I pull up short, alarm crashing through me. He might not want to believe that this trip has anything to do with our town or the people we love, but it's an inescapable fact that it would have an effect on them, too.

But he, of course, senses my presence, the annoyingly observant man. He pokes his head around the edge of the chair, phone hovering away from his ear. I watch him end the call with a tap of his thumb, then eye him eyeing me from my toes all the way up to my hairline.

"Hey," he says warmly, pushing up from his seat.

I look my fill of him in return and immediately understand the slow perusal he did of me a moment ago. Seeing him in thin shorts and sandals instead of his standard boots and jeans . . . I roll my lips together to trap a smirk. Even at the height of summer, Spunes tends to have a chilly dampness at the edges of its days, with maybe a hot couple of hours when it'd be comfortable to rock some sandals and swimsuits in the afternoons. That particular stretch of the Pacific is way too freezing to casually splash around in, especially when the wind will just sweep the sun's warmth right off your skin.

Look at us here, a couple of townies posing as tourists in another state. It sends a bright feeling soaring through me, like maybe we can relax and play the sunny versions of ourselves here, too.

"Cowabunga, dude," I say with a laugh.

He flicks his sunglasses down from his head with a fingertip and a small chuckle. "Brat," he says sweetly, and I heat up another degree. "Which Barbie would you be, then?" he teases.

I slide my own shades on and scrunch my nose. "*Hungry* Barbie."

His hands slide into his pockets and he inclines his head. "Same."

"You're the hairiest Barbie I've ever met."

"All the better to snuggle up with."

My smile falters. The big, handsome bastard has the pedal down on play, and I should probably keep this on a slower, safer route, but I think I'd rather play back.

"People don't typically snuggle their Barbies," I say.

He holds the door open for me to leave. "Hmm. That's a shame."

We stroll out of the hotel side by side into the shimmering

golden morning, sandals slapping against the pavement. The day is already pleasantly warm, the sun bright and powerful in a cornflower sky.

He leads us across the street to a busy restaurant called Café Co-op. It's covered in open windows, lined with flower boxes spilling over with succulents, the whole place percolating with cheer.

By half past eight, though, the mile-long beach across the street begins filling in with people. I spot a crowd lining up outside of the theme park in the distance, sea lions' dark heads weaving in and out of the waves, and gulls circling the pier.

"Let's take it to go?" Ellis asks when we're near the register and he sees me staring across the way.

We amble up to a bench on the pavement that lines the sand a few minutes later, just as we spot another couple getting off of it. The man beams at Ellis and me, nodding at the coffees and to-go bags in our hands.

"Best lattes in town, right?" he says.

"Uh, first one here, actually, but I'm sure you're right," says Ellis, holding his black coffee up in salute. I swallow a laugh at him trying to match the other man's booming friendliness.

The woman smiles softly and snorts. They're both upsettingly good-looking. Tall, dark-haired, and sun-kissed. The man is about Ellis's height at six foot three or four, but the woman has to be around six foot herself.

"Deacon, let them enjoy their breakfasts," she says patiently to her guy, herding him down the steps toward the beach with a quick swat on his rear. Envy zips through me at that little pat. I miss casual affection so much.

We end up watching the couple drift onto one of the sand volleyball courts and pass a ball back and forth for a few minutes.

When she peels off her cover-up, I see she's sporting the telltale bump of a pregnant belly. I feel Ellis tense where his arm brushes against mine.

"Is it hard, still?" he asks. "To see?"

"To see someone pregnant? No—not anymore, at least," I say honestly. "It's . . . It was always harder seeing the actual kids for me, anyway," I admit. "But none of it is anymore. Is it hard for you?"

I can feel him warring with himself over his answer. "No," he eventually croaks. "But I think I—I think I feel bad that it doesn't feel bad. If that makes sense."

I nod silently. It does make sense now. After the fact and after so many years. He was more than happy with one kid. I was the one who wanted more. Who asked for more from him when I probably should have been grateful for what we had.

We finish our breakfast bagels and watch them play volleyball for a little while longer. More accurately, we watch *him* leap and fall around the sand. She, however, gets visibly more agitated each time he sprints and dives for balls that should've been hers. She eventually snaps at him, chucking the ball at his head in exasperation. Their opponents wait politely while he crawls over to her on his hands and knees. He grasps at her hips and pecks kisses to her belly, clearly begging for forgiveness while she tries to resist. She reluctantly gives in, it seems, smiling and playfully tugging at his curly hair. He climbs to his feet and peppers more kisses to her face until she's giggling and shoving him away.

"He's gotta just let her play." I laugh. "She's obviously capable."

"He's just protective," says Ellis. "He doesn't want her to get hurt."

I don't look at him when I say, "She could get hurt crossing the street. You can't predict that sort of thing."

He hums. "They're young."

A laugh gusts out of me. "I don't think they're that much younger than we are, Ellis." And yet I'd wager they're still somewhere near the beginning of their story, and here we sit, five years past the end of ours.

"Have you thought more about letting me read them?" he asks, clearing his throat.

I frown, trying to pick up whatever conversation thread he's got weaving through his mind. "The . . . My journal?"

He nods, but quickly adds, "Or just talk to me about whatever you're writing?"

I attempt a saucy eyebrow lift. "Nosy much?"

His big arms stretch across the top of the bench, the hair on his forearm tickling the back of my neck. "Very," he says lightly, letting his head roll my way with a shrug. "I think it'd be fun. You letting me read them. Like passing notes back and forth in middle school." And now his voice is lower, teasing. *Flirting.* "I'd like to hear about them either way. I forget how much other life there was, I think. All the adult stuff makes you forget."

My notes in middle school would've been absurd. Would've revealed a mortifying level of unrequited pining, back then. *Wren Salem Byrd Wren Salem Byrd Wren Salem Byrd*, I'd scribble whenever the impulse would strike. Like the emotion itself was too much for my body to contain and had to be funneled out onto a page.

"I'll think about it. Letting you read them, I mean."

At his hopeful smile, I suddenly can't bear to sit still, and I jolt up from the bench. "Let's walk," I announce and start marching down onto the beach. I feel him hesitate behind me a moment before the air shifts and I know he's gotten up. I know he senses my skittishness and is suppressing the impulse to soothe it away.

God, all this *knowing* between us is embarrassing and grating. It's disconcerting how much I *know*, and how little I still understand.

"I started writing, thinking it would help me sort of reveal the ugly truth of things, and instead, I keep remembering a lot of good," I admit. I keep my eyes on my sandals as I kick them off at the foot of the stairs. Watch his giant, pale feet do the same. I'm tempted to rib him about putting some sunscreen on them, but his agreeable hum stops me instead.

"I did that for the first year or two," he says conversationally. "I'd try to think about some of the pettier shit I didn't like and I'd end up missing you instead."

My delight is so outsized by this, by this little kernel of something unknown, that I'm afraid of what my face is doing. I take a bounding step ahead so I can turn and look at him while I walk backward. "What petty shit?" I ask. When his expression turns nervous, I add solemnly, "Speak now or forever hold your peace."

He takes three more steps while he considers his reply, adjusting his pace to mine and watching his feet as he goes.

The sand is so much warmer here. Softer and dryer, too. A mile of burnished gold. It feels gentle on my feet but gives more easily than the stuff back home. Spunes's sand is wet, coarse, and packed cold and hard into the earth. Easier to get traction on, though.

"The mystery showers. The mystery showers used to drive me crazy," he finally says.

"Mystery showers? You had a *name* for them and everything?" I ask, aghast.

He smirks. "Deluge of Dread seemed a little heavy-handed. You'd take, like, forty-five minutes and play 'Silver Springs' on repeat, and I'd have to scramble and try to figure out what I did wrong."

I toss my head back with a laugh. I did have a flair for the dramatic when I wanted to, I guess. "Be fair. Sometimes when I was *really* pissed, I'd play Alanis Morissette."

"Oh, trust me, I remember." His throat bounces with a laugh. "I got pretty good at decoding for a bit. 'Silver Springs' was the bad kind of mad. Alanis meant I got on your nerves somehow. Celine Dion was the real mystery. Sometimes she meant you were happy, other times she meant . . . Well. She indicated that it might benefit me to go get Cheetos Puffs and possibly something with both chocolate and peanut butter."

I don't realize we've stopped until I catch my own reflection in his sunglasses, a dozy grin leaping up my face. "It's all coming back to me now," I say.

"Nice one, Byrd," he says lowly. The look on his face makes me feel like it was funnier than it is. He nudges my foot. "But you see what I mean?"

I turn around and continue walking along at his side, a little closer this time. "I get it," I tell him. The fights weren't the bad part. At least we were trying to communicate then, even if I didn't recognize it for what it was, even if I needed to lean into the power of song to channel my emotions. I let out another small laugh when I picture it, and this is when it hits me.

I miss fighting with him. It was when we stopped fighting that everything went cold.

We make our way down where the bank angles toward the water, then turn to our left and walk in a line toward the park, right at the edge where the tide slides across it. Our shoulders brush occasionally as we amble along, listening to the steady sigh and swish of the waves. My attention divides between everything in front of us and the man on my right, mentally sifting through a little piece of our past with me. After twenty-five yards or so, I hear him grunt a laugh again.

"What?" I have to ask.

"You remember when they tried to add some carnival rides at the festival that one year?" he asks, dipping his head toward the park like it reminded him. "They could only fit two on the lawn lot area."

"And one was the world's saddest excuse for a Ferris wheel." That whole summer had been a bust. "I don't think we went together? I hardly saw you that year." The same summer that turned into the autumn I'd written about earlier, come to think of it. "You'd grown like half a foot, and your voice was changing by the time I saw you again. First day of seventh grade."

"Eighth," he corrects. "I remember you that day, too."

"You do?"

He nods.

"What do you remember?"

He makes a warning sound that stretches until it rolls into a laugh. "You don't want to be inside my head, Wren. It's a pretty primitive place to be, especially when I was fourteen."

"I'm not exactly delivering slam poetry over here, Ellis." I laugh. "Please."

He shrugs innocently in a way that says, *Fine, but don't say I didn't warn you.* "I remember you showed up with new assets." He nods at my chest, and I see the planes of his cheekbones turn pink.

The sight of that flush fascinates me. Ellis has licked and sucked and nuzzled my *assets* more times than I could possibly count. He has greeted them like sentient beings and whispered goofy things into them, held them to his ears like they were whispering back, buried his face between them while I laughed. He's napped on them. He's bitten and left marks. The fact that he could still blush over something so known is a revelation to me.

I feel my smile bloom before it turns wistful, loop my thumbs around the straps of my little beach backpack. "You didn't act like you noticed me in that way one iota, Byrd. Not for a few years still," I say.

"You were too good for me," he says without hesitation. He plucks a seashell from the sand at his feet and flings it out into the water.

My steps stutter, a small sigh punching out of me. This was always an issue. Ellis didn't put me on a pedestal. He put me on a shelf where he had to strain to reach me. Like he thought I'd be harder to break. I stayed there because I couldn't risk him seeing me in pieces, knowing he'd take all the blame.

"I wasn't," I say. "I never was."

His brow folds behind his sunglasses, his mouth set in a hard line before it melts into something softer. A distant storm cloud surrounded by gold. "You were," he says quietly. "You still are." He pivots away.

"Ellis." I wait until he turns back to me again. "If that were true then, what's the difference now?" I ask, spreading my arms wide before I let them fall.

He takes two strides closer, careful, intentional, and steady. So close I have to tip back to look at him. "Now?" he says, and I swear I feel his eyes land on my lips behind his sunglasses, his chest near enough to feel his heat. "Maybe now I'm just too selfish to give a fuck." He lingers, his pulse beating in his neck and his lips slightly parting. *Now* I suddenly think he might kiss me, and everything goes white hot beneath my skin. From the corner of my eye, I spot one of his hands flex at his side, like he's just stopped the impulse to reach for me. *Do it, anyway*, the most reckless part of me thinks. *Take it. Remind me what it's like with us. Should I?*

He blinks first, clearing his throat at the same time that I take a step back, breaking the trance. He takes an additional step to put some distance between us again. Carefully putting me back on my shelf.

"I don't know, Wren," he says, voice rusty. "All I know is that it doesn't feel like we're done with each other. Does it?"

No. No, it doesn't. I glance back at the horizon and shake my head.

"Do you want to go to the park?" he asks. He's still a yard away, hands planted firmly in his pockets.

Being strapped into a ride seems like it might be prudent for us both. I feel like my lips have a heartbeat and absently reach up to trace them. "Yeah. Let's go."

CHAPTER 18

WREN

I think if I knew we were taking some more purposeful steps (figuratively) toward a reconciliation, I might be able to relax and quit overanalyzing or flinching at every feeling that clangs through my brain. As we climb the concrete stairs from the beach and step (literally) into the park, an idea hits me.

"Two things," I blurt before I lose my nerve. I've got to be the one to tip myself off the ledge, I think. "What if we share two bad, or petty, or hard, or annoying things a day while we're here? And then we're free to do what we want with the rest?" I turn to face him, body lifting with glee, like bells are chiming and baby angels are singing hallelujah from the perfect cotton clouds.

I love making deals with myself like this, from the mundane down to the big goals. Bargains that keep me moving toward something I *want*. If I put spinach in my eggs, I can also enjoy the cheese danish. If I get the menu for the week laid out now, I can slug away the entire following day and alternate between the couch and my bed and watch nothing but mindless reality TV.

"Let me get this straight," he says, crossing his arms at his broad chest. "I'm supposed to tell you stuff I did *not* like about you, or things you did that I didn't like, and that is somehow supposed to work toward my ultimate goal of getting you back?"

At this bold, blunt phrasing (and with exquisite timing), something rockets upward in my stomach in synchrony with the plummeting Drop Zone ride to my right. Screaming rings through the air like a background track in a horror flick. "Yes," I say, rattled. "But you already promised you wouldn't shy away from the hard stuff, and look what happened when—"

"Done."

"—you told me about the mystery showers, it ended up being a good thing, and honestly, that's what's already happened whenever I journal." His confirmation doesn't register until I've finished my pitch. I swallow. "Some stuff won't be as . . . harmless."

"Done," he repeats anyway. "I gave you one, now you give one to me," he commands. And I might be a little hypnotized by it because I'm already drawing closer to him.

If I can tell him that I hated the way he used to shuffle his bare feet on the hardwood, I can also let myself touch him and have a blast with him on this trip. If I can tell him how I hated his inability to relax on days off, I can also let myself kiss him. Maybe even . . . No. No, I'm flushing and sweating before that particular thought can fully form. My heart is whirring in my chest like the Tilt-A-Whirl at the other end of the boardwalk.

If I can tell him all the ways he broke my heart by holding back with his, maybe I can have my husband back.

I start with something in between. "I wish you'd . . . uh. I wish you'd maybe been better with compliments." *Ope,* it's harder than I thought with him standing there, handsome and determined in his Spring Break Ken getup. It's pathetic how much it's working for me. His shoulders rise on a deep inhale. "I mean I didn't need you to pen letters dedicated to my hair or worshipping at my feet at all hours, and you definitely *showed* me that you appreciated me, at times," I add. "You were great at showing me you appreciated . . . parts of me . . . physically." Jesus. I feel a bead of sweat drip down the back of my neck. "Sometimes it just would've been nice to be told things more often. I'd like to have known what you saw and what was in your head, more often."

"Byrd, you don't—" He reaches out and circles my wrist to pull me out of someone's path. The movement brings us unbearably close again. "You don't have to qualify it. Telling me what you wanted from me. Tell me so I know."

The warmth is doing something to his scent here, amplifying it like an oven would a treat, and my mouth waters just the same. His salt and smoke surrounds me, a vein of something cool running through it that must cling to him from home. His hand is still looped around my wrist. How many bad things was I supposed to tell him before I could kiss him?

"I hated how you'd skid your feet along the floors," I say huskily. It sounds more like *I'd love to run my tongue along your chest*. I wonder if he can see me staring at his mouth through my glasses. The mouth that's pulling slowly into a crooked grin.

"I just wanted you to know I was coming," Mouth says. "Didn't want to sneak up on you and scare you."

I laugh through my nose. "Oh, I could hear you, all right. Through two doors and up a whole set of stairs I could hear you skittering around." His laughter rumbles through him, and my eyes finally break free, drifting up to his. I feel my smile fade. "It was too quiet when I moved, at first," I tell him. I missed it after all.

His smile turns sad. "I didn't play music at the house for two years after you left."

The dull, constant ache sharpens into a knife-twisting pain. I shut my eyes against the force of it, the image of him alone in the house where we dreamed. No music. Only the sounds of his feet on cold, bare floors.

He tugs gently at my wrist. "Hey, no. Shit. Let's not . . . let's not do that." The *not yet* hangs in the air. "The time's past, Byrd. We're here now. I don't want to waste more of it being something that makes you sad."

My free hand hooks his wrist, enclosing it as much as I can, like I can let him know I'm holding on, too. "I don't want to be something that makes you sad, either." We had so much happiness. It'd be a shame not to honor it alongside the tough shit. "I do . . . want to kick your ass at balloon darts, though."

His face is inscrutable. I think it's relief, or maybe gratitude? "All right. Don't go easy on me," he says.

"Never."

He halts me when I move to turn away, dipping his chin close to my ear. "You were made for someplace like this," he says. My body erupts in chills. "With that pile of golden hair and all your golden skin in the sun. I thought I missed your baking . . . That was nothing. I was starving to be near you again."

With that, he slips past me and starts off toward the games, smirking at my stunned expression over his shoulder. "Game face, Byrd. You let a compliment throw you off your game, and I might get excessive with them."

CHAPTER 19

────

WREN

A couple of hours later, Ellis and I are each at least a hundred dollars poorer, dewy from exertion, and two colossal Care Bears richer.

"Here, hold this for a sec," I say, handing mine to him. When I pull out my phone, he obliges me with a surly look, mashing the genial bears' faces against his.

"I can't wait to send this to Silas," I say to the picture, snickering.

He lets out a long-suffering sigh. "What do you want to do with our friends here while we go on some rides, Byrd?"

I snort. "Guess I didn't think this one through."

"Nah. You were pretty singularly focused on victory." He chuckles. "Thought you were about to fight that poor kid at the Top-a-Pop."

"He said two pops got the top prize!"

"Say that ten times fast." He ducks behind one of the bears

like he expects me to throw something at him before he bumps my shoulder good-naturedly.

I let out a little groan. "I was too intense, wasn't I? This is why I don't compete in things." I've told Sage for years that I'm allergic to competition.

"I liked it. Always have," comes his reply. I can't see him from behind the neon-pink bear. I bite my lip in a smile.

Ellis and I veer off and hover near the park exit until I see a family with two girls and offer them the bears. They are elated, and their mother is politely grateful. If she's annoyed to add two more gigantic toys to a clutter of kids' things at home, she hides it well.

I peel my smile away from the little girls and look back at Ellis just in time for him to shutter a heavy look, slipping his sunglasses back into place. "Is it too early for ice cream before noon?" he asks.

Rather than wonder what that expression was about, I aim for fun some more. "I dole out chocolatey-caramel sin before seven, honey. Ice cream is good anytime." I shouldn't have used the endearment. Too bold. His grin over it is downright beatific. "Don't get a big head over it."

"Over what? You flirting with me?" I spot his laugh lines fanning out from his sunglasses. He takes a step closer and cocks his head. Lets his arm brush against mine before he brazenly reaches up and tugs on a wild curl. "Wouldn't dream of it, Byrd. I know it's not like that." His eyes are playful, but the silliness is gone, replaced with an invitation. All while he toys with my hair, testing its feel between his middle finger and thumb.

Oh, it's definitely like that. I see what this is. An exchange. After rounds of games and surrounded by sunshine and cotton candy–scented air, we're both feeling playful. If I indulge him, he'll play back. I let my smile unzip across my face. Hope he feels it like a slow, metallic snick in a dark room.

He abruptly drops my hair and straightens with a laugh, then tucks his hands into his pockets. "Let's go get ice cream. I'll even let you buy, *honey.*"

I think I just got teased.

I nod at the Big Dipper after we secure our cones. "When's the last time you went on a real roller coaster?"

"You mean the hand-cranked brontosaurus ride in the O'Doyle's parking lot that year didn't count?" His throat bobs when he laughs. "Junior year. Gandon County Fair." He looks over his sunglasses at me. "Same night you got the Wrangler." He watches my reaction to this while he laps at his ice cream, spinning it against his tongue. Heat creeps across my collarbone as I try to laugh and seem unruffled. *Same night I got the Wrangler* also equates to *Same night we parked and played Just the Tip for the first time.*

"You think it's bad that we never told Sam he drives the car he was most likely conceived in?" I ask, since I can play dirty, too. He chokes lightly at my side, eyes rounding. "That Wrangler has seen some things, am I right?" I lick my vanilla nice and slow, a satisfied grin hooking my lips. "Do you need sunscreen, honey? You're a little red."

He recovers himself with a filthy look my way. "Yeah, baby, I could use some SPF," he says, low and deep. "Finish up that ice cream and we'll touch up your pretty shoulders, too." He raises his chin like it's a challenge.

I raise mine back. Flick my tongue over the tip of my treat. He bites the remainder off of his and smiles with a mouthful.

"Lunatic!" I cry. "You're gonna give yourself a brain freeze."

He manages to swallow it down after a beat. "Good. My

brain is overheating," he mumbles, throwing his bald cone into the nearest trash bin. "By the way," he says as he leads us toward the roller coaster line, "I looked up some of those questions."

"What questions?"

"You said you were planning on bringing one of those lists. 'Twenty-Six Questions to Fall in Love' or something," he explains.

"And you looked them up?!" I laugh incredulously. "Isn't that kinda cheating?"

He shrugs, all innocence. Entirely unrepentant. "Wanted to get a head start on my answers."

"Ellis Orion Byrd. That *is* cheating!" I squeal.

"Don't care. Wanted to come up with good ones," he states plainly. "Besides, I had no way to know which ones you'd go with exactly. Just did some googling."

Oh, he's diabolical. Stripping himself right down to the truth and laying it on the line. I'm defenseless against this brand of charm. I think of one of Sage's wacky words she used the other week when she described Fisher doing something with homemade whipped cream. *Dastardly.*

"But," he continues. "My favorite one that I thought was interesting wasn't really a question but said to make three 'we' statements that you think are true in this moment, like . . . '*We* are in line for the roller coaster, and *we* are feeling . . . excited.'" He gives me a questioning look.

"Okay." I smile encouragingly. "Go on." His returning expression is so damned vibrant, I bite my lip to stifle what would probably be a girlish giggle.

"*We* are on this trip and *we* know it is early, but *we* are feeling . . . cautiously optimistic?"

The laugh escapes through my nose, and I shake my head at him. "You're impossible."

"To resist? Thank you. We are . . ." He trails off when I lift my bikini tie from where it's digging into my neck under the weight of my chest, seeking relief.

"We are . . ?" I prompt.

"We are what?"

"Uh, you were in the middle of telling me what."

"*Right*," he barks, crossing his arms and firmly tucking his hands into his sides with his thumbs out. "We are . . . genuinely concerned about sun protection. Hand me the sunscreen."

The gruff edge in his tone makes me drop my tie. He makes a faint, strangled noise at the recoil. The line starts to shift forward, so we coast with it until it stops again. We both push our sunglasses back on our heads when we make it into the shade of the building. When his eyes meet mine, I feel it like a flash-zap down my limbs, that moment your brain recognizes you're touching hot metal. He puts his palm out, and I swear it looks like it's shaking. I spin around to cover my gulp.

"In my backpack. Front pocket," I say.

I feel the reverberations of him rifling around, and god, I must be touch-starved because he might as well be bending me over for what this alone is doing to me. The sound it makes when he squirts it into his palm is decidedly unsexy, but it does nothing to quell the warmth purling in every single one of my erogenous zones. I think my eyes roll back when his hand finally touches a spot between my shoulder blades.

He's indecently slow and firm rubbing it in, pressing the tips of his fingers into knots and sliding the pad of his thumb beneath the edge of my tank top, gliding against the muscle beside my spine. When his big hands cup over my shoulders, I hum. When one hand slides up my neck beneath my bikini tie, I go weak in the knees. He massages the base of my skull, and I don't even care that he's probably getting sunscreen in my hair there—it's fucking heaven. I want to lean back into him, want him to cup my breasts and lift and ease this ache, want this same massage on my lower back, loving me while I ride him in reverse—

"'Scuse me," a voice says. Ellis and I jolt apart. "The line is moving," the man behind us adds. He's got his daughter held against his leg protectively and is giving us a horrified look. Ellis and I dart forward to make up ground, avoiding eye contact.

My heart is still racing by the time we're called for our turn, which is also when we finally break. He snorts and I cackle, and if I closed my eyes, it would sound like us as kids, laughing and lust-dazed in the tiny back seat of a Jeep, neon lights from a Ferris wheel glowing in the distance.

When the lap bar comes down, I look at him and say, "*We* are about to go on this roller coaster, and *we* are going to be okay. *We* are happy we're doing it together."

His smile splits wider when he says, "We're okay."

———

We spend another four hours at the park, riding rides, playing games, and sampling a cornucopia of fried foods. After the erotic sunscreen application debacle, things between us stay PG-rated for the most part. When we grab sandwiches from the same café we got breakfast from, he leads me outside with his hand at my back, and I feel the echo of all the earlier heat. We eat our early dinner on the outdoor patio area, nod and smile at the same couple from this morning when they pass by.

"What do you want to do with the rest of the evening?" I ask Ellis when I slurp up the final dregs of my iced tea.

A thought insinuates itself suddenly, and I feel myself tense. I hope he doesn't say, "Whatever you want to do," and put the onus back on me like he once would have. We're good and comfortable and making headway, and I hope we don't fall back on old habits this soon.

He stretches his arms out wide and leans back in his seat, a strip of his stomach revealing itself, dusted in a dark trail of hair. His eyes are brighter against his suntanned skin. They're the same shade as the darkening, dusky blue sky around us, backlit by a lemony sun.

He scratches at his five-o'clock shadow. "I'm not gonna lie to you, Byrd. I'd really love an early night."

I make a joyous noise before it tumbles into a laugh. "God, nothing sounds better."

Well, *almost* nothing sounds better.

Right now, we're sun-cooked and pleasantly full. Sticky with sweat and sunscreen, mildly sore from being shaken around by rides, and tired from riding down memory lane. Optimal sleep conditions.

"And tomorrow's flexible. We can sleep in or hit the pool in the morning before we leave. Whatever sounds good. Aquarium opens at eleven, and it's an hour-and-a-half drive. We do have dinner reservations, but they're not until seven," he says. That leaves us all day.

We FaceTime Sam on the walk back, and my chest pinches at the easy delight on his face, like seeing us side by side excites him. It should absolutely make me wary, but that lonely, hopeful piece of my heart burns brighter at it instead.

God, I'm such a sucker for good feelings, aren't I? Sweet, deep feelings that I lose myself in. I make a living out of doling them out in food form.

And I know our rooms are right next to each other, but when he walks me to my door, it feels like he's just walked me home from our first date. I'm a little mortified by how badly I hope he might try to kiss me. I'm also worried that if he does, I'll lose any remaining vestige of restraint. Self-regulating bargains fulfilled or not, I think moving too quickly in a physical direction might not be wise.

He's bashful now, though, and admittedly, so am I. His hands stay snug in his pockets other than when one of them scratches the back of his neck. None of that earlier swagger or teasing to be found here in this empty hallway. I want to thank him for the day with more than words somehow, so I spin my backpack around before I can second-guess myself.

"Here," I say. "You can read it." I zip the bag shut and return it to my back so I can't change my mind.

He takes my journal in both of his palms like it's something fragile, expression melting into a startled sort of happiness. The sight of it in his big, capable hands—calloused but clean, thick fingers that end in blunted, tidy tips—makes me lightheaded. I feel paralyzingly shy all of a sudden and nearly snatch it back. People consume things I make every day, but this is my heart on paper. He immediately flips it open.

"*OH MY GOD, NO!*" I shout. "Don't! Don't read it in front of me!" I flail my wrists like they're on fire.

He holds it up like he's under arrest or like he knows I might make a grab for it. "All right, all right!" he says. "I'll see you in the morning!" He cocks his head, hands still in the air. "Had fun with you today, Byrd."

"Okay," I titter, caught between groaning and giggling. "I had fun, too. Thank you." The apples of my cheeks are so tight I'd swear they were pulling something up from my ribs.

We laugh at the same time, and I wiggle my fingers in an odd little wave at him just before I try to turn around and am promptly lurched back when my backpack snags on the door handle.

"Here—" He lunges forward and tries to help.

"I got it. We're good." I clumsily liberate myself and shove my key into the slot before I swan-dive through the door and shut it as quickly as possible at my back, falling against it.

I let out a whine under my breath. *Thunk, thunk, thunk* my head against the door.

I've got the biggest, most devastating crush on my ex-husband, and I hope I don't get absolutely flattened by it in the end.

Not again.

CHAPTER 20

WREN

I awake the following day with a kink in my neck and a foggy head.

For being as exhausted as I was, it took me a ridiculous amount of time to fall asleep again. I paced my room, replaying the day and wondering if he was reading the journal. Turned the AC down until I could practically see my breath, took a too-hot shower, then slid into the icy sheets, where I proceeded to toss and turn endlessly. I'm ashamed to admit that I put my ear up to the wall at one point to see if I could hear whatever Ellis was up to next door, then cursed the carpeted floors for muffling his movements.

I let out a noisy yawn and look at the clock on my phone, surprised to see that I've managed to sleep in past nine. I get up and drag around my room, throwing out a few outfit options on my bed with a surly flick of my wrist.

"Guess I'll do my navel-gazing for the day," I say dryly to no one.

When I open the blackout shades and grimace into the sun,

something moves in the corner of my vision over by the pool deck. I have to smash my cheek up against the window and strain to see from this angle, but . . . but it is definitely Ellis, down in the hot tub. I can only see the top of his head and one arm folded on the edge of the concrete rim. But I'd know that arm anywhere, even from four floors up.

He disappears from my sight and "Ouch, shit—" I wince when I bang my face against the glass to try to find him again. He reappears a moment later, though, and *Fuck me*, he looks good. The early sun shining off it makes his hair look bronze and silver. Legs and an ass that I know fill out his shorts deliciously, shoulders so strong and wide they cast shadows, a back that's—

His back. My gasp is theatrical in its volume when I see it.

He's got tattoos on his back. Birds. Five of them, to be precise. All black and white, from what I can make out, but in various shapes, sizes, and poses midflight. He settles into a lounge chair by the pool and the birds are blocked from my view, but not his chest or the strong muscles of his stomach. It's too far to know for sure, but I imagine a droplet of water caught in his belly button trickling down his skin when he breathes. I watch him take a pull from his water bottle before he grabs a book—my journal—off the end table beside him and starts to read.

My heart zings and bounces around the cavern of my chest. This man is *studying*. He's . . . he's taking it so seriously. Not just trying to do what I want him to in order to get us back but learning from before. I rub a slow circle against my sternum and try to figure out why this carves out a fearful edge in me again.

I guess because it's a reminder that we will have to talk about all the lost times, too. "*We're okay*," he'd said yesterday, and he was right. He's okay now, and I am, too. It would be easy to step into these new and exciting versions of ourselves. He's suddenly a man in therapy and has tattoos! Lord knows that running full force with the playful and sexy comfort we rediscovered yesterday would be easier than going through the ugly pieces of our past.

But I *want* those ugly pieces. I want everything I missed in between, too. I want to know when and why he got tattoos. I want to know if someone else has run her hands over them—

—*NOPE*. No, I don't. Oh, thank god he didn't reciprocate my yapping about how I've had sex with other people in the bakery that day. I don't need to know. He can win being the bigger person in that regard. And I know I was never successful at it anyway, but I can't believe I ever even *wanted* to get to a place where I'd have been happy for him to move on. I must've been in denial.

Either that, or time and distance had given me that ability and I've already unraveled all of that in a day. God, I've never had an ounce of self-control when it comes to Ellis. I'm giving myself whiplash.

I realize I've still got my nose mashed against the window and step back from my ogling, determined to get ahold of myself.

I'm a mature, thirty-three-year-old woman who is also in the prime of her life. I might not be in therapy or have tattoos, and I might have a few hard limits as far as that maturity goes. And maybe I've had to take some unconventional routes toward building up my emotional intelligence, but I am self-aware, and I can do this. I can stick to this. I'll write more entries and excavate more memories from my brain. We'll stick to the bargains. Two bad things a day. I'll ask the questions even if they're a prompt from the internet that he's already looked up. I can trust him to respond with honesty and respect. And I can handle myself in a sophisticated, measured way while we do it.

I wipe the drool off the window and start getting ready for the day.

CHAPTER 21

———

WREN

"Do you believe in God these days? Or the universe, or something like it?" I ask Ellis as a bloom of jellyfish bob past. I'm transfixed by the sight of them undulating around the glowing blue water.

It doesn't occur to me that this might feel like a bizarre or random question until he doesn't answer it right away.

"It'd be convenient, wouldn't it?" he eventually replies. When I look up at him, he's staring through the glass portal, just as bewitched.

It turns out the aquarium is the perfect place to get a little philosophical. Like being surrounded by neon creatures that look like something make-believe also means nothing we say will seem any wilder or weirder. Certainly, me asking about his belief in a higher power isn't more whimsical than a seahorse.

It started when he broke the ice earlier, when I met him in the hotel lobby and he'd greeted me with a coffee and a breakfast burrito and said, *"Morning. I hated how you'd make us be the last to leave any social function."* When I froze, bewildered, he explained, *"That was my first of the two things. Trying to knock them out early."*

I couldn't suppress a goofy grin. *"I didn't like how antisocial you'd get sometimes, but I miss how you could unapologetically leave a party or a thing whenever we felt like it. I totally took that for granted. I have not mastered the solo Irish goodbye,"* I admitted. *"Also, I hated when you wouldn't relax on days off!"* I added, cheerfully beaming. *"It annoyed the hell out of me!"*

"How about you?" he asks me in the present.

"How about me, what?"

He huffs a short laugh. "You asked me about the universe and a higher power," he says casually, as if I'd asked how he liked his eggs.

"Oh, that's right." It was one of the questions in the prompt list, but I don't think I have to qualify it right now. We're being equally comfortable and curious with each other, the drive over here filled with easy conversation and a few lingering glances.

I think about my answer and watch another jellyfish drift away. Oddly elegant things with no hearts, brains, or blood, that go on existing and serving a purpose, anyway. "I think that as I get older, I'm okay knowing that some stuff will always be beyond my understanding," I say. "I think it's arrogant to think the stars and moon can affect the tides but not have an effect on me. Some things are just more powerful than we are." I shrug and lift an eyebrow at him with a sigh. "You are a Virgo, no matter what you think."

I expect him to laugh, but he just smiles and nods considerably. "Yeah, yeah, I know," he says, resigned. "I've been converted. I read about it more and believe more in the chart stuff these days." He grins at me. "Virgo sun, Scorpio rising, Taurus moon, by the way."

I smile with open-mouthed surprise. "He knows his big three now," I muse.

"He does," he says. "I know yours, too. Don't always check my horoscope or anything, but I like thinking of the chart stuff as sort of default settings, I guess." He looks away into the blue. "People are the sum of their experiences, and we all have free will, but even if it *is* all made up, I think it's nice to understand a little bit of *why* we all handle shit differently."

That ache I feel around the Ellis-shaped corner of my heart pulses. Yesterday, I got to watch him be playful, and today, he's a different sort of relaxed. Peaceful. He's spent so much of his life spread thin between roles: brother, father, husband, (reluctant) leader. I love seeing him this way, like he's allowing himself to sit and sift through his own thoughts and feelings. I want to tug him into one of the dark alcoves and kiss him like the precious thing he is, but I settle for words, this time, since he's being free with his.

"I like seeing you like this," I say.

He turns, blinking down at me, twin furrows between his brows. He didn't shave, and the two days' growth has always been my favorite look on him. Smooth and thick mustache, unkempt stubble across his chin and jaw, soft lips. Half of him is cast in sapphire blue, the other half in shadow.

He steps closer, a lick of humor teasing his mouth. "It's the sandals, isn't it?"

I snort. "Of course it is," I say sagely. "But . . . I also like seeing you open. You've always been observant, good at seeing things. But you haven't always been so . . . sharing." An understatement. "Not afraid to sound silly, I guess."

His eyes land somewhere near the shell of my ear. "Yeah, well." His sigh ruffles my hair. "I've been going to therapy for a while now. Started a few months after Silas's accident."

I keep my expression carefully unmoved. "Yeah? You like it?"

He scoffs a chuckle. "*Like* is a strong word," he says. "I think it's another one of those things that makes me understand why I'm feeling something, instead of like the feeling itself is controlling me." I can't decipher the look in his eyes while they track a path across my face. "Most feelings, anyway." He nods over my shoulder. "Seabirds?"

"See them do what?"

"Do you want to go see the seabirds, Byrd?" he clarifies, smiling broadly, gaze crackling with mirth. I feel my ears heat and roll my eyes at myself when I turn away. We might be finding our rhythm, but clearly, I'm still a little clumsy.

We round a corner into a brighter section with benches and seating, then silently watch the puffins, common murres, and oystercatchers (who rarely eat oysters, according to the sign) swim and flit around, oblivious to the room crowding around us on all sides.

"Feeding time in five minutes," I overhear a mom tell her toddler, lifting her to stand on the bench in front of her so she can see over the people milling in.

Ellis bumps into my back with a short *oof.* "Sorry," he says into my hair. His hands briefly land on my waist to catch himself, and I'm suddenly aware of every breath sawing in and out of me. "Do you want to stay, or you want me to get us out of here?" he asks. I wish I could turn and see his face, but I think if I did, it'd give the crowd a chance to press in closer and thereby give my hips the chance to push directly into his, front to front. My throat goes dry.

"Let's stay." I white-knuckle the railing in front of me as he's bumped into my ass. He mutters a curse. "It's all right," I say, feigning ambivalence. Hoping he missed the slight tremor in my voice. His hands land next to mine on the railing, caging me in, bringing us flush. I feel him suck in a deep breath and hold it.

"You smell . . ." He trails off. "Fuck, you smell good." He says it on a defeated exhale, like it's some bigger confession ripped from him.

"It's the same stuff I've always worn," I say over my shoulder, bemused. Same lotion, same shampoo, same little dab of perfume. I'm sure the people next to us can hear, and maybe this should be a private conversation, but I don't care.

"I know," he says accusingly.

"I thought you didn't like it anymore. You . . ." It's too much of an admission for me in this moment, when I can feel his warmth through the thin cotton of his shirt against my bare shoulders. When I can still feel where his hands held my waist and the wiry hairs on his knees tickling the smooth backs of mine. I want to feel the hard jut of his hipbones drum against me.

"Smells . . . smells were the worst for me," he murmurs, chin grazing my ponytail. "They hang on the longest, and you can't see them coming, so there's no way to avoid them. Like living with a ghost. I'd walk upstairs and swear you were there sometimes, it'd be so strong, out of nowhere. Worse after it rained, like some old sports injury or something." His low laugh is devoid of any humor. "I replaced the bedding and pillows and our bed still smells like you."

Want and something darker simmer low in my belly and sear up through my chest. There's laughter burbling around us now, and I vaguely register an aquarium employee talking about the birds, but I can't sense anything beyond Ellis's voice and heat around me right now. I close my eyes and see him, too. Him alone in our bed in the dark.

"Town smells like you," he goes on. "From a block away,

I can smell the bakery." The pressure of him increases slightly.
"So, no. I didn't like it anymore, Wren. It made me want things
I couldn't have."

I hold my breath, straighten my pinkie, and touch his thumb,
heart in my throat. He catches it and hooks it with his forefinger. We learn absolutely nothing about the seabirds, merely stand
there breathing each other in. His heart pounds against the back
of my head while mine races behind my ribs, and it's ridiculous,
how intimate it feels. I've tasted the palest skin on his thighs and
know what he sounds like when he comes, yet touching like this
intentionally, no sunscreen or excuses, fully clothed, feels like
something brand new after all this time.

We meander around the aquarium for a while longer. Ellis is
so captivated by the sunfish that I can't stop myself from taking a
picture of him staring at it, a look of awe on his face standing in
the blue light. I send a bundle of otter pictures to Sage, who then
asks me to send one of Ellis and me together, which I ignore.

We eat In-N-Out double-doubles on the way back to Santa
Cruz, our knuckles brushing when we both reach into the fry
tray. When it happens a third time, I know we're doing it on
purpose, which should probably fill me with some sort of chagrin
and not this maniacal glee, but here we are. I surprise a bellow
of laughter out of him when "The Power of Love" starts blaring through his truck speakers, and I practically preen over it. I
round it out by playing the *New Moon* soundtrack in its entirety
after.

"What are you gonna do with your free time?" I ask to cut
through the quiet when we get off the elevator back at the hotel.

"Nap," he says, punctuating it with a yawn. It's comforting to
know that he's not getting fantastic rest on this trip so far, either.

"What's the vibe for the liver-and-onions place?" I ask when I get to my door. "So I know what to wear."

He scratches at his chin and smiles softly. "It's . . . nice. Not overly fancy or anything, but I'll be ditching the flip-flops."

I give him a sarcastic pout. "All right. Sounds good."

"Okay. Yeah," he stumbles, his grin boyish. He rifles through his wallet for his room key. "See you in a few hours."

I'm kissing the hell out of you tonight, I think. "See you in a few hours," I say. "Oh, Ellis?" He pops his head back out of his door. "Can I have my journal back?"

The first time Ellis kissed me was on my sixteenth birthday. We'd been falling back into our regular, more comfortable friendship again over the previous month because for four months and three weeks before that, Ellis had been seeing Serena Lindhagen and had been more distant. To be fair, I had also stayed away. Whenever I saw them on the quad at lunch being affectionate, it gave me acid reflux.

Still, we seemed to stumble around each other a bit more than we used to. I'd catch him staring at me in ways that felt new. A few weeks into summer, we met in a big group down at Founder's Point. All the Byrd siblings were there, even eleven-year-old Sage, whom Ellis wandered off with to collect seashells while the other kids tossed a baseball back and forth. It's never truly hot in Spunes, but that day, there was patchy sun at least. I was lying on a towel on the sand reading a book when Silas and Ian Carver each grabbed me by an end and hauled me out into the water while I thrashed and screamed. I came up sputtering, the water so frigid it knocked the words out of me. I ran back up onto the sand gasping and laughing just as I heard Silas say, "Oh shit," from somewhere behind me and saw Ian take off in the other direction at a full sprint.

Ellis came out of nowhere from the corner of my vision, charged for Silas, and shoved him hard back into a wave. When Silas came up with his palms up in surrender, Ellis grabbed him by the back of the neck and spoke to him with a finger in his face, waves trying to knock them both over and churning around their legs. I couldn't hear what was said over the wind and salt spray, but I watched as Silas's expression went from scared to pissed to mollified.

"Ellis, I'm fine," I said when they turned around and started walking toward me. "They were messing around."

He looked at me, irate. "Did you say stop?!" he yelled.

"Well, yeah, but I think that's a knee-jerk thing to yell when you're about to get thrown in—"

"You said _stop_, Wren. They should have stopped." It was clear he wouldn't budge on this, and I supposed he was right after all. He was breathing heavily, his entire body vibrating.

"I'm sorry, Wren," said Silas.

"It's fine, Si. I'm okay," I said. I looked at Ellis and said again, "I'm okay."

We all gathered up our things and started for the car, I along with them since I wouldn't get my own for another few more months. Micah and Silas bickered the whole way down the beach.

"You just gotta ruin everything, don't you?" Micah had said. Silas pushed him, and he fell into the wet sand. Micah got up and shouldered him back.

"Enough," barked Ellis.

"Each of you hold one of my hands so you don't hit each other," said Sage, stepping between her brothers. They complied even as they grumbled.

We piled into Ellis's old SUV and headed home, but I was surprised when Ellis dropped off all his siblings before taking me. He didn't explain himself, just kept on driving with a flinty expression on his face.

"Why does it feel like you're mad at me?" I asked.

"I'm not," Ellis said softly. He continued staring out the windshield, though. He wouldn't look at me. I was still shivering, and he tried to turn his heater on, but it was an old car and something was broken, so it kept blowing cold air on my skin and making it worse. He pulled over in the O'Doyle's parking lot and started scrounging around in his back seat, looking for something dry to give me. I stared at the way his body shifted beneath his shirt in the movement, the strong column of his throat. When he couldn't find anything and looked at me again, my teeth were chattering. He undid his seat belt and reached over the center console to rub his palms up and down my arms in a rapid circuit. When he watched the gooseflesh fade from my skin and he saw that it was working, he climbed out of the car and put himself in the back seat.

"Here," he said, motioning with his arms for me to crawl back there with him. I went willingly. Let him hold me in his lap and surround me with his warmth. I started to feel like I was trembling for a new reason. When I tilted my head back to look up at him, he ran his thumb along my bottom lip.

"Your lips… They're not blue anymore, at least." I felt his heart pounding against my shoulder. "Bird," he'd croaked. He sometimes called me <u>Bird</u> because my name was one. In a weird way, this always felt like a sign that we belonged together. It felt like he was asking for something with that syllable.

"Yes," I said. And then he kissed me.

It was the best birthday I ever had.

CHAPTER 22

ELLIS

I'm ready a full hour early and go back to torturing myself and wallowing around my room. I can hear her moving around hers next door, and it's toying with all my internal systems. I used to love watching her get ready. The little pouty expressions she'd make in the mirror and the way she'd toss her wild hair. She's got one dimple on her chin that reveals itself when her bottom lip juts out just right. Right beneath the corner of her mouth.

I want all of it back. I want too much too fast.

I wonder if she still likes the same kind of underwear she did before. Smooth and seamless and barely there.

I toss my body backward onto the bed and fist the covers. "Stop it," I growl at the ceiling.

My phone vibrates in my pocket, so I roll onto my side to pull it free from my jeans, and find a text from Silas.

Can you talk?

This asshole knows that now I'll call because otherwise it'll make me anxious wondering. I check my watch. Enough time to go down to the lobby and see what he wants this time. The walls are thin, and I'm not sure I want to risk Wren overhearing. If she catches any hint at how invested Silas is in this trip now, she'll be spooked.

And he has been incessant. It took him cornering me at the wedding after he saw us dancing, but I broke down and told him about the paper on the counter that I found and how I took it to mean that there was something still there between Wren and me. He thought it was a stretch at first, but eventually came around and was supportive. Which turned into *enthusiastic* support.

Which expanded into him driving me insane ever since.

Even before we left, he was calling and peppering me about all my plans. Offering a bounty of suggestions I didn't ask for. Spas and private boat tours and horses on the beach.

I still didn't tell him about the letters from last fall . . . it seems like I'd be violating Wren's privacy in a new way by sharing. More than I already have by doing it in the first place. The only person I have confided in, oddly enough, is Lennon Kirby. After she told me about the horses, I confessed everything. I told her my pen pal was my ex-wife. I told her I still loved her.

"Oh my god, Cap. This is fate," she'd said. *"This was destiny. You are meant to be together."*

I hate that. I want to earn my chance back with her. I want her to *want* me back, too. I don't want anything else to be the deciding factor when it comes to us again. Which is also why I need Silas to keep his antics limited to me.

I hit Call on his name as soon as I reach the lobby.

"Hey," he says lightly.

"What's up?" I ask.

"Not much," he quips. "What's up with you?"

"*Silas*," I growl. "You asked if I could talk."

"You didn't tell me if you could or not."

"*I*—" I cut myself off and move the phone away from my ear, inhaling and exhaling deeply. "I called, Si. I think that's self-explanatory."

"Have you kissed yet?" He's munching on a snack into the phone, talking around a mouthful.

"Goddamn it, Silas, I cannot do this with you right now. We've been here for under forty-eight hours and we've been divorced for five years. I need you to chill. I'm begging, in fact."

A pause. "So, no, then?"

"I'm hanging up."

"No! Don't!" he says, belting a laugh. "Micah wants to know what your Wi-Fi password is. He says you changed it since he was here last and you haven't texted him back."

"I've been gone for two days. He never asked the entire time I was still home. I've been busy!" *Wait.* "Does that mean you're at my house right now?"

"Think he was previously avoiding the internet. And yup!" I hear him opening my refrigerator and shuffling things around. "Sage and them are on their way over, too. Micah's been moping."

"*I haven't been fucking moping!*" I hear in the background.

I run a palm over my eyes. "Why is everyone going to *my* house?"

"Because your patio's nicest and your beer fridge is stocked. Let me know if you kiss her tonight. If I'm willing to lose the friend I can shit-talk you to, then you'd better not muck it up."

"Goodbye, Silas," I drone.

He hangs up without a reply.

I rake both hands through my hair. They're all going to know what this trip is really about, and they're all going to be extremely invested. Shit. I'd better not muck this up.

I glance at the clock over the front desk counter; 6:15 now. Only fifteen minutes to go. But just as I get up to head back to my room and pace some more, I see Wren slip into the hotel bar. She's wearing a flowery, low-cut dress that falls just around her shins. Sandals that tie around her ankles. A groan sticks in my throat at the sight of those little leather bows.

She orders a drink at the bar, and I watch her turn it in circles against the wood. I wonder if she's nervous. I come up beside her and lean onto the bar, let myself inhale the perfume I've always loved. Like caramel and something floral I wouldn't know aside from recognizing it on her skin. Jasmine, maybe. A spice underneath it that's her.

"Come here often?"

She smiles into her chardonnay before she takes a gulp and looks at me. Big brown doe eyes and a full wide mouth in a heart-shaped face. Hair down and tumbling around her shoulders in a riot of waves and curls.

"Had the same idea, huh? A drink to level out the nerves?" she asks.

I shrug lightly. "Something like that." I order an old-fashioned from the bartender when he comes by.

"Since when are you an old-fashioned guy?" she says, cocking a brow.

"Was I not before?"

"Nah-ah. Beer, or a Jack and Diet only."

"Hmm." I frown. "I'm not sure, then, honestly."

I can't read her expression or the gleam in her eye when she says, "All sorts of new discoveries to be made."

When we step outside to wait for our Uber a little while later, the evening is bright and cool, the sunset blazing pink in a briny sky. When I look at Wren, I have to put a palm to my chest just to keep myself from reaching for her. Shimmer on her eyes and gloss on her lips. A fresh tan line that cuts its way over her collarbone. A little gold necklace sits at the base of her throat and winks in the light.

She tilts her head with a curious look my way, and I'm captivated—downright enthralled—by a curl that skips and dances against her cheekbone. I think of all the times I didn't say everything I wanted to and regretted it later, and what she said about my compliments.

"I'm having a hard time not touching you," I admit. "You are . . . you're more beautiful than ever, Wren."

She blinks heavily and steps into me. I stop breathing when she reaches up and puts her palm to the side of my face. I nuzzle it and kiss the heel, my breath picking up too quick again.

"You can touch me," she says. I rest a trembling hand where her neck meets her shoulder and trace my thumb along the line of her throat when she swallows. "Let's just take it slow."

Her scent envelops my senses, soothing something frantic in me. "I like slow."

Her smile blooms, my chest inflating the more it grows. "I know you do."

She holds my hand during the ride over to Capitola, and I feel like I am honest-to-god being tickled under my skin, glee crackling and sputtering in every vein of my body. Fireworks all over. I thread her fingers right back through mine the moment she slides out of the car when we get to the restaurant.

"What's this?" she asks when we walk hand in hand to an overhang covering a small platform. "Where's the entrance?"

"Down there." I walk her to the ledge at the border of the deck so she can see the restaurant hugging the cliffside below. "We take a little cable car ride to get down to it." Lanterns glowing with tea lights line flagstone paths that weave through full, lush gardens surrounding it. The building itself looks like someone's craftsman-style mansion tucked up on the rocks. Beyond and below are tide pools, the whites of foamy waves still visible in spite of the fading sun. Diffused yellow light shines through the paned windows that cover its multiple floors. There's an outdoor fireplace on one of the side patios. Globes of string lights sparkling, too.

She gives me a flat look, pursing her lips. "*That* place serves liver and onions?" she clips.

"They will," I say innocently. "I called and asked. Pretty sure they thought I was a prank caller when I did. Honestly, Wren, I just wanted to take you to a nice dinner. If it's too romantic, then I guess I won't even say happy birthday to you tomorrow to make up for it, but, I promise, it's not as fancy as it looks and—"

She kisses me. She's kissing me.

It takes me a second to get my bearings. I'm frozen for a moment, with one of her hands clasping mine and the other cupping the back of my neck so she could pull herself up to me. I boomerang in and out of my body before it comes together.

She's kissing me. Her lips are on mine after five long years. Five hundred years. She's kissing me.

I'm home.

CHAPTER 23

WREN

Well, I lasted a little more than a day.

But then he had to go and stand there explaining himself over this beautiful place on this flawless, pristine night. Had to stand there in a charcoal button-up that matches his eyes, dark jeans clinging to strong legs. Sun-kissed face full of hard lines and angles despite being the softest man I know. I'd noticed a few new graying strands of hair in his cowlick and the way the ends of it flipped out against his neck like duck tails and I just couldn't help myself anymore. He's worked so hard. He's trying and he's earnest, and I somehow forgot just how disarming and sweet. I don't know how I could have ever forgotten all these parts of him. *I've missed him I've missed him I've missed him* looped through my head, and I had to bring my mouth to his.

He's shocked stiff for a moment, unmoving, and still a quiet whimper escapes me at the feel of his lips. Soft and firm and mine. I taste one with the tip of my tongue, and that breaks him out of his stupor. His hands crash under my hair, and he angles my head, a coarse sound swept out of him when he slots my top lip between his. I nibble at him, and he devours me. I recognize this exact taste. I know when he's going to adjust the angle of the kiss before he does it. He hasn't made another noise, but I can feel a million thrumming inside his frame, an undercurrent of electricity ready to spark. I scratch my nails farther up his neck to tug in his hair and *there*, there's that sound I love. A gravelly hum I lick at with greedy strokes of my tongue. I feel his whispered *fuck* like a smack between my legs.

I pry him away by his hair when I catch a glimpse of the little red cable car ascending back up the tracks.

"Ellis—" I say, muffled when he pounces back onto me and gently drags his teeth against my bottom lip. I let out a high, reedy sob. "Ellis, the . . . the reservation." He's on my neck now, sucking at a spot beneath my jaw that makes me squirm. Returns to my lips with an indistinguishable murmur.

"*Ellis*—" I try again. "Dinner. Oh god," I laugh-moan when he manhandles me, tilts my head back by my hair, and dips to lick a perfect wet stripe up the center of my throat.

"I'll cut out my own liver and cook it for you myself," he speaks into my lips. "I'll fucking forage an onion."

My laughter makes him wilder. He sips at my mouth like he wants to absorb it.

"I don't, *oh*, I don't—Ellis. *Ellis*." I'm panting. I'm nearly too far gone. "Ellis. Either order us a ride back to the hotel right now or take me to dinner," I command.

He goes rigid under my palms, prying himself off me with a small wet pop. He's still cupping my face, glazed eyes wild and searching, one side of his hair thoroughly mussed. I make the critical error of letting my body bow into him and feel how hard he is. How full and thick and big and—

"Dinner," he rasps. My jaw snaps shut into a pout, and a low noise whisks out of him. "Slow," he grits.

"Dinner," I repeat, swallowing forcibly. "And taking it slow," I say. *God, whose shitty idea was that?!* "You've got a four-minute cable car ride to get that under control," I tack on, letting my eyes dip to his impressive erection before I thumb some of my lip gloss off his bristled chin and step out of his embrace.

The cable car is big enough for four average-sized people but does not have an ideal amount of space to accommodate our current predicament. He visibly struggles to regain control, his eyes dancing between my lips and neck and chest before they meet my stare and he groans anew.

"Byrd, we're not going to make it if you keep looking at me like that," he says, agonized. Almost plaintive.

"How am I looking at you?"

"Like you really might eat me alive. Like you're devising plans. Like you might let me get under that dress and get my hands full of you and find out if you're wet." I bite my lip, and his eyes fall shut, nostrils flaring. "Wren, please, baby, I really need you to turn around or something," he begs. When I do as he asks, he makes another helpless, throttled sound. "That's not any better," he mumbles, his gaze on my ass like a brand.

This is how Ellis ends up spending three silent minutes in a cable car facing away from me with his forehead pressed against the glass.

By the time we've descended the hill and reached the broad double-door entry, his condition has resolved itself. His hand is still tentative when he reaches for me, fingertips barely pressing into my lower back like he's worried if he touches me any further he'll ignite again.

A host leads us down a grand staircase and into a spacious room he tells us is known as the Redwood Hall. It's a converted patio with floor-to-ceiling windows on three sides, a coffered ceiling dotted with chandeliers, and unfettered views of the night sky and ocean beyond. We're seated at a corner table tucked right up against the glass, and it feels like we're floating. Candlelight flickers across his brutally handsome face. When our stares catch and hold, his eyes fall limpid and warm. Everything goes calm, stretching into something thick and sweet.

"Hi," he says, a promise in his gaze.

"Hi," I say, knowing how good it would be between us. Knowing, by exquisite firsthand experience, how he'll take care of my body and needs. Knowing makes it no less anticipatory, but it does help me scrounge up some patience.

"I thought of some questions on my own," I tell him. "Things you couldn't have looked up beforehand."

His quiet snort and grin are self-effacing. "All right," he replies. Our server comes by and drops a basket of bread between us before telling us the specials and sliding drink menus onto the white tablecloth. When he leaves again, Ellis picks up where we left off. "Let's pick out our meals first?"

"Oh, so you're *not* getting the liver and onions after all?" I joke incredulously.

He husks out a laugh. "*We* are in this magical restaurant, and *we* are going to order something good."

"*We* also need to learn when to let a joke die, don't we?"

"Maybe we do," he says, eyes flicking over his menu before they drift back to me. "It's always better when you make things last, though."

There's a whoosh in my ears, like invisible hands placed invisible seashells up to them. I wriggle in my seat and study my menu with a shaky breath.

"Apparently, this place has some famous orange rolls they reserve for brunches," he says, trying to ease us into safer territory.

"I made orange rolls a few times last summer," I say, a little sad that he missed them. "You didn't have to avoid the bakery for all those years," I add, even though we both know that before the last few weeks, I wouldn't have wanted that. "I mean, you could have come in. At least to visit Mom."

"Wren, I see your mom at least once a month. Usually more."

I gawk at him. "What?"

"Who do you think mows her lawn still?" he says. "Or took down that tree when it started leaning too close to her place?"

"She didn't tell me."

"Because you would have tried to take care of it yourself. And we both know you've been busy running Savvy's pretty much on your own the last few years." His eyes go warm. "It's yours, just like you always wanted."

I study my nails and fidget. "It's still Mom's. She started everything."

"And you grew everything and made everything greater. Which is what you always do. You can take anything and make it into something better, Wren." He blows out a breath. "And yeah, I am still suspicious, now more than ever, that you dabble in witchcraft and put magic in your baking. But you also create community. Why do you think Martha gives you so much shit?" His grin tilts. "You're, like, her main competition for head woman in town. I didn't come in because I didn't want to take away from that for you."

My mouth turns down, but I feel myself blush. "You wouldn't

have taken away from it," I say. It would have been hard to see him more, but maybe I would've gotten used to it. Maybe we wouldn't have lost all this time.

He looks at the table and shakes his head. "Yeah, I would have. Would have made it less relaxing for you, anyway." He sighs heavily. "You wanted a family, and you made it there," he says. "I'm amazed by you."

God, it's disorienting, how forthcoming and open he's trying to be. I feel like my lungs are blooming. "It was big of you to never make it feel like I didn't have you guys, still. Your sister and your brothers. You never cut me off from that family, and I'm grateful."

"We both know they wouldn't have allowed it," he says. "You're still a Byrd."

"I am," I say proudly. His entire body seems to lift in response. "And we both know that they're as great as they are thanks to you."

We go easy on each other after that. Eat our bread and order our meals and drinks, sharing polite conversation and speculating on what everyone is up to back at home. We annihilate a baked Brie appetizer with jalapeño jelly and herbed crostini.

When we talk about the influx of tourism in Spunes, I ask, "Do you think Spunes will ever be one of those places that makes people turn seasons into verbs? Like, 'Well, we *summer* over in the Oregon headlands, but you can't beat Aspen in the fall?'"

His chuckle makes me feel unjustly clever. Making him laugh is inebriating. "Isn't Aspen a winter town?" he asks, brow creased.

I shrug. "No idea. Are we boring for not knowing?"

I wonder for a second why something hungry passes over his face when I ask this, but then I realize the implication of that "we" . . . like we exist beyond this trip in a real and present way rather than in the past or in the hypothetical.

"Because we haven't traveled?" he says, then answers himself. "No. I don't think we're boring just because we've had to work for most of our lives and happen to like where we're from. I don't think it makes us simple or boring to have been busy being . . . immersed in our days or our obligations. I know *you're* not simple, at least." A smirk plays at the corner of his mouth.

My cheeks warm. "So . . ." I work up the courage to ask what I want. "You read it, I'm guessing. The journal?"

He nods. "Thank you for letting me. I liked—loved getting to be in your head." The candlelight dances again and makes his eyes spark. "I'm sorry about the vows. I should have tried."

I feel my expression waver. "I didn't think of that as a bad memory, Ellis. You told me what you were feeling in that moment and it wasn't something rehearsed or premeditated, and it meant more to me because of it."

"I know, but . . . I could have tried. That was the point, right? Finding a compromise. Even if I couldn't say them publicly, I could have written them to you. I could've tried, and I don't know why I wasn't willing to back then. Seems so fucking stupid now." He sits back in his chair, his lashes splaying against his cheeks. "You were my best friend and I still kept shit too close to the chest sometimes."

"So did I," I confess.

His eyes move up to mine again before he blows out a long sigh. "The silent treatments. That's my second thing for the day."

"Worse than my cryptic musical showers?" I say wryly.

"You avoided fighting with me, and I think I avoided fighting with you, too, Byrd," he says, his smile turning sad.

He's right. I never knew how to fight with him. Not only because I didn't grow up with two parents to witness or learn from, either, but because of everything Ellis had always been to me. How do you tell the man who's always wanted to take care of you that you resent how much you need him? I never wanted to be a broken mess to the person who'd spent his life managing everyone else's. I didn't want to be angry at him, not when I didn't always understand why I was angry in the first place back then. And no one teaches you what to do when the person hurting you is still *good* to you. He wasn't off cheating on me, he was an excellent dad and cared about our home and well-being. It feels silly and selfish to say, *I hate that you're working so much and it feels like you'd rather not be here with me, like you'd rather be anywhere else,* when that person's work consists of saving homes and lives. It was easier to convince myself that the growing distance between us was all in my head. I'd thought we could love each other through our hard times, but maybe we should have fought our way through them, too.

"I promise I'll fight with you more," I say. I'll fight *for* you more, too. "Even if things don't . ." I don't want to finish that sentence.

"I'll fight with you, too," he says, grinning genuinely now. "Even if things don't."

"We robbed ourselves of makeup sex, didn't we?" I say. We've done our two bad things and spoken some truths. I'm not going to overthink flirting with him the rest of the night.

He coughs on his water a little. "I have heard great things about it, but I never felt robbed in that department."

I smile into my wine and take another drink.

We take our time savoring our meals after that. I relish watching him eat. I let myself luxuriate in the simple pleasure of eating a meal and having a conversation with him again. I remember how I used to look forward to this all day when we'd moved into our house and out of the Byrds'. Sam was a toddler and would get put to bed at an early hour, still, and for a while, it felt like these meals were the only time we got to be us again, rather than Mom or Dad or baker or firefighter or whatever role we played for other people.

"What did you want to ask me earlier?" he says at some point when our plates are cleared. He pours an ice cube from his empty drink into his mouth and crushes it in his back teeth.

"Hmm," I say, a raspy hum. The alcohol and food have me feeling toasty and brave. "Is there anything we never tried that you wish we would have? Is there anything in particular we did that you think about?"

His pupils dilate in the dim light. I see his pulse hammer at the base of his throat. Watch his Adam's apple roll. He swirls around his highball glass before he tosses back another cube.

"So that I don't misread this," he says, careful and dark, "do you mean sexually?"

"Yes."

An unsmiling nod. Another crunch. He swallows.

"I just think about making you come," he says, simple and gruff. And I know that's exactly how it'd be. Filthy, raw, no-nonsense. "But I think about tying you up, too. Binding you, somehow."

Air escapes me, my nipples pulling so tight they sting. I can't make eye contact with the waiter when he drops off the bill a moment later. Can't even look at Ellis when we leave. We separate in the cable car again, each of us with our hands behind our backs against the glass like we're keeping them restrained. When he grabs my hand in the Uber back to Santa Cruz, my breath hitches. I feel every circle he traces against my skin like he's teasing my opening.

It is humbling, how desperately and how quickly I want him this way. How much effort it takes me to walk in an even-measured stride across the lobby when we get back to our hotel.

I am a panting, wanton wreck by the time we make it into the elevator. He slams a fist on our floor number when the doors slide shut, and dives for me. We're a frenzy of needy sounds and obscenities and desperate, grasping hands. Sloppy, erratic kissing and too-hard bites. I shamelessly grab him by his ass and hook a thigh around his hip so I can grind into him where I need him. He buries a primal grunt into the valley of my chest.

We miss it when the doors open the first time on our floor, and he has to blindly reach around until he slaps the open button again. And then we're ping-ponging into the hallway until he presses me into the wall between our doors.

"My place—" he says, punctuating it with a hot kiss and a feral grin. "Or yours?"

I growl out an ugly moan and throw my key at him. He eagerly shoves it in and slams it open with a bang before he's hauling me into my room behind him.

"Fuck, it smells like you in here," he groans.

I garble something and chase him with my mouth.

"I just gotta make you come. Just once. Please let me," he says.

"Yes. Yes, that's the idea."

"No, but, I just—ah—you said no sex. I'm not breaking that on night one."

"*What?!*" I'm sure I should feel some sort of embarrassment for how appalled I sound. He makes a sound in the back of his throat and cups my jaw in one hand.

"No . . . sex. Not this first night. Going to do this right."

"God, I don't care. I just need—" A knot that matches the one in my core tangles in my throat, and I'm at once inexplicably confused and desperate and aching.

"I know, baby, shh." He kisses the corners of my eyes, the high planes of my cheekbones, the tip of my chin. "I know. I need, too. I need *you*. Let's . . . let's just slow down one notch."

I will my breathing to even out, let him wind me down with slow, drugging kisses while he sways us side to side. I tremble harder the more tender he is, emotion refusing to abate.

"Are we stupid to do this? Is this a bad idea?" I whisper. Am I stupid to want to risk this so quickly again? Are we doing this right? Where'd we go wrong before?

"No, I don't think so," he whispers back. "We're just us."

For a second, I think he's just confirmed our stupidity. We *are* us. Two small-town nobodies that got knocked up at seventeen and eighteen. It certainly wasn't the smartest thing anyone's ever done. But then I realize he's just right. We're what we are and what we've always been to each other. The alchemy of our bodies and the way my skin still remembers his is a part of that. He said it himself before: he's altered my very DNA.

"You're shaking," he says, heartbreakingly gentle. He cradles my head to his shoulder while one palm pets me from my nape to the base of my spine. I idly recall the same way he comforts Bud and wonder if he'll pat me on the rump, too. "Are you okay? It's just me, Wren." That's exactly it, though. It's Ellis. It's been five years. It's been too many other men's arms and not a fraction of this even if you compiled them all together. It's been disappointment after disappointment and feeling emptier and emptier, wondering if there was something *wrong* with me. If something broke inside me. Every step I take with him gets me further away from those lofty ideas of comfort I had and closer to *this*. This overwhelming, gutting, soul-rendering feeling is so dangerous. And I'm watching myself dive for it with so little caution.

"Let me kiss you some more," he says against my temple. Like he needs it just as much. "Let me take care of you. Please."

I nod against him, and his stubble scrapes my cheek. He rewards me with more kisses along the line of my jaw, under my ear and down my neck while he walks me backward, until I'm softly pressed to the wall. His tongue dips into the hollow of my throat, and he blows cool air there before he continues across the shelf of my collarbone. When he reaches my shoulder, he swirls his tongue against my skin before he delicately slips the strap of my dress away, inch by painstaking inch. He lets it hang at the top of my breast for a beat, and I hear him swallow, like he's preparing himself to reveal that part of me. I lift my shoulder and let it fall away before he has the chance.

"Fuck," he whispers before he runs his lips back and forth across my nipple. "Fuck, I missed you." The pure emotion in his voice sears through me.

He slides the other strap down, lifts both of my breasts and molds them together, wetly kissing each of them before blowing cold air on them and watching them tighten more. He rubs his whole face across their surfaces, his nose and lips and even his brow, like he's lost in the sensation. Like he's utterly fascinated by them, like they're his every lurid dream come to life. My arms are still trapped against my sides by my straps, and my lower half is still pinned to the wall by his. My hips tilt, searching for something, and he's there like he knows, pressing his thigh between my legs and lifting me up the wall, perfectly applying pressure where I need it most. I rock slowly at first, until I can feel the edge of what I'm chasing. And then I torque and squirm and grind and gasp and slur helpless, beseeching words when he tugs at my nipples with his teeth. He builds it, stokes it in me until I feel like I'm aflame, desperately and clumsily circling. All while he goes on sucking and flicking me with his tongue.

"You gonna come like this?" he rasps, awed. "Can you get there with just my knee? Fuck, I bet you're wet. If I touch you, I'm done. I'll come in my pants like I'm sixteen again." He's amused at how needy we both are. Moaning at my whimpering and chuckling at my breathy, high sputter of a laugh. I let out an agonized, teeth-chattering sound when he abandons my chest and grasps at my hips to rock me against him harder. "Yeah, you're gonna come like this," he murmurs resolutely. I feel my underwear slip to the side and I'm bare against his jeans. I mutter some nonsense about his pants even as I ride him harder. "Yes. Make a fucking mess," he says.

He sinks his teeth into my shoulder and works at me, lifting, tilting, dragging me until every sensation coalesces into one blistering, incandescently long release. He takes me through every last pulse, whispering praises into my neck, kissing my breastbone before he deftly plucks my arms out of my dress straps and wraps them around his neck to carry me to the bed.

He lays me down carefully and cups me again, twisting languid kisses into my skin and sending little aftershocks shimmering through me. I let my fingers roam along his scalp and touch his serene face. His eyelashes fan out against his cheeks while he goes on enjoying himself.

"I missed you, too," I say, chest still rising and falling and sweat cooling on my skin. His eyes open and meet mine. "So much." When I toy with the top button of his shirt, his hand envelops mine and holds it still. He slides up the bed to kiss my mouth. "Can I touch you?" I ask.

"I'm a feather stroke away from coming already, Wren. I just wanted to—*oof*—what are you—shit." His eyes roll back when I palm him through his jeans, and he grabs my wrist again. "No, honey. I'm serious. First time I get to be with you again, I would really like to make it last."

"How do you think putting this off until tomorrow is gonna help?" I muse.

He exhales a laugh and rolls one of my nipples playfully with his palm. "Because I'm going to go back to my room now where I plan to masturbate furiously," he informs me.

"Can I at least watch?" I say.

His eyes stutter closed. "*Jesus Christ*, you're trying to kill me," he groans weakly.

When he extricates himself from my limbs and bolts to his feet, I lean up onto my elbows and pin him with a coquettish look, my dress still tangled down around my waist. His hands bracket his hips before he roughly adjusts himself in a way that makes my mouth go dry. His fingers thread over the back of his head while he stares down at me, visibly enduring a battle within himself, biceps bunching and flexing. I lazily slide a thumb over a nipple, and his plea is downright grief-stricken.

"*No*," he abruptly says—yells—and I jump a little. Which makes him cycle through a half-worded apology that melts into another mewl when my tits bounce bawdily. "I'm doing this right. We're taking it slow. I'll . . . I'll see you in the morning. Checkout is at eleven, but we both know we'll be up before dawn, so just text me when you want to get breakfast. Or come

by. Or send a homing pigeon. Tap Morse code against my door."
He bends himself in half to plant a firm kiss to my mouth. "I—"

His eyes widen and his lips pale. Mine do the same when I
realize he was about to say *I love you.* I quickly stretch up to kiss
him again and pretend I didn't notice.

"I'll talk to you in the morning," I say, forcing a smile.

Emotions drift over his face like a time lapse of a storm. He leans
in for one last kiss. "I'll talk to you in the morning."

I try to push it out of my mind when he leaves. I shower, go
through an entire skin-care routine, brush my teeth, and admire
all the marks he left in places. I tell myself it was an easy slipup.
Just because he fell back in time on one routine phrase doesn't
mean we're doomed to fall back into our darkest time altogether.
For the most part, it works. I have genuine butterflies when I
finally lie down to go to sleep.

But . . . they're heavier than butterflies, with different wing-
spans and speeds. More like birds.

CHAPTER 24

———

WREN

I lever up in bed in my dark room when I awake, after finally getting a solid night's sleep. I grab my phone to check my notifications and see that I've got two emails from Ellis in my inbox. One that was sent right at 7:00 the night before, like he scheduled it in advance because he knew we'd be at dinner. Then one from a little after midnight. I open up the earlier one first.

From: ellis.byrd@gmail.com
To: wrenbyrdbakes@gmail.com
Subject: Journal

(I tried to write this the way you did where I wrote about you distantly, but my brain got tongue-tied (lobe-tied? Sounds gross). Anyway, it's me responding to what you already wrote so I hope this is okay for me to do it like this and write TO you.)

Wren,

We just got back to the hotel after a long, fun morning
at the aquarium, and I want to start by saying thank you
for graciously allowing this old man to take a nap. I'm not
going to be able to reply to your journal line for line in the
same lovely, thoughtful way that you have, but I figure if
I let my thoughts unspool, something coherent will come
together.

I would like to start by defending my first compliment to
you. Your eyes do remind me of a cow's. They're big and
dark and hypnotic. They're lined with pretty eyelashes and
have irises that seem to take up most of the room. They're
the kind of eyes you can get lost in and the kind you want
to tell your secrets to because you know they'll stay safely
hidden.

I think when it came to you and me later on, you were
always so in tune with my thoughts that I took it for granted.
I started forgetting to share them out loud. Sometimes I'm
just lost in my own head, Wren, and I forget to tell you that
I love the little lines that bracket your mouth. They were
on full display yesterday when we rode roller coasters and
when you won at those overpriced, rigged carnival games,
then again this morning when you watched the otters play.
I love that dimple under the corner of your bottom lip that
pops up when you pout or when you concentrate. I've
noticed that your hair is lighter over the last few months. I
need to remember to remark on that later. Shit, I'll probably forget. Did you do something different, though? Is it

my imagination? I will do my best to get better at compliments.

As far as vows go, I plan to apologize tonight, but I'll say it here again. The point should have been to compromise. I could have written them. Put them on paper for you to read. Given myself time to get my thoughts out right. Even if I couldn't speak them in front of others, I could have tried to give you something you wanted while still honoring myself.

Reading your journal and being in your mind made me feel all sorts of things, but mostly awe. We all talk about Sage seeing what people need and her empathy, but it's clear to me that you've always been the same, Wren. You're indomitable in every way when it comes to the people you love. I'm grateful you saw me. Thank you. I think your friendship made it so I could look back on my childhood and not only remember Mom dying or Dad's flakiness and that constant instability. We talk a lot in therapy about my parents, and it probably sounds a little stupid when I say that I wasn't expecting to, but the truth is, I wasn't. I expected to learn how to fix me, not *why* I am how I am. I've always been scared to talk about the things I resented because they were still good parents and good people. It used to feel like I was only remembering them in a negative light if I did that, but I'm learning how to hold space for more than one feeling.

There's something you and I have never talked about when it comes to them, too. Actually, there are a lot of things you and I never talked about. I think it's strange when people act like there's no room for secrets or keeping anything (excluding nefarious shit) in a marriage. I've known you my whole damn life, and you still surprise me.

Anyway, back to my story . . .

I know I never talked to you about all the details behind the fire in our first barn over at our old house (Sage's), and how it was started. It always seemed irrelevant. You already know that it was caused by a propane buddy heater that got tipped over—probably by some sort of mouse or a feral cat. What you don't know is that my dad had an old TV with rabbit ears and he would take that old propane heater out to the barn to watch that TV in peace and quiet. Didn't matter that we had a much nicer TV inside the house where the rest of us were, he wanted to be by himself and wanted his peace. I don't fault him for that, but . . . Wren, I can't tell you how many times my mom nagged him about not falling asleep out there and not leaving that buddy heater in the barn when he would come back. It was almost *every time*. When she was alive, he'd amble back and grab it, but later on, he'd just turn it off and leave it to save himself the load. I couldn't understand why someone would forget something they were reminded of so consistently. It was like that for a lot of things. Practice and game schedules and anything that required adhering to a schedule, neither of them prioritized. I know that they were unusually good at living in the moment, and maybe because they came home and started having kids later in life, they'd already adopted that policy on not sweating the small stuff, or something. Not even small *stuff*, exactly, because they were good at making mundane things feel special, but more like the responsibilities of life. And if they wouldn't sweat that, who would, I guess? I got tired of being late all the time, or feeling like something or someone was being forgotten. That feeling when you're leaving for a trip and can't remember if something was left on or unlocked, or if Macaulay Culkin was still in the attic? I felt like that all the time growing up. I think their lackadaisical approach to life only amped up my need for order.

Part of me thinks that's why Dad tried for so long to put out the fire himself. Why he inhaled so much smoke and gave himself a heart attack. I still don't know how I feel about that. Embarrassed that he might have been embarrassed? Mad that he couldn't just be responsible in the first place, especially since he'd been reminded so many times?

For all that I prioritized regular life responsibilities, structure, and plans, I have realized over the years how little room I left to make other plans, simply for fun. I recognize how that stuff fell onto you by default, and I'm sorry.

I really don't want to end this there and want to talk about some brighter things. Because, Wren, I really do feel brighter than I have in years. The last two days felt like they lasted a century in the best way, and this trip isn't even halfway over. I'm not a writer, though, and don't know how to make a smooth transition here. (Hold for awkward pause??)

I don't remember the first time we met, but my memories started to get stronger right around eleven. I know we've briefly touched on this before, but you were the inspiration for so many of my first inconvenient, ill-timed, and very accidental boners. I remember feeling fucking alarmed by how out of control I felt, frankly. I think that's why it took me so long to let myself own my real feelings for you when we were sixteen and seventeen. I'd always thought of myself as some perverted, untrustworthy creature who hardly deserved to be your friend, let alone more.

I remember when your voice changed for me, too, when the way you said my name felt like a hook under my ribs. When we got together and would make out between classes and I was sure that happiness was stuck in my teeth for everyone to see.

I can't wait to see you tonight. I'm going to try to nap now, and then if there's time to kill, I'm going to head down to the pool on the off chance that you'll be down there, too, and I'll get to leer at you in your bikini.

I can't wait to see you.

From: ellis.byrd@gmail.com
To: wrenbyrdbakes@gmail.com
Subject: Thank you

Thank you for kissing me tonight.

After a very dignified squeal into my pillow, I flick on the lamp and pack up my things, excited for the next leg of our journey.

CHAPTER 25

WREN

My phone is already busier than it ever is with the standard birth-day notifications, but I quickly scroll and find a message from Ellis telling me he's left a coffee outside my door.

Memories of last night hurtle through me at the same time I see all the names of the people I love on my phone. It feels like a gentle nudge from the universe to be careful, to remember that we have a regular life and home to go back to, the same place and people who had to pick up the debris of us before. But when I remember the easy intimacy Ellis and I rediscovered yesterday and the bare pleasure in his eyes even after he took me apart, I want to rebel against all of that caution and grab the rest of this trip with both hands.

Thank you for the coffee, I text Ellis. **I slept in**

Good. Happy birthday, Byrd. If you need time to get ready I'll go grab breakfast and drop it off?

You don't have to drop it and run :)

Three dots hover and disappear. Come back again and disappear again.

If we want to get checked out of here on time, yeah I do

———

I continue to be a disordered mix of edgy and exhilarated as I get ready for the day, but the moment I see him in the lobby, all my circular thoughts wind down.

I watch him catalog every inch of me as I make my way toward him. He starts at my favorite worn-in cowgirl boots, then drifts over my white flowy skirt, lingers on the slope of my hips like he's remembering how they filled his palms while he drove me over the edge. I see him sigh, and I'm not sure if it's in relief or resignation when he traces over my top. It's a simple black knitted thing that ties across my chest, a triangle of torso on display. I can already feel him taking it off. I see it when he clocks the little strip of a whisker burn he gave me at the edge of my neckline. His jaw clenches tight before it relaxes into a heady grin.

"Hey, birthday girl," he says. It sounds like the first time he's used his voice today. He lifts two of my bags from my shoulders and loops them onto his own. "Ready to keep going?"

"I am."

It's a forty-five-minute drive into the Santa Cruz mountains to get to where we're headed, and I'm scheming up more questions and torturous, sad-girl playlists, but the outside world interrupts as soon as we leave the parking lot.

Sage calls first to wish me a happy birthday, followed by Sam and my mom. Then comes Silas, who lingers on the phone.

"*Sooo*, what are you guys up to?" he asks, singsongy. I frown over at Ellis, who scowls at the phone.

"You're on speakerphone, Silas," he informs him, which makes me lift a brow.

"We're just driving to our next stop," I say. When he's silent, I ask, "What are *you* doing?"

"Driving to Beaverton with Micah to use the Sluggers tickets I got him for Christmas."

"You're making him go to a baseball game? Christ, Silas." Seems a bit insensitive given that Micah is in a rough place with the sport right now.

"*What?* He was still playing when I gave him the tickets. It's circus ball, anyway. Not regular baseball."

"It's a *joke*," I hear Micah spit. "And happy birthday, Wren."

"Thanks, bud," I say. But I'm stuck remembering how I had to fake being sick to get out of last Christmas. After Thanksgiving . . . it felt too fresh, and I couldn't handle the idea of more togetherness so soon.

The first two years after the divorce were like that. For me and Ellis both, I think. Holidays and family gatherings were too damned uncomfortable for everyone. Getting to a place where I could handle being in proximity to him again without the hurt affecting everyone else took a lot of work.

Work we might've undone in the span of a few days.

Silas starts arguing with Micah about how circus ball is more entertaining than traditional baseball, and I quickly hang up before their bickering has a chance to bring my mood down any more.

"You okay?" Ellis asks.

I heave a sigh and study him. He seems more well rested and peaceful than he's been in years. "Just being neurotic about taking it slow or moving too fast." I look down at my phone and the background picture of Sam with an arm around Sage and me. The deeper we get, the bigger the climb to get back out if we can't make it again.

He grabs my hand on the center console and intertwines his fingers with mine. "I told you before, I like slow," he says. But then he plants a kiss to my knuckles, and I feel it somersault down my arm until it tingles across my chest and in all the places he kissed the night before.

"It's just too easy to fall right back into what we know is . . . good," I say. Incendiary, life-altering, explosive, and good.

"*Good*, huh?" he says, a smirk bending his lips. He knew exactly where my head went. "I get it and agree. But it's your birthday, and I'm at your disposal, however you need me. If you want to talk, we'll talk. If you want to write, we'll write." He beams, laugh lines spreading. "If you want to use my body, I won't hold it against you."

"Think you'd have to hold something against me to get me off," I say, and his grip around my hand squeezes tighter. "But." I've got a brilliant idea. New rules. "What if we say we can't do anything we've done before?"

"Meaning?" He licks his lower lip.

I can't resist teasing him a little. "Meaning, we couldn't pull over and fuck in the back seat—"

"Jesus, Byrd."

"—but last night was the first time I came on your thigh." I give him a slinky grin. "We could get creative." Somehow this is another justification in my brain.

His jaw works in fits. "I have always appreciated your creative-thinking skills," he grits. I'm not sure if it's his palm or mine starting to sweat where they're pressed together.

"Thank you. They've served me quite well in the past. I was a big fan of yours last night, too."

"Then it's a deal."

"Good," I declare. "Now pipe down so we can listen to my birthday anthem." I hit Play on my phone and turn the volume up. He grins at the road and kisses the back of my hand again.

———

The switchback road that leads us up to Montetesta Ranch is lined in soft, wheat-colored grasses that sway in the breeze, the occasional California poppy bursting through, plus a medley of cypress and other evergreens. The climb feels never-ending, until it finally crests and deposits us at a two-way stop. To the left and in the distance is the manor I saw from the website, and according to the sign in front of us, to the right lies the guest cottages and tasting room, where we also check in.

The tasting room is a condensed version of the manor; white stucco with black trim and terra-cotta tiles on the roof. A deck littered with tables and chairs wraps around it on all four sides.

"Reservation for the Byrds?" asks a woman from behind the counter when we stroll in. She looks like she's barely older than Sam. Emilia, according to her name tag.

"Should be two reservations, but yes," says Ellis at my side. When she pauses wiping down the glass in her hand and gives us an owlish look, I can predict what's coming next.

"You called and updated your reservation to one cottage . . . ?" she trails off, eyes darting back and forth between us.

Ellis and I turn to each other. "*Silas,*" we say in unison.

"I'll text him," I say, but Ellis shakes his head silently, already pushing Call on his phone and walking out.

"Sorry," I say to the girl. "We'll need to change it back to two cottages, if that's all right."

She grimaces. "We had a waiting list for this weekend. I called the first name on the list already."

I shut my eyes. This is *fine*. No big deal. I already had designs on hooking up with him, anyway. This isn't an insurmountable problem, exactly. I'm not going to lie to myself and act like this is the Thing that will make me prematurely jump my ex without appropriately addressing the issues we're unearthing on this trip.

I would have last night.

"Silas and Micah swear it wasn't them," Ellis says, stepping back into the room.

"Sage wouldn't do this," I say suspiciously. "You don't think . . . ?"

He gives me a quizzical smile. "You think he'd try to *Parent Trap* us?" He laughs. "Now?"

I try to call Sam to find out, and it goes to voicemail after two rings. "It doesn't matter, anyway," I say with a sigh. "They're all booked up now."

"Should I take you to the cottage, then?" asks Emilia. "You'll have a few hours to settle in and explore the grounds before your cooking class."

"*Cooking* class?" I struggle to keep the annoyance out of my voice. I bake six days a week, and as much as I love what I do, I'm not exactly gunning to spend my birthday in a kitchen. Still, I realize Sam probably thought he was planning a nice surprise and I try to recover. "That'll be fun," I say, faking a smile.

We climb back into the truck and follow Emilia in her golf cart over to the rows of cottages. They're tiny. We're about to be squeezed from all sides. It's dramatic, I know, but it feels like the last forty-eight hours might've been as successful as they were because we had space to separate, too, and I'm suddenly worried the extra pressure could crack us.

When we step onto the small porch with our bags in hand, Ellis looks over at me and says, "We're okay," with a nod.

I realize I'm holding my breath, and I blow it out on a nervous laugh. "We're okay."

It's his turn to laugh anxiously when he unlocks the door and steps in. At least 75 percent of the room is occupied by a bed.

CHAPTER 26

ELLIS

I'm less than okay.

I guess the good thing about being irritated with Sam is that it softens the whole missing-him thing. It's safe to assume our entire family all know exactly what we're doing here and are in cahoots at this point.

I don't want to be pushed by them—or by any outside forces, for that matter. I want us to stay in control.

Still staring at the bed, I ask Wren, "Do you really want to do a cooking class?"

I feel her eyes on me, but I can't take mine off the stupid bed. "Sure," she says, her voice high. It's the same voice she used to switch into around Sam, too strained and too careful. "Sam planned it, so."

I look at her now. So pretty it stings. I spot a freckle on the bit of her waist that's exposed by her scrap of a shirt and force myself to blink away. "Byrd, Sam's not here. No one's here. There's no one running plans but us. This whole thing is . . . *We* are taking the wheel here. Plus, it's your birthday."

She blows out a big sigh. "Then, no. I do not," she admits, smiling at whatever pleased expression lifts onto my face. "Now you tell me a truth. Are you freaking out about this? About any of this?" Her gaze bounces around the room.

"Yes."

The rosy flush on her face disappears, and her eyes flare wider. "Wait, you are?! I expected you to say no and platitude me!" She stabs a finger into my chest, and I stop myself from grabbing it and biting it. "Why are you freaking out?"

Because I want to spread you wide on these pristine white sheets and taste you. "Because I can practically touch both ends of this room with my arms spread, which means you're close enough to touch no matter where you are in here." *Because I hate that I lost you for half of a decade and I need this to be perfect more than I've ever needed anything, ever. I'm struggling not to grab you and kiss you and fuck you until we both forget the time we lost. Until we both forget our names.* "Because it's a big and fast change to be this close, and I don't want anything to go too fast between us. Because I want to do this right, which also means that on a day that is not your birthday, we will need to keep going through the bad stuff, too, and that scares me because I've loved finding all the good memories and good things we lost. Because, unless I sleep in that tub on the back porch, we will presumably be sharing that bed, and I haven't heard you snore in, like, five years." *Because you make up half of my soul. Because as desperate as I am to be near you, to be inside you, I'm terrified that having you this close again will also remind you of all the parts of me you wanted to leave.*

Her face is frozen in surprise. "That was . . . a lot of truths."

And not even the half of it.

"Except I don't snore," she says, rolling her eyes.

Yes, she does. In soft, disjointed little growls that I used as my personal sound machine. "Dare you to tell me why you're freaking out," I say.

She softens, brown eyes glowing. "Dares now, huh?" She eyes me sharply like she's filing that away. "And all of the above."

The only thing between us is the suitcase at her feet. The outside of my thigh is touching the edge of the mattress. It would be so easy to tip over onto it. "At least we're still on the same page, then? Seems like a good sign," I offer.

She grabs the suitcase handle and rolls it behind her with a precise flick of her wrist before she steps into my chest. I can feel my heart in my temples. "Do I get a dare?" she asks.

I gulp. *Coax. Convince. Gentle. Don't go too fast. Don't blow past all the important shit you need to get through.* "Be good, Byrd," I say, but it comes out a begging wheeze and sounds a lot like, *Have mercy.* "But yes, you can have your dare."

Her smile unfurls slowly, her eyes never leaving my mouth. She cups my jaw in her fine hand and drags her thumb across my chin. I feel it in my cock. God, the way she smells. I want to bury my nose in that hair.

"I dare you to get a little day-buzzed in the tasting room with me, then haul one of those premade platters I saw in there out into the vineyards so we can have a picnic together," she says, smile beaming. Before I can chuckle and agree to this, she adds, "And then let me take advantage of you a little bit."

"Shit," I breathe, shutting my eyes against the near-painful surge of blood racing south. "Wren, that was, like, three dares."

"Keep the change," she sings. "You can use two of them on me later." And with that, she slides herself past me, taking care to rub her chest across my ribs.

I groan. "You've gotten meaner," I tell her, thoroughly tortured. A little amazed.

"Good," she says sweetly. "Maybe I want you to be mean back."

She glides out the door still grinning, and it takes me the entire football field's distance to the tasting room to walk off the semi.

CHAPTER 27

ELLIS

It is disturbingly easy to get drunk wine tasting.

A little more than an hour after Emilia sits us at a table on the covered patio overlooking the vineyard and the big house in the distance, I'm good and buzzed.

"It's the tiny sips that get you," Wren muses. "Especially when they're tasty and you wanna toss 'em back." She demonstrates.

"Is that it? I keep downing the ones I don't like to get it over with quicker," I say, snorting a laugh into my glass.

Other patrons have slowly joined us over time, too. A few families mill around on the hillside lawn area that slopes down to the edge of the vines. Mostly, it's other couples at nearby tables on the deck, and one in particular that I think is fueling our consumption.

"—on the nose, pear, with crushed rock, fresh grass, lychee, and honeydew," the man says. Some people look more like animals than people to me, and I swear to god this one's a ferret.

I might be approaching drunk.

I catch Wren's eyes, and she mouths *What the fuck?* with a nod in his direction. I shrug. Beats me.

"On the palate, it shows vibrant flavors of tropical fruit and citrus. Really a remarkably bright finish," he adds. Should we applaud? His partner merely hums her agreement.

He pours his next glass and sniffs loudly into it before he swirls it, tips it back, and swishes it around his yapper like snooty Listerine. Right down to how he spits it back into a metal canister.

"Lovely perfume of Daphne. Freshly sliced apples—"

"*I bet they were days old*," I mutter out the side of my mouth to Wren. "*Old, wormy, NON-sliced apples.*"

"—and Anjou pears. Finishes with jasmine tea and a drop of honeysuckle. Definitely a Burgundian aging technique. SUCH a velvety mouthfeel."

"*I'll give you a velvety mouthfeel*," says Wren into my ear. I give her my best scowl over my sunglasses. This evil woman cannot make me get hard while listening to Ferret Face. Her full lips slip into a grin, and I hook my foot around her chair to haul her a few inches closer.

Ferret moves on to the next wine. "*For fuck's sake, do you think he's training for something?*" Wren whispers. The light puff of it against the shell of my ear sends chills up my arms.

"—a touch of pine and forest floor," I hear Ferret say. Wren mouths, *FOREST FLOOR??* And I laugh silently. "That complex oak just explodes on the tongue, doesn't it?"

Wren bursts into a fit of giggles, and I choke on my water. "Yeah, we gotta get out of here," I manage.

We grab a bottle of her favorite thing we tried—the champagne—plus one of their to-go platters with meats, cheeses, and nuts, and a borrowed picnic blanket that they have available before we head for the vineyard. I pop the bottle open and pass it to her when we're a safe distance into the maze. She takes a hearty sip, licks her lips, and says, "Mmmm. I'm detecting notes of grape." Which surprises a shout of laughter out of me.

She halts and I look down at her to find her expression serious. "I missed that," she says quietly, almost like it upsets her to acknowledge it. "I missed making you laugh like that."

Probably it's all the tiny sips of wines, but a variety of different feelings are making me feel drunk on them, too. She's the same woman I've always known. Same big, glittering eyes. Same wide, full mouth. Sharp jaw, smooth neck, wild, rioting curls I couldn't call *smooth* or *round* or *wavy* because they're all of it. But I'm disoriented looking at her now, nonetheless. I feel fucking stricken.

"I missed it, too," I say, voice ragged. I'd said it to her last night, too, but I also realize she was topless at the time and maybe she thought I only missed her half naked, specifically.

"What're you thinking about?" she asks, intrigued by whatever my face is doing.

"You, naked," I admit. To her flattened look, I add, "And how I missed making you feel anything. Turning you on, making you happy. Even missed annoying you." A new flavor on the palate—Ferret would be impressed—but there's an undercurrent of something bitter I can still detect, too. Like some small, pathetic part of me realizes how much power she has over me. How much she owns me. I've known I belonged to her since I was six, in one way or another, no matter the years I resisted it beyond being friends. I've never felt like I deserved her back.

The rest of me is a brute that wants to take and push and claim again.

I pull the plastic water bottle out of my back pocket and chug it. My pickled brain has no business getting this complex.

She chews over what she wants to say and continues walk-ing, the ground crunching quietly under her boots. We've gone far enough that we're tucked between two tall hills striped in rows of vines, only the tops of the surrounding buildings visible. "Strange that it doesn't feel like it's been five years," she says, tak-ing a pull from the champagne bottle.

I hitch the blanket higher on my shoulder and snort. "It felt longer," I say sullenly.

"Were you happy?" she asks. "I mean, like, did you get to a place where you were okay? Where you were able to feel happiness?"

I choose my words carefully. "I think so, yeah. I'm not naturally exuberant or anything to begin with, but . . . In comparison to those last years, once I got out of the thick of it after the divorce, I felt lighter again, I guess. What about you?"

"Yeah," she says tightly. "I felt happiness. It was just different."

"How?"

She huffs out a frustrated breath. "I guess . . . Like feeling the sun shining through a window. It's sunshine and it's there and it's warm, but it's not the same as feeling it on my skin."

I reach out for the champagne, and she hands it my way. I let the bubbles fizz through me, that mild, refreshing sting. And then I kiss her.

I kiss her because there's no glass or walls or miles between us right now. Just her and her glowing skin and her full lips that taste like sweet, bright grapes. I kiss her because she's kind and clever and so pretty it takes my breath away. She's mine and I'm hers, and all my life's greatest happiness can be traced back to her, so I kiss her because I want to, and forget the rest.

It starts out frantic, licking wine and groans off each other's tongues. The champagne bottle thumps against her thigh while I cup her face with my free hand. It quickly turns into something languid. Scratchy sighs and slow tugs. I become hyperaware of all five of my senses. I hear the noises that catch in her throat, hear birds chirping. I feel the softness of her skin and skate my thumb along her jaw. I taste her. Feel myself clench and flex where her hands press into my arms and back. When I pull away, I watch her eyes open, heavy and slow. See it when her pupils contract, irises like brandy here in the bright day. Her smile battles with one corner of her mouth first, before it sprawls out to the other. It's like watching a sunrise lift across her whole face.

"Let's go back to the shack," she says dreamily.

I shake my head. "Picnic," I say.

She lifts one dark eyebrow at me, and I let myself thumb it. "It's my birthday," she reminds me with a sassy tilt of her chin.

"I know it is. That's why I want to get my hand up your skirt and play with you until you come," I say. And then I step back and lay out the blanket. "I've never done that in a vineyard before."

Her chest rises unevenly. "You can't always get your way, you know," she says, primly lowering herself onto the quilt. She stays propped up on her elbows, and her knees shift beneath her skirt, parting slightly.

"I know, Byrd," I say, heart drumming hard in my chest. I stretch out beside her and lean onto a forearm, planting a kiss on her bare shoulder. "You said you wanted me mean."

We both watch my hand slide up her shin, bunching the skirt up with it. I pause when her smooth, tanned kneecap is revealed, and I spot the two-inch scar beside it.

Shortly after she and Sam moved in with me and my siblings, she'd been down on her hands and knees helping Sage with a school project, using an X-Acto knife to cut through poster board for something I can't even remember. She was cutting toward herself and got a little stuck, pulled too hard, and sliced into her own skin. There's another faint scar in her hairline from when we were in third grade and I dared her to walk across the top of the monkey bars. There are two more scars on her stomach. One from a cesarean when they cut Sam from her, where I watched her split open and saw a whole life pulled out. Another vertical scar from an emergency laparotomy when she had a ruptured fallopian tube, terminology that was burned into my brain when I was stuck in a cold, clinical room waiting for her to be out of that surgery. So many of her scars are related to me. It's a struggle to breathe around the emotions billowing in my lungs.

"If this is you being mean, I don't think I'll survive it when you're nice," Wren says. When our eyes lock, she frowns sharply. "What's wrong?"

I fight to swallow and shake my head. "I'm just happy you came here with me," I say, throat tight. Fingertips tracing over the scar on her knee. "I'm just happy I get to be with you again. Right now, I mean. I know it's not . . . I know you haven't decided anything. I just thought I never would." I also plan to never drink wines again if they make my mood this unstable.

She wraps a hand around my neck and pulls me down to her lips. I let half my weight settle onto her, and I swallow her quiet groan. I go back to tracing patterns on her skin with my fingertips.

"So soft," I say, then hiss when she palms me through my jeans.

"You're not," she says into my mouth.

I tease a path up her thigh, let my knuckles brush across her panties, blood surging through my veins at the heat of her. I slide my palm down her other thigh, massage my way back up and over in a circuit until she's writhing and panting. Small, bitten-off sounds slip out of her against my chin.

"*Please*," she says like a curse.

I think I make more noise than she does when I finally touch her. Blazing hot, and "So fucking wet." Wet and lush and perfect. She curls a fist in my hair and tugs. It's second nature, knowing what rhythm and pressure she likes. *Like whisking, but with your finger*, she'd once described it when we were younger. I smile against her neck at the memory. She chases my mouth with hers, and all of it, it's all coming back to me. I know how she'll start to circle a little and how she'll get super quiet just before, like she senses it right in front of her and is concentrating on getting it. She'll clench her eyes shut until she's about to tip over, and then *there*, she opens them and looks right at me with a low hum that I'll feel vibrate all the way through her.

"Get it, baby," I say, watching her come apart in bliss. She does, another little anguished sound leaving her in a hot, breathy plea, and it's the most beautiful thing I've ever seen.

She's still pulsing against my fingertips when she reaches for my zipper, and I ache so badly I can't think of any reason to say no. "We're going to have to steal this blanket," I say, panting before she's even freed me from my jeans.

"Not if you come in my mouth," she says, and I think I black out.

We've just wrestled my pants down my hips when the sound of feedback blares over a loudspeaker from somewhere. "*We need Wren and Ellis Byrd up at the main house*," a voice says. "*Wren and Ellis Byrd*," it says again, drawing out each syllable. It's like the time we got called into the principal's office senior year because we got caught by a teacher making out next to Wren's locker. "*Class starts in one minute.*"

CHAPTER 28

ELLIS

Apparently, it wasn't safe to assume we'd be left to our own devices if we didn't show up for the cooking class.

We end up hoofing it to the manor house after they summon us through the sound system one more time, fixing clothes on the way and following the signs pointing to the cooking class and the thumping sounds of music blaring.

I'm about to tell Wren that I'll cover us and let whoever the host is know that we won't be participating, when a tiny woman comes flying around the corner in a cloud of white, gauzy material, her arms wide and her smile wider.

"They're here!" she croons toward the room she's just left, which makes the room erupt in a cheer. She turns back to us. "We've been waiting for you!" Her smile is as white as her slicked-back hair and her linen pants. She dances her way back into the room, gesturing for us to follow.

"I'll tell them we're not staying," I say to Wren. I have to shout a little over the music.

"We'd better just do it!" she shouts back. "I'm curious now."

We round the corner to a long, tiled room with four separate islands complete with stove-top burners, sinks, and counters overflowing with ingredients and cookware. One wall of the room is lined with photos that showcase the grounds during various phases of construction, another is filled with cabinets and a gigantic refrigerator, and the last has a huge set of accordion-style doors that are open to a patio with an iron railing.

There's a group of eight mingling and swaying together in one area of the room; half of which are wearing something that states BRIDESMAID. A girl in a white sundress wearing a crown and a veil shimmies her way over to one of the guys in the group. He takes a swig from a flask before he passes it to one of his buddies and intercepts her, dropping her into a dip and kissing her. The rest of the room applauds accordingly.

The white-haired woman is doing some sort of salsa with an equally linen-clad man at the front of the room, and standing stoically off to the side are Ferret and his partner.

"Oh no, our nemeses," Wren says into my ear.

I refrain from groaning. I don't think I can handle anyone going on about a "bright finish" right now.

"G'day, everyone!" calls our hostess from the front, turning down the music volume from a remote. "I'm Bernadette, but please call me Bernie, and this here is my partner, Robbie, but please call him Bob. As you might've guessed, we are from Australia. Please don't ask us to say 'aur naur' or anything of Cleo or condensation, as this is the one and only time we will mention it." She claps loudly.

"Right, then," says Bob. He launches into a brief history of the place and when they built it. It's lost on me because I'm a bit stuck on the bachelor-bachelorette party, who, upon closer inspection, all appear to be fucking *blitzed*.

"First things first," calls Bernie. "Mingle about the room and introduce yourselves. Let everyone know why you're here, what you're celebrating, what have you."

Wren and I share a commiserate look. "I know you don't want to meet new people, but . . . ?" she says.

I'm not sure I'd like anything other than to finish what we started in the vineyard, but I'll muster up the social energy. "I can summon some manners," I say. "Keep a wide berth around the maid of honor, though. She's, without a doubt, hurling before the end of today."

"Oh, for sure she is," Wren agrees. We watch the girl's chin rear back with the force of her belch, skin going a shade greener.

"I reckon this isn't their first stop of the day," Bernie says to Wren and me, nodding toward the group with Bob tucked into her side, a genial grin on his sun-weathered face. "What are you lovebirds here celebrating, then?"

"We dropped our son off at college," says Wren.

"And it's her birthday today," I add.

"Surely you're too young to have a kid in college," Bernie says to Wren, genuinely perplexed.

Wren looks my way with a knowing smirk, and we end up grinning at each other like no one else is here. Like there are no groomsmen talking about hitting some sort of wine bong called a *porrón* in the opposite corner and like Ferret and his partner aren't mean-mugging the rest of us. We turn twin, politely subdued expressions on Bernie and Bob, and raise our brows patiently. The same timing and same looks we mastered when Sam was little.

We learned early on that we didn't owe anyone else explanations about our ages.

Their smiles stiffen, and the bride from the bachelorette party stumbles over to nudge Wren with her elbow. "Older men, though, am I right?" she says, tilting her chin my way in explanation. I look over at her fiancé, who does, in fact, appear to be older than she is, by more than a decade if I had to guess. And she thinks Wren can relate?!

Wren makes a good show of trying not to laugh before it bursts out of her.

"How much *older* do you think I am?!" I ask the bride indignantly.

Wren wails another laugh, and the bride blushes. "Oh shit, I'm sorry," she says. "You just, well, you look—" She grimaces and shrugs apologetically.

Wren finishes chortling enough to peck a placating kiss on my chin. "You just have a very distinguished look about you," she says.

I feel like milking it and want her to kiss me again. "You mean tired and old," I grouse, trying to look stern. "Haggard."

"Handsome," she corrects, smiling softly. She quickly kisses the corner of my mouth and scratches a hand through my hair. I feel like purring.

The rest of our classmates have gone back to socializing among themselves when Bob claps from the front of the room.

"All right, everyone," he starts. "As we covered, Bern here and I are Australian, living on this replicated Italian villa we get to call home, growing French grapes on Californian soil. *So*, naturally, we will be cooking Indian cuisine today!"

Ferret raises his hand, then speaks out before he's called upon. "Do you have a pairing list to accompany the meal, or are we just supposed to wing it?" he asks.

"Uhhh, drink whatever you'd like to, mate. There's beer in the fridge, too," says Bob.

Ferret looks like he might have an aneurysm. His partner looks asleep on her feet, rocking back on her heels. I bet for all his sipping and spitting, she's been consuming.

I have a sinking feeling this entire debacle is about to get ugly.

"Everyone needs to divide into three groups," Bernie explains. "One will be in charge of samosas, one will be making a variety of chutneys, and the last will be assembling keema. There are no vegetarians or diet restrictions here, yeah?" We all sound off our nos. The maid of honor yells out, "*Naur!*" obnoxiously. "Right, then," says Bob, sharing a long-suffering look with Bernie before continuing. "Everyone, divvy up! Only rule is y'can't stay in a group with the partner you came with! I know, I know. Very sad. But the goal of this class is to mingle. To mix it up and do something fresh. Feel free to put your spin on any part of your dish you'd like, but you'll find instructions are in the binder at your island, along with all the proper tools you'll require."

This new bit takes me from mildly irritated to flat-out annoyed. I don't want something fresh. I don't want to mix it up. I need to be back with my wife as much as humanly possible and spending this time wisely. I'm officially pissed at Sam.

"Wanna sneak out?" I try, leaning into Wren.

"If they tracked us down earlier through a property-wide sound system, you think they'll let us ditch without a fuss now?" She chuckles. "I'm hungry, anyway." She swats my ass lightly before she struts off toward the samosa island, immediately wrangling the groom, the maid of honor, and Ferret's partner to her station.

I'm pouting. I love when she gets bossy in a kitchen.

Of course Ferret moves to me first. Dammit. The bride and a barely coherent groomsman join us.

"Bear," Ferret says, holding out his hand for me to shake. Fuck, that's not going to be easy to remember.

"Ellis," I reply with a worn-out sigh, taking his clammy palm in mine.

I learn that the bride's name is Tabitha, and the groomsman (who is also the best man) goes by Schwartz.

Bob turns up the music again just as Bernie comes dancing around with a tray full of shots.

Great. This is definitely gonna get ugly. I take one, salute Wren from across the room, then toss it back. If you can't leave them, join them, I guess?

Schwartz starts reading the directions for the spicy pineapple chutney with one eye shut. I start pulling ingredients out of bowls and grab a cutting board and a knife, moving aside a pair of gloves that was haphazardly thrown in with the pineapple.

Tabitha's fading fast all of a sudden. After apologizing to me a few more times about comparing me to the Crypt Keeper and leaning into my shoulder drowsily, she's now swaying to Michael Bublé and drinking from a tumbler with a penis straw. Fer—*Bear* is completely off task and useless, gone hunting for "an aged Riesling" because "anything else might as well be bilgewater with this meal." I am the soberest, so I grab the knife and get to chopping. Pineapple first, then the chilies. Tabitha and Schwartz start bickering about what he is and isn't allowed to talk about in his best man speech while they absentmindedly eat the diced pineapple straight from the bowl. I slide it away and chop a bit more, then cut up the onions as quickly as I can. I've cooked in a firehouse for years and have never desensitized my eyes to the damn things, so of course they start to water in the process. I wipe at them with the back of my wrist and wrap up the rest of the cutting that needs to get done so I can make a quick trip to the bathroom and not leave my dead-drunk team unsupervised with knives.

A spot under my eye starts burning when I've taken care of my business and start washing my hands. I swipe at it with a little cool water and get back out into the kitchen. Christ, someone started playing "Sweet Caroline." We've descended into chaos. Bob and Bernie look out on the group fondly, like this is any regular old Sunday to them.

The maid of honor is now fast asleep, slumped in a chair on the patio with her head hanging limply, shoes cradled in her lap. Wren's all business, making her still-upright teammates laugh and smile. She's got everyone in a line putting together samosas and has some already cooking in a fryer.

Shit, my eye burns again. It starts to water. I wipe at it again and it gets worse, right before the other one starts to sting, too. I rub at them harder, and suddenly, it's like I poked at hot embers and stirred up a flame.

My heart starts to pummel in my chest, panic ratcheting through me as the pain picks up. The sting is immediately too raw to open either of my eyes at all and I don't know my way around this place, so I don't know what to do or where to go.

"Ellis?" I hear Wren ask when I bump into an island and curse. Tears are still leaking from my eyes despite being clenched shut as tight as I can keep them. "Ellis, what's wrong? Are you okay?"

"No. I don't know what happened. My eyes are on fire. I . . . I can't open them." As soon as I say this, I feel a tingle in another place.

The absolute last place I want to feel a burn.

It ignites the moment my brain acknowledges it.

FUCK.

CHAPTER 29

WREN

Ellis is doing a potty dance.

I'm sure there's a better way to describe it, but that is all that comes to mind at the moment. A very large, very grown man's version of a potty dance.

He alternates lifting his knees and slightly crossing them, sputtering out a litany of curses. His eyes are still clenched shut, and his hands continuously ball and spread at his sides.

"Oh no!" Bernie yells, fluttering over here in all her linen. I guess she said *aur naur* again after all. "Did you not wear the gloves?!" she asks Ellis, a horrified look on her face.

Ellis turns toward her voice, but he's angled about a foot off in the wrong direction. "The gloves weren't in the instructions!" he says helplessly.

"Ah, fuckin' hell, mate. You touched your eyes, I take it?" says Bob.

Ellis pivots toward me. "Wren," he says, a deep, broken growl. Oh, I've got to get him out of here.

"Mate, you didn't touch your doodle, did you?" Bob adds.

"The gloves were for the peppers! You don't want those touching your skin!" Bernie cries.

"No shit," Ellis says through his teeth.

The maid of honor lets out a loud sob from her chair, the bride and another bridesmaid crouched in front of her and deep in conversation. One of the groomsmen is peeing off the balcony. I keep hold of Ellis's elbow so he knows I've got him. He keeps stretching a palm in front of his crotch like he's dying to grab it. The skin around his eyes is an angry red.

The wine guy comes bounding into the kitchen, bottles held aloft in his hands. "Found it! I've got the Riesling and the perfect chardonnay!" he declares.

I turn back when I hear the unmistakable sound of vomiting. Maid of honor has finally begun to purge her demons, directly down the front of the bride's dress. Bride stands up on shaky legs, then runs to the edge of the balcony and retches next.

Some of the samosas start to smoke, and Bob runs over to the fryer. I grab ahold of Bernie with my free hand and hold her in place before she can flee.

"What do I do about him?" I ask urgently, nodding up at Ellis.

"Ice cream!" calls Bob over the smoke detector that starts going off. For a second, I think he's said *ass* cream and I am about to rip into him about his ass not being the issue. "Gotta flush his eyes out with water, but ice cream will break it down off the skin!" This time, I hear it through the accent.

Bernie scuttles over to the freezer and flings it open, grabs a carton, and lobs it at me.

"Let's go," I say to Ellis, tucking his hand in mine.

"No!" He rears back. "What if it's still on my hands?" he says. And right then and there, it's as if whatever piece of my heart I was trying to reserve is slingshot straight from my chest. The fact that he can stand there with his dick and eyeballs on fire, liquid streaking down his face from the corners of his eyes and his nostrils over his mustache, and *still* think of me . . .

He can have whatever he wants from me again. Everything is his.

"Here, honey, hold on to my shirt, then." I put it in his hand and lead him away.

We make it safely out of the house and down the stair pathway we came in that leads into the vineyards. We make it about a quarter of the way before he has to stop.

"Holy *hell*, this fucking hurts, Wren," he says dizzily. He tries to open his eyes and hisses, more tears spilling free. He briefly braces his hands on his knees before straightening again, shaking out his legs one at a time and squatting like he's trying to get air up his jeans. The condensation from the ice cream is streaming down my arm.

"Come on, honey," I say gently. "Let's get back to the room as quick as we can."

He lets out an awful whimper. "I can't believe that *this* is the reason you're saying those words to me right now," he says.

I put the end of my shirt in his hand again and march on, determination lengthening my stride. We cut over a hill straight to the enclosed back patio of our cottage. I have to rifle through his pockets for the key to unlock it, then shut the slatted wooden door behind us. When I turn on the water for the outdoor bath, he flinches.

"It's just water so you can flush out your eyes," I explain. I guide him to his knees and slowly push his head beneath the running faucet, rubbing circles on his back while he tries to blink into the water. After a few rounds, I ask, "Any better?"

He blinks rapidly, shaking his head. "Not really. I gotta do something about my dick, though," he pants.

My entire chest aches at seeing him this vulnerable, knowing it's killing him. "Here, stand up. No, don't touch anything. Let me," I say.

His hands hover out at his sides, his jaw working. I peel off his shirt first. Feel my entire body flush at the sight of his naked torso. His nostrils flare. "I can't believe this shit," he whispers. "I cannot believe I don't get to watch you undress me right now."

Because he's said it so mulishly, and because there's nothing to be done for it, I aim for humor. "There were easier ways to get out of the class early, you know. You didn't have to go through all this trouble."

A soft snort is his only response.

"Are you okay if I take your pants off?"

He tries to open his eyes and winces again. "I don't think I've ever been less okay, Wren," he says miserably. "Oh, fuckfuck-fuck, it's worse."

I make fast work of undoing his belt. "It's getting worse because you're getting hard." Very, very quickly. Impressively quickly. The metal of his belt clangs against the wooden deck at our feet.

"Please. Don't say *hard*," he says, toeing off his boots and socks. "Actually, shit, nothing's gonna help." He gets visibly more frantic. His eyes dart around rapidly behind his lids, his hands flailing at his sides, and I know—I *know* that it doesn't speak well of me as a person that I let myself take a good look at him, but when I do, I feel my own sort of throbbing burn, from my head down to the soles of my feet.

I pick up the half-melted ice cream carton and stick his right hand into it. He immediately scoops some out and brings it to his other palm, where he hesitates in front of where he's gone fully erect.

"I forgot . . ." I say to myself, my voice distant. I forgot how big, thick, and built he is, everywhere. That impossibly wide chest. "You're a little hairier than I remember," I remark. Still not gray anywhere other than around his temples, though. His hands rub together, vanilla bean melting through his fingers, but they don't make any move to soothe his grievously hard cock.

"Wren," he says raggedly, head shaking side to side and his entire body flexing. "I swear on everything. I swear on my life I wouldn't ask, but I'm s-scared to touch it in case there's anything left on my hands."

I should consider hesitating. I don't. I reach in and wet three fingers in the ice cream and carefully slide them along his flesh. A noise from somewhere deep inside him echoes through his bones. His skin feels like hot silk here. I tip the heavy length of him up more so I can spread some around the whole thing. "Thank god it wasn't rocky road or something, am I right?" I say, lightheaded.

He rumbles out a laugh that cuts off in a whine. "It's helping, at least." He swallows heavily, shifting his weight on his feet, hands dripping ice cream onto the deck. I'm careful not to pump him, and still he's . . . he's painfully solid against my fingertips, a bead of moisture at the tip.

"Ellis, you have to try to soften, I think." My swallow is audible.

"I'm trying," he says, then tries to slit open an eye and promptly shuts it again. "But I can still hear you and smell you, and I think my body just, ah fuck"—he grimaces as his cock twitches eagerly—"knows you."

It's the most erotic thing I've ever seen, his shaft glistening with melted ice cream. I can't decide if I want to dissolve into a fit of hilarity, hug him and comfort him, or fall to my knees and lick him clean.

"Here, get in the bath and wash off while I look up what else we can do," I say. I help him step in, and he lowers himself into the tepid water. "We'll do another round with the ice cream if we need to."

He grips the edge of the tub stiffly, big body squeezed in tight. "Could you just . . . Would you mind just leaving me here for a bit?" he asks. "Alone. I think I'll be able to calm down if I don't know you're right there."

I mark the hard set of his mouth and the lines between his brows. His still-clenched eyes and his white knuckles on the lip of the tub. It's clear how much he hates this, being exposed and vulnerable and not in control this way. But it's more than his need to calm down. He wants to hide, too.

"All right," I reply quietly, then walk back inside and sit on the bed.

I google remedies for "pepper dick and fingers," which, unsurprisingly, yields mixed results. Once I figure out the correct terminology is "capsaicin burn," I'm on the right track.

I try not to let myself be hurt or bothered by him wanting to conceal himself—his pain from me. I'd like to not make it more meaningful than it is.

I do, anyway.

It's just that it's aggravating how hypocritical this is right now. Every time we take a chance and lean into trusting each other, we come out stronger by the end of it. It's pulling away, withholding our hurts that destroyed us before. Being too damn *careful*. Since I let myself commit to this trip and its objectives, I haven't withheld much of anything.

And I get it. I do. He's in pain. I can practically hear the thoughts churning in his head. He's put in so much effort to plan this, to make it go just right. He's been committing, too, but he's also been in the driver's seat. Today has been out of his control since we checked in, and now things have gone awry, and he's trying to take back what he can.

Well, fuck that. We haven't come this far just to come this far.

I dig into my toiletry bag to find the bottle I need and walk back out onto the porch.

He's managed to get his eyes open, now, and cuts me a wary, bloodshot look.

"Getting better?" I ask.

He nods. "Getting there."

"Let me help," I say.

He closes his eyes like he's stung and lets his head fall back, exposing the long lines of his strong throat. "Let me hold on to a shred of my pride, Wren. Please."

"No."

Now his eyes fly open and find me again. I untie my top and let it fall away. He whispers a curse.

"Oil apparently helps break down the chemical from the peppers, too," I explain, nipples tightening under his stare.

"What are you doing?" he asks, his voice rough with longing. "You won't fit."

I let my smile heat. "What'd you say to me the first time I said you wouldn't fit? We'll make it work." I peel down my skirt and panties and step out of them.

"Wren."

"I'll go slow. I'll try not to make it hurt. If I hurt you, tell me and I'll stop. I think those are all things you said to me, too."

"Fuck, baby." He's breathing heavily now, running a wet

palm over his mustache as he tries to make room for me to step into the tub, water trickling over the edge in the movement. I stand between his knees and watch him drag his gaze over every inch of me slowly, like he's committing me to memory again. Some of my bravery wavers when I kneel, as I try to be graceful about it and end up needing to scooch and wriggle closer to him, wedging myself between his legs.

He stays utterly still aside from his chest rising and falling. The water licks up and retreats below his belly button with each exhale, the proud head of his cock resting there, too. I squirt some of my shower oil in my palm and ask again. "Let me help?"

"All right," he rasps.

I let my hand slide beneath the water and lean forward to kiss his neck. Feel his hitching sound against my lips. I feel myself tremble a little, too. The oil seems to stay on my hand beneath the water, but I keep it careful and slow, letting my fingers slip against him gently. I catch the corner of his mouth with mine, wrap my hand around his cock, and give him one long, gentle tug. "Okay?"

"Yes," comes out of him with a soft, graveled gasp. He idly thumbs one of my nipples.

"Ah-ah-ah," I chide, which makes him go back to holding on to the tub. I'm sure he assumes I'm worried about any residue burning me, but I simply need to take care of him for once. Only him. I hold him a little tighter and notice that the smooth slide from the oil's faded away. "Come inside with me?" I lean back and ask.

His heavy-lidded stare moves across my face, a hand lifting instinctively before he puts it back down. I wipe a droplet of water from his mustache. "I don't think we can," he says, a little mournful.

"I know," I say. Even aching like I am, I'm not brave enough to test having him inside me. "I have another idea."

I feel his soft grin like a twinge in my chest. "All right," he says.

I grab the shower oil before he lets me lead him out of the tub, back inside the little cottage shed, a trail of wet footprints in our wake.

The distance from the back door to the bed is nearly nonexistent. I turn and sit at the edge of the mattress, bringing him closer to me by his hips and holding his gaze with mine.

"I thought of something we've never done." I grab the oil and let some dribble down the center of my chest, everything cinching tight in my stomach when his mouth falls open and his thighs lightly quake. "Come here."

He stumbles closer and cups the base of my skull in his hands, weaving into my hair and pulling so he can bend down and kiss me. The motion makes his cock draw a path down my front, and I let out a moan into his mouth.

He keeps one of his hands in my hair and watches himself when he grinds back up, where I squeeze him tight between my breasts.

"God, Wren," he says, still glued to the sight. I can't look away from him watching, or from the lust and the adoration on his face. I keep pushing, plucking at my nipples when he thrusts up against me again. My hips writhe against the sheets, and his grip in my hair curls tighter, his thrusts picking up. "Squeeze me, baby," he begs, sliding over slick, warm skin, the muscles in his thighs straining. I lose any awareness of time, marveling at his face and his closeness again. At the cadence of his breath and the friction of him hot and hard on the skin over my chest. "Can I?" he asks with a rough gasp.

"Yes. Make a fucking mess," I say, repeating his words back to him from last night.

His brow folds in amazement and relief right before he pulls back and comes with a truncated groan, some landing on my chin below the corner of my lip. I wait for his eyes before I swipe my tongue across it, which makes his neck arch back with another deeply satisfied, harsh sound. He rocks against me once more before he bends to kiss me again. "Thank you," he says, kissing my forehead after nipping at my lips. "Let me grab a towel, I . . . I got a little in your hair, too, I think. Sorry."

I wrap my hand around his wrist, where he's still cupping my head in his big palm. He brings a thumb around to trace along my jaw, and I couldn't care less if it ends up burning there. "It's okay," I say, softly laughing. I feel like my whole body is humming, like I needed this as much as he did.

We end up in the teeny indoor shower together. I kiss the tender pink skin around his eyes, and he washes my hair, laughs slipping out of us and our hands lathering over one another. We keep the kissing and touching as chaste as we can manage, but I still feel like an exposed nerve ending by the time we towel off.

I have no idea what time it is or where my phone might be, but the sunset shines rosy orange shapes through the gaps in the blinds as I pull on one of Ellis's shirts. Something about the feel of it on my bare skin and his scent in my nose threatens to make me cry. I should manage my wet hair, but I catch him looking at me from the bed, bare-chested and smiling gently in the sherbet light, and I decide I'd rather slide in beside him now.

Even as I tuck myself into the crook of his shoulder, he keeps the hand at my back pressed to the sheet or his shirt, careful not to touch bare skin.

"Does anything still hurt?" I ask.

"My fingertips feel a little raw and my eyes still sting, but . . ." He sighs. "Everything else is better."

I grin against his chest. Everything really is better in this moment with him.

Hope, hope, hope goes that pulse again, desperately hoping nothing will change. Or that everything already has? I'm not sure either way, and I fall asleep happy.

CHAPTER 30

———

WREN

I awake to Ellis's mouth on my bare hip, his shirt tucked up around my waist.

"You okay?" I whisper sleepily as he slides down the bed in our dark room.

"Starving," he murmurs back. "You keep making these little sounds in your sleep." My breath hitches when his tongue coasts over to my inner thigh and he gently bites me. "Yeah. That sound," he says darkly. He kisses a path down the outside of my thigh, and I roll onto my back, legs pressing together. I feel myself start to shake half a moment before he does, and he immediately stops.

"What is this?" he asks, so quietly I almost convince myself I imagined it. "How come . . . how come you start shaking before I touch you now?" He takes his hands away, and my throat pulls tight. "That's new, Byrd. Is it . . . is it me? Am I too . . . ? It feels like you're scared."

He sounds scared. "It's not you," I say, still hushed. "It is you, and it's not." He lays his head on the pillow beside mine, and I can just make out his face in the dim light. The temptation to lean over and kiss him until we're too needy to have this conversation is there. But he gave me his exposed moments last night, and I'm going to give him mine now.

"I think," I start, then pause to swallow. "I think I was just so used to what sex was like with us. I was always so comfortable. And . . . and I don't know, Ellis." I put a hand over my face. "You're sure you want to hear about this?"

"I want everything," he says plainly. Not whispering anymore.

I take a deep breath and blow it out slowly. "There are some stone-cold weirdos out there. And I'd only ever been with you, so I didn't know anything, I guess. It just. Wasn't like it was with us. With anyone else. I was never *not* disappointed. And part of me kept thinking it was me. Like, maybe those years when we were trying . . . maybe they took the sex out of sex, and I was ruined or broken somehow and I'd never get to enjoy this again." A stupid tear escapes, and I turn my face into the pillow to wipe it away. There are some things I still can't say out loud. Like how every single time I felt someone's weight settle on me, I thought about someone else feeling Ellis's weight on them. How, the first time I slept with someone else, I cried so hard I gagged. I can't even remember his name now. "I am scared," I admit. "I'm scared this isn't real. And terrified of how badly I want it to be."

He's still and quiet at my side, his chest lightly nudging my arm with every inhale he takes. His forehead comes down to rest on my shoulder, and he kisses the side of my breast through his shirt. "I'll be right back," he says.

I scowl into the room, the bed jostling lightly when he gets up and walks to the door in his briefs. "*Seriously?*" I ask his retreating form. "*That's* how you respond to everything I just said?!"

He pauses in the doorway, limned in a twilight sky. "I have a lot to say about everything you just told me, Wren. I'd like to resolve some of it with more than words." And with that, he slips outside. I hear the truck door open and shut, and I'm sure I'm still wearing an indignant expression when he comes back in with a smile and something in his hand.

He climbs onto his knees on the bed. "I can't go back in time and fix everything, baby. I would if I could. I've spent so much time wishing I could erase mistakes . . . And I hate that we lost five years together." He crawls closer, something still clenched in his fist. "But we're here now."

I'm still miffed, but intrigued. "Explain."

He dips, laughing against my stomach and dragging my shirt up a few inches with his teeth. "We're getting a lot better at our explaining, aren't we?" He kisses my scars. "We can talk. We can write. And maybe we can tie you up and you can come on my tongue enough to make up for some of the times you weren't taken care of." His tongue circles my navel, and I start to pant.

"Since you're begging," I say. There's no bluster in it when it's as breathy as that, though.

I feel his laugh stirring through him. "Oh, I'm begging. I'm so hungry, Byrd. Please."

I sit up and peel off my shirt, and he chases me with a frantic kiss. Before I can tip my legs apart, he's got a knee braced on either side of my hips, big body hovering over mine.

Watching him focus on his task makes my thoughts go liquid and drippy like hot fudge. He's quick and eager about it, muscles shifting beneath his skin and sending shadows dancing across him. He takes a flat, soft strip of rope in his fist and loops it behind my neck first, before crossing it over my front between my breasts, bending down to lick my nipples lazily. He brings it back around and starts to braid and knot it in a complicated pattern, stopping just above my belly button before it splits and goes around each ankle, then each wrist, and weaves it back through the middle. He briefly surveys his work before he gingerly tugs on the tail end of it, pulling my ankles an inch wider and a quiet gasp out of me as he does. His smile goes molten.

He walks on his knees back down the bed, pulling the rope a little more the farther he goes, spreading me more and more.

When I'm wide enough to accommodate him, he wastes no time bringing me to his mouth. My thighs close a fraction around his jaw, and he gives the rope another rough tug, my heels digging into the sheets. He kisses my clit like he kisses my lips, soft, adoring, devouring. Like he's missed me and can't wait to hear me and taste me and see me in every way. He hums encouragingly at every noise I make, every writhe and circle.

"Do you still like—" He takes his thumb and pins my clit to the side, lapping at me in one specific spot, at one exact, maddening angle.

I mutter a string of garbled curses.

"Yeah. You still like. God, I love it when you cuss." He rubs his face against me in that unpracticed, hungry way of his, his stubble rasping against my most delicate skin, and I let out a guttural, desperate noise. "My sweet baker with a filthy mouth. I missed you so much."

He makes a beseeching sound against me and goes at me again with his tongue, strong and slick and so damn familiar. My body bucks off the bed, and he brings a palm to press me down.

"I need it, Wren," he says, almost apologetically.

He stays at my clit tirelessly, keeping me spread and close until I'm moaning and cursing and thrashing against him. I spiral up impossibly high and shatter into sparks and he never lets me down, only changes his angle to come at me again and pushes two fingers up into me with a groan. "Again, honey. Need to feel it."

I sob an incoherent sound and fall apart again, clasping around his fingers greedily and trying to twitch away, everything too sensitive on my skin. He gives me a moment of reprieve, kissing and nipping at my inner thighs.

"Five years," he grits. "I think we can start with five."

CHAPTER 31

WREN

Ellis is still asleep when I hear my phone vibrating. It's a good thing, too, because when I slide out of bed and take my first step, my legs wobble dramatically. Can't go giving him a sixth reason to be smug.

I find my cell under the corner of the bed, then quickly dress and pad quietly outside, just in time for Mom to call again.

"Mom?" I say under my breath. It's barely after 6:00 A.M., so I don't yet have a grip on my panic reflex.

"Hi, sweets," she says in a singsong voice. "How's it going?"

"Mother, are you okay? Is everything at the bakery all right?"

She tuts into the phone. "Oh, shoot. Did I call too early or something? I didn't even look at the time, I guess. I just barely got to talk to you yesterday, and I wanted to hear about your birthday. I want to hear how the trip is going so far."

Savannah Meridian is polite to a fault. Not a chance she forgot to check the time. I stop in the road and squint suspiciously out over the pond. "Fucking hell, Mom. It was you?"

"Me, *what?*" she crows.

"*Mother.* Did you change our reservation?"

She's silent for five seconds too long. "I mean, for goodness' sake, Wren, you're on a trip with the man to decide if you should get back together or not. You might as well sleep together!"

"*Wow.*"

"And it sounds like such a lovely trip he's planned, sweets."

"Are you my pimp or my mom?"

"Oh, now, don't be crass."

"This coming from the same mouth that just implied that I owe a man some action for taking me on a vacation?!"

She sucks her teeth and makes an exasperated sound. "I said *sleep* together. Figure out if you can stand to share a space again. That always seemed like the worst end of the deal to me."

I start walking again, pulling my denim jacket tighter around me. "First of all, does *everyone* know that's the real objective here? No one believed us about the casual friendship celebration trip, huh?" I say.

"Not for a second, dear."

"Right," I say. "But then . . . Does that mean you're hoping it *won't* work out?" I start to chew on a nail. She's always adored Ellis, but she's also never tried to foist her feelings on me about the divorce. She understood it, encouraged me to maintain a healthy co-parenting relationship, and otherwise minded her own. Only since she met her *man friend*, David, last fall has she started to let a few opinions loose. I just figured she didn't like the idea of me being alone when she wasn't anymore, not that it specifically had anything to do with Ellis.

I hear her set a baking dish down hard. "Of course I want it to work out," she says snappishly. "Of course I was hoping a little . . . *mixing the batter* might help you two work out a few things."

"Could have gone my whole life without hearing that euphemism."

"That boy," she growls. "That *man*," she corrects herself. "That man is the best sort of good. He's the kind of good that doesn't want to be seen or fussed over with accolades. He's a man of action."

"Oh, we're back to action, are we?"

"Wren Salem, don't be glib with me right now," she says, and I'm shocked by the strictness in it. "I understand why you split before, mainly because I understand not wanting another person to have any influence over how you go about your life. I understand that marriage is highly inconvenient at best, and it's paralyzing at its worst."

"Most people would argue that marriage is convenient," I say. Sharing money, meals, responsibilities.

"Most people are fucking idiots," says Mom. I gasp playfully. A curse is a rarity coming from her. "All I know," she continues, "is that you are both the sort of people who deserve all the best things, who deserve to be taken care of, but I don't think either of you ever got to know how, because you were both always taking care of other people, or maybe . . . maybe in your case, it was that you had to take care of yourself because I wasn't around more."

"Mom, no."

She cuts me off with a long sigh. "Trust me, sweets. I know I didn't always provide the best example, but I think you can and should have everything you've ever wanted. Let yourself have it. Don't be afraid to go after it again."

"Mom, that is exactly what you showed me," I say. "You were the best example when it came to that."

She sighs again, but it's laced with frustration this time. "I showed you that I didn't need a romantic partner in life because I knew it was the safest bet, relying on myself and no one else.

But even I had to ask for help from people sometimes, Wren. And no, I didn't lack for a full life without romance, but . . . I'd had my heart broken once too many times and made all my decisions based on fear of it again thereafter," she states. "Since I met David, I've seen that. And I've regretted it. But you've always been braver than I am, Wren." She chortles. "Hell, even with what you bake, you are! The things you try sometimes!"

We catch up on the bakery after that, and she assures me things are all running smoothly.

"Busy for this time of year, though?" she observes, sounding a little harried. "You might have to hire more people when I'm gone."

I don't pull on my end of that conversation thread. She's down to partial days on the few that she comes in, and I'll be just fine when she officially retires. I'm on enough of the local counties' recommended vendors lists for larger events, and the seasonal influxes are reliable, too. I can afford to hire more staff. While I'm excited to be able to call the place mine, I've got no reason (or right) to push her out too quickly.

"It'll always be Savvy's, Mom," I tell her.

"It won't, sweets, and it'll be better for it," she says. "New beginnings are best when you get to pick and choose what you carry over from the old."

"*Subtle.*" I laugh. "What happened to not putting a burnt cake back in the oven?"

"That's *cake*, babe," she says. "But think of all the things that only get better after they've been burnt. Caramelized sugar, flambéed bananas, flambéed apples, for that matter . . . ooohhh, a Basque cheesecake . . ." She trails off just as I hear a strange rubbing sound and spot something blow up from the vineyards and into the road before me.

"Hey, Mom? I gotta go."

CHAPTER 32

—

ELLIS

When my eyes slit open, daylight is blazing through the room, and a sunny Wren is sitting cross-legged on the bed, chin in hand and watching me sleep.

"Apparently, you snore these days, too," she says. "Good morning."

I close my eyes and growl appreciatively. "Must have been extra tired."

She gives me a sympathetic cluck and ruffles a hand through my hair. "You did work very, very hard last night. I've got the beard burn to prove it." I can hear the blush in her tone.

"Yeah?" I blindly grab at her ankle and lift up her skirt to see. She bats my hands away.

"Nah-ah, we don't have time for that. We've gotta pack up, and we've been invited over for breakfast at Bernie and Bob's, who also comped our stay. I ran into them on a little walk a bit ago." She escapes my wandering hands again and glides off the bed.

"Hey, Byrd?" A yawn rolls out of me and I stretch. Something crackles in my knee.

"Yeah?" she says, trying to manage her wild hair.

I sigh happily at the sight of her concentrated pout in the mirror. "Why is there another man in our room?" I ask.

She grabs the inflatable doll propped up against the wall beside her and spins around with him. "Oh, do you mean him?"

"Mm-hmm."

She gives him a jovial shake. "When I was on my walk, he came drifting across the road on the breeze, like some sad tumbleweed of depravity," she explains with a sigh. "I didn't want him to end up in the pond or for some sort of animal to choke on him or something. Between this and the groomsman I saw passed out on one of the porches, my best guess is that the other cottages are occupied by the bridal party."

I'm still slow on the uptake, I think. "What sort of animal is gonna choke on a whole-ass inflatable doll?"

She gives a bratty scoff. "I mean if it, like, popped or something," she says. "Why, you jealous of my new friend?" She hugs the thing a little closer.

I'm so happy I feel sick, actually. "Wren, I can still taste you in my mustache. I can't think of a single person on the planet to be jealous of right now."

Her mouth falls into a little O and her eyes go round, cheeks and chest blushing a pretty pink. "We need to go to breakfast," she says, husky and unconvincing. At whatever my face is doing, she adds, "I mean it, Ellis. We haven't eaten since yesterday afternoon. We're supposed to be there already," with a laugh.

I unfold myself from the bed and scratch at my chest. When

I catch her ogling me in my briefs, I lift a brow at her like a final offer. The color on her cheeks heightens.

"I'll be outside," she clips, rolling her suitcase behind her.

———

Breakfast ended up being a delight. For Wren and me, at least. Bob and Bernie intercepted Tabitha and her future groom somewhere and wrangled them and their crew into joining us, and I got to be smug over the fact that, after calling me old, the *youngsters* all looked like they didn't think food would ever be good again. Meanwhile I was upright, feeling great, and wolfed down my omelet and fried potatoes with enthusiasm.

We're now more than four hours into our five-hour drive time (predominantly spent in companionable silence or, if you're Wren, snoring softly), and it's flown by with ease.

Which, naturally, has started to make me uneasy.

It's just that we're headed for the last stop on our trip, and that means decisions have to be made for where we go after this, for what we are after this. Are we . . . dating? Are we together, but going to live separately? It's a weird concept to wrap my brain around when that house I still live in always felt like it was possessed by her. Maybe I'm getting too ahead of myself, but it feels like it's my last chance to prove something. I know it's not rational. I know that all our real tests are still at home waiting for us, folded in between the daily regularities of life.

But it's all the mundane stuff that I can't wait for again. That's what this trip has made me realize the most. Like having a candlelit meal with her in a beautiful, romantic setting made me remember how special it was to share a meal at our kitchen table, or even standing up and eating over the stove. Laughing with her drinking champagne in a vineyard made me miss laughing with her in our backyard, sitting on lawn chairs and sharing a beer and a bag of salt and vinegar chips between us.

I want her sad music playing in our house and her shit all over the bathroom counter. I want the chance to be lazy with her on a day off. I want our boring life back.

She lets out a happy hum from the passenger seat, arching and knuckling the muscles in her back in a way that does something very distracting with her tits. I grip the wheel a little harder and stare out at the road.

"We should go through some more questions, shouldn't we? The ones we didn't do. I only had the one made-up one designed to seduce you," she says, tracing a line down the arm closest to her.

"I'm in. You'll have to read them off."

She snorts. "Of course you're in. You already looked them up."

"If it helps, I had no answers for most of them, and there were plenty of them left that I am still nervous for you to ask."

Her head tilts in the farthest corner of my eye. "Fine, then. I'll just try to pull up a more obscure list."

"Go for it, Byrd."

"Do you have any hunch how you'll die?"

"Oh, so we're keeping things upbeat today."

She's chuckling. "It was the first one I saw. Let's pick a different one."

As much as I'd like to prove I'm game for this and show that I'm committed to these things, that's the last question I want to think about. I've always had this lingering, buried feeling that makes itself known now and again—like some sort of recurring nightmare I can't forget even when the dream itself bleeds away. I can't remember the details, but it still leaves me edging panic the whole day after. I've always carried this illogical fear that everyone I love will die before I do. It's not exactly a hunch, but that's all that question brings to mind. And I think . . . I think if Wren goes before I do, my body would probably give out. I can't imagine I'd be long for this life.

"All right. Here's a new one," she says. "What's your greatest accomplishment?" We chuff a single sound in unison because we both know our answer.

"Sam," I say, anyway. "For all our faults, we're good parents."

She blows out a dramatic breath. "Okay, enough with the weepy ones. Let me find a happier one." She clicks her tongue, scrolling on her phone. "All right. Complete this sentence. 'I wish I had someone with whom I could share . . .'"

I scratch the back of my neck awkwardly. This is one I tried to come up with an answer for that didn't sound overembellished and couldn't. Oh, well. "Er, everything," I say nervously. "I know that sounds corny, but really. I've sorta learned to be fine with being alone when it comes to a lot of the big, shitty stuff that takes up more space in your head than it should. Taxes, taking care of the house." She smiles when I look at her briefly. "I miss sharing a bed, and not *just* for the reasons you think." I turn back to the road. "I, uh, started sleeping on your old side for a while because it felt like the mattress was caving in on mine."

When she's still quiet, I look at her again and find her eyes shining. "You could have bought a new mattress," she says through a wet chuckle.

No. Too many memories on that one. Maybe we'll get to buy a new one together. "What about you? How would you finish that sentence?"

"Everything, too," she breathes. "Everything, everywhere. I want to be able to call someone and share what I'm worried about or puzzling over at any given point during the day again." I grab her hand and kiss it. "Sometimes just sharing helps, even when the other person can't fix it." She says the last part very pointedly. I guess I do have a tendency to jump in and try to fix things. "I want to do this kind of stuff more," she goes on. "Trips. Going places, even if they're not far. It'd be nice to share that with someone."

"We should . . . we should try to do this more." It's such a casual thing to say when it's meant to be anything but. *Make plans with me forever*, I mean. *Hitch your life to mine again and we'll go places. We'll share every plan, every heavy thing together, and all the good stuff, too.*

Through the speakers, the phone instructs us to get off at the next exit, and I almost think she's not going to respond.

"I agree, by the way," she says. "We should try to do this more."

I nod a little too animatedly. This is where the old me wants to dive in and ask if she wants to move back home and be together and maybe even remarry me and if I should book another trip and for exactly when. I swallow down the urge and recommit myself to what's been working so far. Taking it slow. We're only ten minutes away from our last stop.

She looks at the questions again. "What's your most treasured memory?" she asks.

I saw this one before, too, but didn't have to consider my answer. "Sam's fifth birthday party," I say, grinning.

"When he sat in his own cake?" Wren laughs.

"Yeah. It was a perfect day."

I feel her studying me. "What made it a perfect day?"

The road curves sharply through redwoods that get taller and taller the farther we go from the highway. It gives off the illusion of the day passing in a sped-up video, the sky getting darker around us the thicker the forest grows. "I just remember feeling light, I guess," I say. "Sage had just graduated and knew what she was doing next. Silas had started at the fire department with me. Micah was doing great in Double-A and was home from spring training for a few days. I guess I felt like I could relax with them a little more, like all of a sudden we were all our own people and had made it and I didn't have to worry as much. Getting everyone through high school was like . . . like my primary parenting role with them was coming to a close." I remember it being a rare sunny day. We'd just moved into our house and hardly had any furniture, so we kept it to a small family party in our new yard. We played lawn games and barbecued. Sam was in a phase where he would do anything for a laugh, even to the point that it got obnoxious at times. Wren brought his cake out and put it on the picnic table we had at the time, and before we could even light his candles, he'd jumped up to the bench, felt everyone's eyes on him, turned around, and sat on it.

We all stood there with our mouths gaping. But then I started to laugh at the complete absurdity of it, which made everyone else join in. The cake was unsalvageable, and no one cared.

"I remember being happy, and I remember it being easy to be happy that day. I think that's why it was perfect," I say. "What about you?"

She falls quiet again, pensively staring out her window. "I'm not sure. I have a lot of those. When I think about it now—when I make myself think about all of it, I remember feeling so much happiness. So much that I feel fucking mad that those things weren't big enough to outweigh the bad stuff at the end." She raises her hands, shrugging before they fall back to her thighs with a small clap. "Like, I don't get it. Why'd we let the bad stuff win?"

My nose stings and my throat knots. "I actually have an answer for that," I manage to say. "Per my therapist." It comes out stiffly, but I feel like credit should be given where credit is due.

"Tell me."

I clear my throat. "Because when it comes down to it, on a physical level, feeling happy doesn't take priority over surviving," I say. "We're programmed to remember the bad so that we know what to stay away from and how to keep going. That's why the shit that hurts stands out in our minds. That's why holding on to the happy takes work."

Her eyes are wide and her lips press together tightly. "What's your worst memory?"

My lungs constrict in an instant. "Wren." I don't know how to put that sort of helplessness into words. The real fear that she could die. The guilt I couldn't explain that went with it.

"Ellis," she says, wobbling at the edges. "We have to talk about it at some point."

But we're pulling into the parking lot now to check in. "Let's get unpacked and get out of this truck first. We'll go on a walk," I say.

"It's the last time we can stall on it," she says.

"I know. I know it is."

We get out of the truck and head to the counter and check in. Neither of us is surprised to find out that we've been switched to a single tent reservation. We smirk at each other and take the map with the directions to our tent location.

It takes us another few minutes to get to our site. An off-white canvas tent with a wooden deck out front and a little chimney popping up from the top greets us. Past it, I can see that the dense trees give way to a clearing that narrows into a trail leading out to a rocky beach.

A few notifications start chiming from both of our phones when we pull in to park. We must not have had service deep in the woods. My phone was the one hooked up to the Bluetooth today, and I forgot that I have the Read Text setting option on, so it's jarring when Siri reads out, "From Silas, to you and Wren Byrd: This time, it was me."

Wren cocks a brow at me with a crooked smile. "The tent," she says. "Kinda excited to tell him we were going to, anyway. Wipe the smug look off his face."

Before I can reply, Siri starts up again. "From Kirby," the robotic voice says. "Did you tell her yet?"

I feel the blood drain from my face. I watch it leave Wren's.

"Tell me what?" she asks.

CHAPTER 33

WREN

It's the way his expression goes sheet white with fear that makes me feel like my windpipe is shrinking.

"Why is there a woman texting you and asking you if you've told 'her' something?" I ask, struggling to swallow back air. Using my voice feels like blowing on a whistle.

His head does a small shake, and he blinks hard. "Wait, how do you know that's a woman's name?"

I'm actually a little grateful he's made this utterly stupid remark. Now I can feel momentary rage instead of soul-crushing dread. "Is that seriously what you're asking me right now?"

"No, I mean, she is, but—"

"Who is she?"

"Wren, she's just a friend. I swear it." Realization dawns over him. "Thanksgiving. That's whose text you saw."

I start to pant, heart in my fingertips and in my throat and temples and everywhere but the place it should be. "So she's a friend who texts you on the holidays. A very attractive friend you've maintained since *last fall*?! Are you fucking serious right now? What is this? What is this, Ellis? You'd better tell me right fucking now."

"She's a friend," he says calmly. Because that's what he's capable of. Staying calm in the face of life-altering disaster so we can move through it. I want to throttle him until he's as rattled as I am. "She's a friend who I confided in about you and me. After Silas's accident, I . . . I . . . She's like ten years younger than I am. She's a kid! I did some work on a campaign fire when the rest of the crew took time off over fall, and that's what I know her from. She's just a friend, Wren. I swear on everything."

"Then what the hell does she know that I don't? *'Tell me'* what, Ellis? Tell. Me. What."

"*That I still love you*," he gasps, his eyes falling shut. "That I still love you. I was worried telling you too soon wouldn't be fair. I needed to tell you the right way. I needed to show you the right way."

I want to say it back. I want to say it back, but I'm still scrabbling. "But you could tell someone *else*? You could talk about everything with someone else before you could tell me?" I ask. There's not enough room in this truck cab for everything I'm feeling. I'm out before I'm even aware that I've made the decision to be and he's right behind me, his car door shutting right after mine and his steps coming for me.

"Stop." I hold up a palm. I know if I look at him I'll lose my nerve. "My bad thing for the day. It's the last one I'm going to do because it's worse than all the rest. But the thing I *hated* . . . that I still *hate*. Is how you didn't trust me. Not now, and not then, either."

The way his breath sounds when it gusts out of him again lets me know he's holding back tears. I keep my eyes closed. "What are you talking about?" he croaks.

God, he's been trying so hard, but I know it in my marrow that I'll have to drag this out of him, and I don't know if I have the strength. "Did you ever want another baby?" I ask.

I hear his heel skid on the packed earth. "We tried for three years. After the ectopic, they said there was a higher chance of it happening again. You could have *died*. I wasn't going to risk it."

"Did you ever want another baby?"

"Wren. *Byrd*." The hitch in his voice claws at me. "I wanted to give you everything you ever wanted. Ever."

"Did you ever want another baby, Ellis?"

"I wanted you to be happy."

"*Did you ever—*"

"*No*," he says, the syllable ripped from his chest. And now I open my eyes, just in time to see his face crumple before he wipes a palm across his mouth. The rest comes barreling free. "No. I didn't want to take care of *anyone* else. I was *tired* of trying to hold all these pieces of myself together all the time. Too fucking tired to take on more!" The billows of his breath get ragged. "I wanted to make you happy, though. I'd . . . I thought I'd *robbed* you of so much, Wren. Of more of a life! I felt like I'd trapped you into it with me in the first place, however accidental it was, getting pregnant so young, I still felt like I'd robbed you of something. At the very least, of getting to experience *that*, getting to feel excited and prepared for a baby. Having to do it when we were kids was fucking *hard*. I couldn't stand the idea of taking anything else away from you."

I shatter, all my fissures expanding into one jagged, flooding canyon. "You robbed me of *YOU*! Don't you see how not telling me how you really felt robbed me of *you*?!" I wail. "Three years, and I felt every single day. I *felt* you pulling away. You worked more and more. You were quieter and quieter. You retreated and retreated and retreated. And I thought it was because you were *sad*. And you didn't want to go to therapy then. Didn't want to talk to someone else back then. And you wouldn't talk to *me!*"

"You wouldn't talk to me, either!" he cries. Angry tears hit the dirt between us. "You'd get *silent*, too, and most of the time, I couldn't stand the thought of pushing you, knowing how disappointed and upset you were. Every fucking month."

"I thought—" I gulp back a shuddering breath. "I thought you were disappointed in *me*."

He looks horror-stricken. The moon and stars are so bright I can see every line of his expression. "*No.*"

"I know it's not reasonable," I say. "I *know* it's not the truth now. But at the time when I was drowning in everything else? That's how it felt to me. And I started to resent it." I have to pause to let out a sob. "I started to resent you. How much I needed you. How much I wanted you. While you could just pull further and further from me. And then . . . and then, Jesus Christ, Ellis. Three *years*, and then three *days* after my surgery, you tell me you're done?! You're getting a vasectomy. I felt like you'd backhanded me. It was your choice. Just like what we decided to do when I got pregnant with Sam was mine. But right then and there, it was clear to me that you'd never wanted to in the first place." I quit struggling against the tears and just let them fall. "After everything. Everything we were to each other, to know that you wouldn't trust me to care about what you wanted? And then things started with Mom, who'd never needed anyone before, and nothing felt *fair*, and I just . . . Everything made me angry. All the time. And I hated who I was. I started getting short-tempered with Sam. I hated going to work. I hated that I *couldn't* hate you. When I said I wanted out and you didn't fight me at all, I thought I might, but the closest I ever got was hating myself. I couldn't hate you, couldn't even stay angry with you." Another burning sob. "Because I know you. I know what kind of man you are." I stab a finger at him. "I. Love. You. I would choose *you*. Over everything! Over everyone." He's a statue other than a rogue tear tracking down his cheek. "I still would. I still love you." I put both hands over my breastbone like I can hold my heart in place there, the cage of my ribs not enough to keep me together. "Whatever you want from me, Ellis. It's all yours. It's always been yours."

He reaches me in a single stride.

He's not gentle, and I'm grateful for it. I'm grateful he's as messy and out of control as I am for once. He circles my wrists and tosses my hands down to my sides, his mouth replacing my palms. He kisses me hard there, right against the bones of my chest. I feel it like a volt rattling through my frame. My fingers come back up to curl in his hair when his teeth scrape against my clavicle. I let out a small cry against his jaw when he nips at my neck, at the way his grip leaves my waist and tightens around my hips. His mouth chases mine and swallows down every sound after that. My spine bows, our stomachs pressing into each other, the metal of his belt biting into my soft skin. For the million and one kisses we've shared, I've never felt like this. I want to be in him and for him to be in me. I want to *be* Ellis. I want him to *be* me. I want to be one single body and spirit, and I want him to feel what I feel for him like air in his own lungs.

"I'm sorry. I was blaming myself. I thought I was killing you, because I didn't want it the way you did, and then when you almost . . ." He chokes back a sound. "I'm sorry," he rasps against my lips, his hands in my hair now. Cupping my jaw now. Around my throat now. His lips are salty with tears. "The worst had happened before. My mom getting sick. My dad. Sometimes the worst really does happen and I knew it could happen again. And I thought it was my fault and I just—I shut down."

"I'm sorry," I cry back, our noses sliding across each other and tongues licking into our mouths. I can feel the heat still coming off the truck engine beside me and I don't care that a tent is right there on the other side, I want him to fuck me into the ground at our feet. I don't think anything is more important than having him moving inside me as soon as possible. I'm practically climbing the length of him, blindly trying to strip off his clothes. He hauls me up and wraps my thighs around his hips and starts toward the tent. My shirt hits the deck before we make it inside. He lets me leave the kiss to yank off his.

And then I'm laid down onto a soft bed, white canvas above me and white sheets all around me, a glowing lantern strung up in the peak of the tent. Everything a clouded blur other than him. He's peeling off my shorts with quiet determination and pushing down his pants, and then he's there, naked and glorious above me.

"I have to tell you more, Byrd," he says gruffly, his eyes black and greedy over every inch of me, following the path of his hands. "But I need you so bad" comes out of him in a whispered breath. "I have more I need to say."

"*Later*," I say. "Say more later." Right now, I want him to take and take and take. I spread my legs, catching his hand at my thigh and guiding it where I need him. We both groan when he slips against me. When he feels how wet I am. "I need *you*."

He drags himself over me, kneeling between my legs, his entire body trembling. He's achingly hard. Has to push himself down to notch against me. Tears I can't bother to be embarrassed about slip from my eyes when he nudges the head of his cock inside me.

"Don't be gentle," I say, voice tight. "I won't break." If living without him this long taught me anything, it's that.

He doesn't move right away. He's lost in thought, eyes roving over me with so much adoration it makes me ache. I've never felt more beautiful. He shapes me with his palms; from the abundant swell of my hips to the sharp dip of my waist. His hand spreads wide over the flat of my stomach. He traces the shimmering stripes below my belly button and all my scars with his fingertips.

I writhe and try to pull him deeper, but he's brutally stubborn, even as he holds himself there, shaking with need. He thumbs my clit lovingly.

"You wreck me," he murmurs. "God, your pussy's sweet. So pretty all over. My memory never did you justice." He finally pushes forward more, and I start to pant.

"I'm—" His eyes shiver closed. He grunts and slips in another inch, a tremor racking through him. I let out a tight gasp. "I'm not gonna last, baby. I should get you there first." I can see the skin at his throat beating wildly. He moves like he's going to pull back.

"Don't you dare leave me," I say, digging my heels into his back and arching off the bed. I use my thighs for leverage, fucking myself up onto him. A low whine escapes me at the perfect pinching stretch.

He finally lets his control slip. Grabs my hips with bruising strength and slams the rest of the way home, his head falling back with a tormented groan.

The sight of his heavy-lidded gaze watching himself thrust in and out of me does more for me than it should, I think. He tries to go slow, and I try to urge him faster, riding up to meet him at the hilt. I can't catch my breath. It's pushed up out of me each time he fills me again. My hands come up to soothe my nipples, and he stops to bend over me, wetting them with his mouth, his tongue and teeth between my spread fingers, then balances himself on a forearm so he can kiss my mouth and neck. His free hand starts at my thigh and skims up my body until he grinds against me at a particular angle that makes my spine bend off the bed with a gasp, and then he's cupping the back of my neck while he works me over. I feel his thighs quaking against the backs of mine each time he stills, as he relentlessly tries to be gentle and slow. A strangled sound leaves him when my nails rake down his back and I feel a pulse start to thrum in my core, and God, I'm so needy for him, I feel *made* for him. My skin was meant for his hands. My core was meant to hold him. Meant to grow for him and make a life for him once. My strong thighs were meant to cradle him to me and hold a piece of him forever. His DNA altered mine, and our souls shaped themselves for each other. Everything in my body and being welcomes every part of him, and fuck, I'm going to come like this, I realize. I'm going to come, and I want him with me in every way; I'm desperate for him to fall apart.

"Let me have it," I beg in a throaty whisper. "Please."

"*Fuck*," he growls. When his eyes clench shut, I see a tear leak out of one.

He hooks one of my legs higher, pressing my knee up before he starts rutting into me, hot and hard and rough and fast, his control dissolving and his hips snapping against me. It's too much. It's too much of everything, and I don't care. I'd take on anything for him. He's stunning when he's unleashed.

I come with a shock, sensation shooting up my spine in a torrent and his name leaving me in a rush. When my eyes open again, his are on me, wide and drunk on bliss.

"Wren," he says raggedly. "Can I?"

"Yes," I tell him, a little sob stealing it at the end. "I got you." I reach up and try to hold on to his arm and end up scratching against him again, our skin slick with sweat.

He immediately comes, and it's devastating. It's broken

groans and him chanting my name into the skin inside my knee. It's his heat pouring into me and his strength thrumming against me. It's his pulse synced with mine. It's bare, raw love shining through his glassy eyes and into my own.

He keeps one of my knees wrapped around his hips and tilts us onto our sides, still inside me, his strong arms around my waist. I bury my face in his neck and let his pulse beat against my lips, our chests fighting for space against each other as we try to catch our breath. I can't tell if we're crying or laughing or if we're both doing both, our bodies vibrating with whatever this charge is between us, like we've finally returned home to our rightful ports. I run my hand over his chest and the dusting of coarse hairs there. He pets me down my back in the same pattern, kissing my temple and nuzzling against my curls. I try to adjust into a position that won't make my spine hurt tomorrow, and the movement angles his still-hard cock in a way that surprises a moan out of each of us.

He circles his hips a little and turns his face into mine, making a gritty sound against my cheek. "Need two more minutes. Then, again," he says.

My laugh cuts into a satisfied hiss when he does it another time, but my indulgent brain is already making calculations and plans for doing this often, and the last thing I'm willing to risk is a UTI.

"Ellis?"

"Mmm?"

"Where's the bathroom?"

———

We end up throwing on clothes and walking down a short trail lined in solar lights leading to the shared bathhouse between our site and the one closest to us (originally our second, which looks to be vacant still when we spot it through the trees). The bathroom itself is fancier than any campground bathroom has a right to be. Heated concrete flooring, slatted pine doors with iron fixtures and hardware. Two stalls in addition to two showers.

I turn on one of the showers after taking care of my other human business, and Ellis watches me raptly when I strip and step into the stream.

"Is it even a campground bathroom if you don't need quarters for the shower?" I ask, laughing. I feel carbonated. Giggly and buzzing and pleasantly sore. "This has better water pressure than my house."

He leans against the door, folding his arms and crossing a foot over another. I can see the outline of him growing hard in his sweats. "Better than our house?" he asks.

I lean my head back and act like I need to think about it. "Hmm, actually, no," I say, turning and letting it spray me down my front. "Our house is just as good."

I squeak in surprise when I feel his hands on me from behind. I spin around in his arms. "What are you doing? You'll get wet!"

"That's the idea," he says, letting the water rain over him and soak through his clothes. "You said *our* house. Does that mean you'll move back home?"

I press my lips together and my body tighter against his. "For the water pressure?"

His head cocks with a predatory smile, and he rakes his wet hair back. "For everything we can do in a shower there," he says. I'd been trying for coy, and I think I walked right into his setup instead. "How about I remind you?"

CHAPTER 34

WREN

It smells like home.

It's the first conscious thought I have the following morning. My eyes are still closed, and my other senses are the ones to come alive first. I smell the earthy-sweet spice of the redwoods around us, the campfire I presume Ellis has started in the ring outside our tent, the salty dampness of the ocean nearby, and Ellis's scent on the sheets.

I hear the crackling of that fire and a few distant birds chirping, and farther off, I hear the ding of a phone. My face rustles against something when I turn into my pillow, and I crack open my eyes. An origami bird with one wing worse for wear after I inadvertently rolled over it awaits me, *Open me* written on its neck. I smile and yawn at the same time, eagerly unfolding it. The first thing I see is my hastily scribbled signature in the corner.

After pushing me back against the tile last night, Ellis went to his knees and hooked my legs over his shoulders before bringing me to his mouth. He took me to the edge on his tongue with cruel efficiency twice before he'd stopped and toyed with me, leaving me bereft.

"Do you think you'd move back into our house?" he asked me after the second time.

"Ellis." It was half-growl and half-plea. I could feel the vibrations of his voice inches from me, but it wasn't enough to tip me over that edge. I tried to push against him, and he held me firm. I peeled my head off the tile and gave him a filthy look. *"I was planning on saying yes, but right now, I've got half a mind to—"*

"Would you sign something? Put it in writing? Have your people call my people?"

"Your people are *my people,"* I growled.

He laid a featherlight kiss against me like a sweet little *please*, and I tried to chase it, but he pulled back and gave me an expectant look. *"Yes,"* I whined. *"I'll sign something, just—"*

"Good," he said. He held my eyes and spit on my clit. *"You belong back home with me."*

He proceeded to make me feel exceedingly agreeable thereafter, and we jogged back to our site in the dark. After he followed through and made me sign a statement saying I'd move back, we made love one more time. We lay naked in bed under a pile of fluffy covers after, drowsily touching. Only the nighttime birdsong and crickets singing around us.

"So," I'd asked, my eyes half-closed. *"The tattoos?"* I traced the outline of one of the wings as he tucked a pillow under his cheek, his lids blinking heavily.

"Just wanted something permanent," he'd said. *"Something that can't be erased, even when everything changes between all of us."* He'd laughed through his nose and shut his eyes.

"One of them looks suspiciously like a wren," I'd murmured.

"*Nah. That's just a tit of some kind,*" he fibbed sarcastically, not bothering to open his eyes. My laugh seeped away the last of my energy, and I drifted off.

Aside from my sloppily scribbled agreement, the rest of the note says:

You looked too pretty (and you were snoring too loud) to wake. I was getting tempted, though, so I took myself on a walk to the camp store to grab us coffees.

I love you, Byrd.
—El

I hear a phone go off again from somewhere, so I reluctantly unearth myself from the covers and go hunting for it. I hear it again and realize I left it in the truck yesterday. By the time I get to it, I see I've missed Micah's call a third time.

His name pops up before I can hit Call on his name, and I quickly swipe to answer.

"Micah?"

"Hey, Wren," he says, relief thick through the phone.

"What's wrong? Everyone okay?"

"Yeah. No, yeah, we're good," he says, and I blow out an annoyed sigh. "I just need to go get my baseball stuff from your place. I can't stand it anymore."

"God, Micah. You scared me."

"Sorry for the power calls."

I laugh. "All good. You know where my spare key is?"

"Still under the gnome?"

"Yep. All the stuff is in my safe in the garage. Let me know when you're ready to write down the combination."

"K. Hang on." I hear him moving around and rifling through the drawers at Ellis's place. "Jesus, what grown man has this many pencils?" he mutters to himself. "All right, I'm ready."

I fire off the combination to him and hang up the phone, which is when the playback hits me. *What grown man has this many pencils?*

". . . *living my life in pencil, because I don't think I can get shit right the first time.*"

". . . *did some work on a campaign fire when the rest of the crew took time off.*" Which was last fall.

"*I want to be connected with my wife again.*"

"*Just wanted something permanent. Something that can't be erased.*"

"*El*"

"*L*"

CHAPTER 35

———

ELLIS

I take the trail slowly back to our campsite, thinking I'll let Wren sleep in, so I'm surprised to find her dressed and ready to go on our hike when I get back. She's lacing up her boots, a small backpack set up beside her on the stairs outside the tent. I pass her one of the coffees I snagged, and she smiles softly at it.

"Thank you," she says. There's something a little shy in her expression. Uncertain?

No. I'm determined not to get too deep in my head about it after last night. Not when I know my own nerves are heightened today.

"Welcome. Good morning." I bend to give her a brief kiss. Grin at her messy hair thrown up in a bun.

"You ready?" she asks.

"Sure. No rush, though. We can finish these, if you want?" I hold up my paper cup.

"I'm feeling pretty wired, actually."

"Oh, uh, all right." My heart gives a little stuttering kick. "Yeah. I'll just grab my pack."

We head out silently a few minutes later, and I try to steady my nerves and root myself in everything surrounding me. There are a lot of things here that feel reminiscent of home. There are the epically tall trees that get scragglier the closer we get to shore. The rocky, dramatic cliffs on either side of the beaches. The shifting, spotty sunshine and the salty-thick air. *Hard-water air*, my Mom always called it. It can warp wood and weather stone, but that's the stuff that builds character. When something can withstand it, you know it's better made.

We come to a narrow rope bridge over a rocky creek, and I hesitate because it looked sturdier in the pictures I saw online. Wren pushes past me and starts to cross it without pausing, though, and my feet carry me behind her automatically. Push and pull. Where one of us leads, the other one will follow. At least I hope. I hope she'll let this tie between us stay now.

We coast over a small bracken-covered slope, and I hear the waterfall before we see it. We round another corner, and there it is, gushing over the mossy rocks like a veil and ending in a misty cloud below. It smells earthy and damp in a way that grounds me, makes me ready for this final, hard conversation. When I turn to her, she's already sat herself on a rock and is looking at me. Her hair is wilder here in the spray, but the look in her eyes is indecipherable.

"Wren," I start, then have to swallow hard. "Last night, when I said I had more I needed to tell you, I . . ." I realize it would be easier to show her, so I slide off my pack and unzip it, squat down, and start digging around for what I need.

"Looking for these?"

The bag drops with a thud, and I look at her, at the stack of letters in her hand. "Wren."

"I wanted to see if you were going to tell me," she says, so quietly I almost miss it under the sound of the rushing water. "I just figured it out this morning."

I feel my brow crease. "I don't know that I like being *tested*, baby," I say with levity I don't feel. Her expression only gets sterner.

"*I* don't like feeling deceived. Or feeling like the last to know. I realize now that you were pretty clever about not outright lying to me, though, weren't you?" She moves to stand, and I slip to my knees—kneeling, because I don't trust my legs right now. "I want you to tell me what you need to tell me, Ellis. I—" Her chin quivers, and she inhales deeply. "I can't see you trying to manipulate me. Tell me why you didn't tell me before." Her shoulders drop, the envelopes wobbling against her thighs.

My hands start to shake, and I need to press them into my legs.

"At first—" I croak. "At first, I lied to myself and convinced myself I could just find out about the horses and get you what you needed. And then I just wanted . . . I just wanted to *talk* to you again, even if you didn't know it was me. But then everything came pouring out, and I realized how I still felt and that I hadn't been brave enough to own up to everything. For that alone, I thought I didn't deserve you. I thought I'd stolen that link to you again and . . ." I work at clearing my throat and force myself to hold her gaze. "Do you remember when you asked me if I believed in something like fate? Well, the truth is, I don't want to. I hate that fate or chance or fucking luck can get any of the credit for us finding our way back to each other. Not this time. Not when we've worked so hard. I don't want it to be because we got pregnant that we ended up together. I shouldn't have needed my stupid brother and his friend to toss you in the ocean for me to kiss you for the first time. I hate—" I have to blow out and take in a steadying breath. "It terrifies me to think that I might've let this life go by

without finding my way back to you. Never again, Wren. I promise. Never again. I'm not letting you go. And if you're mad at me
about this and if you think I kept this from you to manipulate you
or something, I'll spend the rest of my life proving it to you that I
didn't, if you'll let me. If you won't have me back anymore, then
I'll find you in the next life. You are the only thing that makes me
believe in that. In something bigger than myself. The way I have
felt about you has been the only thing that's felt like . . . like it
can't be contained in one body or lifetime." She hasn't moved, and
I fight to swallow my building panic. "I only stopped the letters
because I knew I had to get my shit together, Wren. And maybe
I still don't have it all figured out, but I'm working on it, and I'll
keep working on it. I'll keep going to therapy. I'll go with you
if you want to go together. I'll talk to you about everything. I'll
listen about everything. Talk my fucking ears off, baby; I'll beg
you to every day if I need to. I'm *begging* you to fight with me,
do anything with me. Just be with me." I blink, and hot tears slip
down my cheeks. "I saw that paper on the counter and I couldn't
wait a fucking minute longer. I knew part of me still lived in you,
and I couldn't let it die. I would've done way worse than keep one
last secret a little while."

She's quiet for too long. "Quite a speech," she eventually says.
Tears spill from her big brown eyes.

"Yeah, well . . ." I can't tell if she's angry or sad or what she is,
and it's making my pulse go insane. "I've had a long time to think
about it. I just . . . I wanted you to choose this."

She comes closer. "Are you done?" she asks.

I stare at her again. "Done what? Talking?"

She shrugs, her chin bouncing chaotically now. "That, too,"
she says, breathing out a single, teary chuckle. "But are you about
done trying to prove yourself?"

"I don't know," I say, heart in my throat. "You tell me."

She closes the distance between us and slides to her knees, laying her hand against my face. I start to cry like a fucking kid again the moment she touches me. I reach up and hold her palm tight to my skin.

"I wanted it to be you, anyway," she says wetly. "I *wanted* it to be you." She coughs out a tiny cry that I feel in my chest. "But then I saw that fucking text on Thanksgiving, and I misread everything and oh my god, Ellis, I panicked. I thought you'd moved on, and realized I'd stayed there, still loving you somehow. I panic-dated! It was awful!" Relief collapses me into her, and I wipe at her tears while mine flow freely. We laugh, and our teeth clink in a frantic kiss. "I'm so sorry I misread it all. I'm sorry I didn't realize it sooner."

"Hey, no. No, baby," I tell her, my rough laugh a little hysterical. "It sure as hell wasn't you. My timing has been shit for a lot of things. And I'm sorry you panic-dated. If it's any consolation, I died a little every time I heard about it."

Her head falls back with a wail. "Some of them were so bad! I should be so mad at you."

We're both laughing again. "That's okay, baby. Be mad at me forever," I say. But then she kisses me sweetly and it feels like forgiveness.

"Thank you. Thank you for doing this. For making this trip happen," she says. The high tightness of her voice has me kissing every corner of her face. When I get to her lips again, we lose a few minutes. "Would you be offended if I asked you to bring me home a day early?" she asks, punctuating it by nipping my jaw. "I want to come home now."

I can't help it—I break into a full-bodied laugh. Hugging her tight around the shoulders like she'll keep me from floating away, I say, "I'd move into the truck with you just to live with you again," I say. "Care if we take one more little segue, though? It's the last thing I wanna do."

One last thing to get right.

CHAPTER 36

———

WREN

We hold hands the entire way back to camp, then past it when we decide to go grab breakfast at the restaurant. We're both starving after only focusing on our other appetites last night. I think I can't let go because, just like he said, the thought that we could've missed out on this makes me feel a bit unsteady.

Ellis and I share a platter of waffles and split a hearty omelet between us, swapping plates or cutting pieces and forking them onto the other's. It's like remembering the steps to an old dance.

"So, I've been wondering," he asks me. He automatically cuts the perfect corner off his waffle and puts it onto my plate. "Did you ever talk to anyone about the letters?"

I offer a melancholy smile and a shrug. "No. It wasn't like they were romantic or something, but . . . I don't know, I guess they felt intimate still?"

"Hinting that you looked like a goblin was pretty racy," he snorts.

"Ha." I pour him some fresh coffee from the press at our table. "But again, no. Even if she could sometimes pry a little bit out of me, I was pretty careful with what I talked about with Sage. And yeah, Silas is just downright nosy, so he had no qualms about asking if I had date plans and stuff, but . . . I don't know. They always put on a good face about things, but I couldn't talk to them about much without feeling like I was making them disloyal to you or something," I say. "Plus, you know Sage. If I'd mentioned a pair of horses potentially caught in a fire, she'd have gone and looked for them herself or something." I laugh but look back up at him when I notice he doesn't.

"I'm sorry you felt like you didn't have people you could talk to," he says. He drags my hand over and kisses the base of my palm.

I shake my head, not sure if the tears springing up are happy or sad. "What about you?" I say. "Did you have people you could talk to?"

"I let it slip to Kirby, and that helped. Her cousin was the one who found out about the horses. But as far as the rest of them . . . my family." He sighs wearily. "All these years, I just . . . I just assumed they were closer to you than they were to me."

It's my turn to sigh. "In a way, maybe. But mostly, I couldn't do that to you. You hardly ever got the chance to just be their brother, let alone their friend."

He continuously massages circles into my hand with his thumb. "I'm trying more with them. To loosen up, worry less. Be their friend instead of managing them and hovering, I guess. Sometimes I feel like the least fun brother." He chuckles wryly.

"Ehh. You are," I say, my shoulders jumping in a small shrug. "But you're the *most* fun for me."

"Yeah, well. I provide a different sort of amusement for you," he says, mouth tilting in a crooked smirk. "They don't always share things with me like they did with you, and then I find myself not sharing things, too, and it makes me wonder why we don't all trust one another more. And sometimes I just think I put a damper on their fun." He adjusts in his seat uncomfortably. "Even the bride at the winery thought I was an old man after taking one look at me."

"She was on her fourth winery of the day and hammered, Ellis. Your brothers and sister don't have any less fun with you. And it's not that they don't trust you, either. I think they just . . ." I try to find the words. "You've always taken on anything for any of them. For any of *us*. It can be hard to feel like you deserve that kind of love. It gets hard to share your burdens, especially with the one person who's always tried to relieve you of them. It happened with me and you, too." I kiss his big knuckles and touch his empty ring finger. "I bet if you confide in them more, they'll meet you in the middle," I say, which is when something occurs to me. "Do they know about your tattoos?" He shakes his head, and a happy sound pops out of me. "Silas is going to lose his shit." They all will, I'm sure.

We finish breakfast and stroll hand in hand back to our site before we pack up the few things we'd unpacked. I feel on the edge of giggling the whole morning. He sprawls in a wooden chair in the corner of the tent, legs braced wide as he watches me get ready, his gaze heady. I throw on a midlength sundress and strappy, comfortable sandals for the day. When his eyes heat and his jaw starts to tick, I decide to ask him to take everything off again, which ends up costing us an hour and leads me to have to start the process all over.

"Ready?" he asks. This time, after I've strapped on my sandals. "Just one more stop."

"All right. I'm ready."

The little town of McArthur-Burney is painted green and orange and teeming with music, tourists, and merriment of all sorts. Food trucks and bar carts line the streets, every old brick building covered in Irish regalia and signs that advertise their annual festival. There's an outdoor stage in a nearby park with a band playing on it and a trio of young girls river dancing.

"This is so random," I say delightedly to Ellis. "But great. I love it."

"Is it random?" he asks, suspiciously nonchalant, hands sliding into the pockets of his jeans. When he looks down at his boots, I notice the color flagging his cheeks.

"Oh my god," I whisper, coming to a stop and staring around me before I look back up at him. "You . . . the letters. When I talked about traveling?" The warm beach in Santa Cruz. The Italian villa; a replica of one and in California, sure, but as close as I've ever been to drinking wine on an Italian villa. And now he's brought me to an Irish festival full of dancing.

He smiles shyly. "Sorry I couldn't get you to Europe, Byrd, but even if this didn't go the way I hoped, I wanted to give you what I could," he says. "Even if you never put it together, at least I'd have known."

I curl my hands in his shirt and tug him down into a desperate kiss. Tongue and teeth, short whimpers and low hums, oblivious to the crowd walking around us on the sidewalk. A few people whistle and clap until we break away, softly gasping in the space between us, his forehead pressed into mine.

"This was better. All of it was better," I eke out. That *hope, hope, hope* that's been beating in my chest blares into a symphony of love and joy.

"I have mixed feelings about the pepper burn," he says, thumbing my cheek. "But of course it was. It's us."

The sun starts to fade, and we slip into a bar, aptly called the Burney Stone, overflowing with music. The walls are all brick and fieldstone, with wood-beamed ceilings, a raised stage at the back of the room holding a different band from the one outside, and a sizable dance floor packed with people spinning around, linking arms, skipping and stomping to the beat.

Ellis pulls me out onto it immediately, and I have a fit watching him hop his big body around. We only take breaks to collect water from the bar and catch our breath when we're both sweaty and disheveled. I catch him staring at me as he crunches down on a piece of ice, and he looks as invigorated as I feel. Bright stare, bright smile, flushed face. Young and alive and real. His bottom lip glistens with melted ice, and I push up onto my toes and lick it off. He smiles, and I lick at that, too, just as the band takes their bows and filters off the stage.

The lights go dim, and different music starts to play from whatever sound system they've got in here. Popular, mainstream hits combined with oldies in modern arrangements. Ellis and I watch as the dancing starts to change. There's no more skipping. All that quick jouncing rolls into smooth waves.

"One more dance before we head out?" I ask, already beckoning him over my shoulder and walking that way. He comes willingly, more people ebbing onto the floor around us. The temperature lifts until it's just short of stifling, but the crush of undulating bodies makes me feel braver, like there are too many other people for the spotlight to be on us this way. I hardly recognize any of the crowd members from earlier, faces all a puzzle of shadowed hollows in the dappled lights. The red glow of the room matches the warmth in my veins, feels like it might even be emanating from me as this beat moves through me, too. It's a slow swat punctuated by a grinding twang, a vibrating thrum in my core that matches the one I feel in his chest when I drag my hands down it. I can't make out his expression, just see the muscle flex in his jaw when I slide and press myself into him, his hands tightening on my hips and his fingertips digging into my ass. I turn in his grip, ring my arms around the back of his neck. Watch his hands glide down the front of my waist to clutch at my hips again. His chin tucks into my neck, and I know the view down my dress is making him wild, can feel it when I circle and arch against where he's stiffening.

"Be good, Byrd," comes his deep timbre in my ear. He presses against me again like he can't help himself.

I let my head fall farther to the side and catch the ends of his sweat-dampened hair in my fingers. Feel a throaty hum crawl up from my chest when his lips skim back and forth over the curve of my shoulder. I smile at his hiss when I grind back and catch his hard cock in a perfect tug, right between my cheeks.

"You're killing me, baby," he groans. God, I'm totally sober and entirely too drunk on this. I can't believe I'm dry-humping my ex-husband on a dance floor like we're at junior prom. He's killing me right back. A low, needy tug starts to pulse between my legs. My heart kicks up when he lets his big palms drift down to the tops of my thighs, galloping when he teases me, and brings them right back up. Down, spread, squeeze again, heat unfurling in the same rhythm. The moment his fingertips finally touch my bare skin, I snap. I spin and bring my mouth to his for one hot, wet kiss. Hook my fingers through his belt loops to keep him close and drag him off the dance floor into the dark hallway.

His lips are back on mine in a second, eating at my sounds. "You're so goddamn beautiful, Wren," he says, half growling, half panting before he forgoes air and steals mine in a kiss again. "You sound like you fucking ache, huh? Need my help?" he asks.

"Yeah. Make it better."

He walks us deeper into the alcove and props me up against the wall. His eyes are black, his hair a mess. He's glimmering with sweat and deliciously out of sorts. "Take it out, baby, see what you did to me," he says. He's impossibly hard and hot in my palm. "Wrap your legs around me—yeah, fuck, I love your thighs." He pets them up and down before he tucks my underwear aside and buries himself into me in one long, hard thrust. I can't stop a tight whine of surprise, the breath plucked right from my lungs. "Too much?" he asks. "You okay?"

"Yes," I sigh. Yes, too much, and I've never felt more right. "It's . . . good." Having some part of him embedded in me is so inconveniently essential.

I feel his grin against my neck. "Good. I'll make it so good for you if you're quiet. Think you can do that for me?" I nod incoherently and moan when his hips tip up impossibly more, my feet dangling helplessly behind his strong thighs. "Dirty girl, that wasn't very quiet."

I plant a kiss into his jaw. The infuriating man lifts me so slowly I feel him hit every nerve. What I'd thought would be fast and rough turns slow and . . . still rough. But desperate and tender, too. He finds a steady pace, his forehead against my temple and his bruising grip around my thighs. The only sounds are the music filtering in from the other room and my quick puff of breath each time he nudges into me. I let myself feel every part of him I can with every part of me. The bunch and flex of his powerful shoulders and biceps under my hands. Hard thighs and hips beneath mine, keeping me where he needs me while he fucks me into the wall. The mile-wide chest I feel wholly protected by, like anyone could come around this corner and I'd still be safe. My orgasm spills through me, something molten and quick and consuming, and I have to bury my strangled noise against his collarbone. His rhythm stutters.

"Wren, shit, can I—"

"It's okay, it's okay. Yes, I want you to." A fresh wave of heat blooms at the idea of walking around full of him. Him knowing I'm a mess of us both beneath my dress.

That pulls a deep, bitten-off groan from him, and then I feel him coming, everything going taut before he relaxes in degrees, hips still occasionally thrusting even after he starts to soften inside me.

He pulls himself out, agonizingly slow, then keeps me braced against the wall while he slips my underwear back in place with a loving pat.

His arms are still shaking under my hands, and his breathing is still labored. I hug him against me like I'm reminding myself that this is real again, that we've really come back to one another. He lays a kiss to my temple.

"I love you, Byrd."

I kiss his chin, then his lips. "I love you."

CHAPTER 37

─────

WREN

Ellis and I end up sleeping for a full eight hours in a rest stop parking lot after we leave McArthur-Burney. We cover another hour's distance under a star-speckled sky, then park, fold our seats back as much as they'll allow, intertwining our hands on the middle between us—like otters trying not to drift away.

We wake up at the same time, groaning and each making a series of miserable noises. We raise our seats up and give each other sidelong looks. I feel stale and sticky and preemptively tired from the work I'll have to do to tame my hair. Ellis's hair is smashed down on one side, and half his face has an imprint on it from sleeping on his palm.

"Get us home, honey," I say.

"Happily," he replies. "Three more hours."

We keep the music low, and by silent agreement, we don't make any stops, intent on getting back to where we belong.

A little over two hours into it, Ellis pierces our quiet bubble.

"How do you want to tell everyone?" he asks. "*What* do you want to tell everyone?"

I cock my head thoughtfully. "What if we didn't for a while? Just to make them a little crazy." I pinch my fingers together. "We could say something annoyingly vague that they'd be forced to respond respectfully to. Something like, 'We're still figuring it out,' or, 'We're taking it day by day.'"

His snort of laughter is adorable. The combination of it and his bedhead makes me feel like we stepped back in time somehow. "How long do you think we could drag that out?" he asks.

"A week, tops."

He grins at me, all boyish happiness. "Then yeah, Byrd, I'll sneak around with you."

It's not any of the beautiful declarations or gestures he's made for me in the last five days, and yet the sight of him right now, rumpled and content, sends an implosive chain reaction through my chest. I feel every bit of it in this truck cab, all the memories of every version of his face I've known, all the times I've fallen in love with him in some new way. Him at six, alone in a classroom and studiously tracing the letters of the alphabet in pencil before any of the other kids had even arrived. Him in middle school, awkward and gangly and gentle and sad. Him in high school, filled out in his body but restless in his own skin, the friendship between us growing hungry with longing. Him, sitting in the passenger seat of my Wrangler when I told him I was pregnant. The way he jumped to apologize to me and the fear in his eyes, the way he immediately assumed responsibility, like it was somehow only his doing. The strength he showed when they told me I needed an emergency cesarean after thirty-six hours of laboring. At eighteen, he'd been more of a man than any of the ones I'd ever known. How, even as he went pale at the sight of them cutting into me, he kept talking me through it all, telling me he couldn't believe what I could do. Telling me I was a miracle, that I was powerful, that he hoped our baby would be just like me. I'm grabbing his hand across the console when I remember how he'd rarely put Sam down in those early days. I'd had to playfully lecture him about tummy time and not wanting the kid to end up with a flat head from how often Ellis carried him tucked into his arm like the world's cutest football. I remember the first time we slept together after having Sam, and how I'd started leaking breast milk and immediately bawled from mortification. He'd laughed warmly and licked me clean, milk and tears alike. He managed to make me feel womanly and sexy right then.

I remember when he taught Sam to ride a bike, the way he'd pumped the air with his fists and jumped up and down. I fell in love with him anew when he came back to the house with a sobbing, skinned-kneed Sam in one arm and a kid's bicycle in the other. His mouth set in a grim line when he told me, "I got so focused on teaching him how to go that I forgot to teach him how to brake."

I fell in love with him again when he told me he'd bought an industrial mixer for the bakery. We hadn't even closed on our house and we were not supposed to be making any big purchases, but he didn't care. He needed a new car more than I needed anything, but Savvy's only had a few countertop mixers and a hodgepodge of equipment before then. He was adamant about supporting my dreams, about supporting me at every turn. He wanted me to make the place my own as much as I could.

And this? This love that I feel for him again is something brand new, like some charred marshmallow skin peeled away, exposing a fresh, gooey, unmarred center. I'd keep getting heart burnt for the rest of my life with him, knowing we can find a new layer underneath. Until every bit of us runs out.

For how many words we've used to help us through this to get here, from writing them to finally sharing all the ones we held back, they all fall short when it comes to what I feel right now.

"Hey," I say. He turns away from the road to face me, eyes crinkling at the corners. "I love you."

We beam at each other, his smile staying put when he has to look back at the road. It stays put even when he brings my hand up to his lips. "I love you, too." We pass the sign welcoming us home to Spunes. "We made it," he says.

We did.

We made it.

"Ellis?"

"Mmm?"

"I don't want to wait," I say. "We have to tell Sam, first, obviously. But I don't want to wait to tell everyone. I don't care about the pressure or any of it." He's mine again and I want everyone to know it. I want him to feel found and chosen by me, as much as I feel by him.

His eyes flick to me briefly again before he looks over his shoulder, flipping on the blinker and pulling the truck over so quickly I screech. We're still recoiling from being thrown into Park when he takes my face in his hands and kisses me hard.

"Good. I don't want to wait, either," he says.

"Let's call Sam."

"Okay," he says, laughing eagerly. "Do you want to talk about how we should tell him? Anything specific? What should we say?"

He's still got my face in his palms when the words burst free. "Marry me."

His expression softens in shock, and my mouth goes dry in panic. "What?" he asks.

"Or not, I don't know. I just—"

"You can't take it back!" he says defensively. He starts pecking kisses all over my face. "Haven't you ever proposed before?"

"I'm"—peck—"out of"—peck—"practice."

"You have to give the other person time to adequately freak out," he informs me.

"I didn't give myself time to adequately think about it before I asked!" I squeak.

"You didn't ask, you *demanded*," he says. "I have no choice but to say yes now."

"Really?" I say, even as he's flipping up the center console and pulling himself closer to me, his stubble scratching at my cheek. "We don't have to. We could just be together."

"No. I want the whole thing this time. I want to make you my wife again. We deserve a celebration."

"Good." I laugh. "I want Sam to be there. I want you in a tie."

"I want you to have a pretty bouquet. Not just a pen and a paper." He pulls back from my neck to look into my eyes. "I want to write some vows."

I kiss his chin. "I do, too."

CHAPTER 38

ELLIS

I'm not the least bit surprised to see that my siblings, along with Fisher and Indy, are all at my place when we pull down the driveway. I'd only texted Micah to give him a heads-up that we were coming back early, but I figured he'd tell the rest. Wren and I share a look, then unload ourselves from the truck, moving like our limbs are lead. We school our faces into flat, regretful expressions when they start approaching us.

"Heyyyy," Sage calls. "So happy you're home?" She says it like it's a question. I almost cave when she gets closer, and I can see the disappointment in her eyes. She hugs Wren first, then makes her way over to me. "Drive go okay?" she asks in a strained voice.

Micah has already crossed the front lawn, too. Only Silas hangs back on the porch with Indy and Fisher.

"So, did you have a good trip or not?" Micah asks.

"*Micah*," Sage growls.

"What?! Let's just get it over with now, all right? They

came home a day early, so clearly it didn't work out, and that's fine. They need to know we still love them, right?" he asks, crushing Wren to his chest in a hug. "We can all move on with our lives."

I catch Wren's eye from where she's being suffocated in Micah's arms. When he steps away, we study one another from our opposite sides of the gravel.

I cross my arms and kick at a loose pebble with my boot. She lets out a sad sigh.

And then we take a step toward each other.

I let my arms fall before we take another.

And another.

And another.

"I think we nailed it," she says just before she bumps into me, and I turn her in my arms and lower her into a deep dip, crushing my mouth to hers.

I'm not sure who screams, who whistles, or who claps, but for a crowd of four, they're all loud as hell.

I disappear into the feel of her lips, the scent of her mixed with all the smells of home, and it's like I've finally come alive under my own skin again. The version of me I was meant to be, misshapen heart finding its matching piece. By the time we come back up for air, we're being circled in a hug by everybody.

Everybody but one.

"Where's Silas?" I ask.

Wren and I walk hand in hand around the side of the house until we meet the backyard. Silas is sitting in a lawn chair with his face in his hands, a beer bottle dangling from a finger he's got curled around the neck.

"Si?" says Wren softly.

He shakes his head at the sound of her voice, and now I get

it. He's overwhelmed. I know what it is to feel too much, even when it's happy.

Suddenly, he jerks up from the chair and a sob wrenches out of him, and his arms are stretching to hug us both. He cries into my shoulder, and I laugh and cry with him.

"I knew you wouldn't fuck this up," he says, muffled in my shirt.

"I'm glad I made you proud, brother," I say.

"It's about fucking time!! Dammit!"

Wren makes a soothing noise and pets the back of his head.

"Hey, Si?" I ask.

He lifts up and steps back, sniffing aggressively and wiping his face. "Yeah?"

"Will you be my best man?"

He points the hand holding the beer at me. "Now you're just being an asshole," he says with a violently wobbling chin, just before he hugs me once more. "But no, actually, I won't," he adds. He moves away again and bares us one of his shit-eating grins. "Because I'm *ordained* now!"

"Oh, Jesus, Silas. That was a little presumptuous, don't you think?" Wren scolds.

"I am bored out of my damned mind most days, anyway, right now, so no, I don't," he says. "I can't wait to have a sister again!"

"What the hell?" says Sage. Micah tugs her into a sideways hug.

"I mean another one," Silas says, shrugging her off with an eye roll.

"Did you guys tell Sam?" asks Indy from a few yards away, Fisher's arm slung over her shoulders.

"Yeah," Wren says, smiling broadly at me. "Yeah, we did."

As soon as we decided earlier, we FaceTimed Sam right then and there from the side of the highway.

"Hey, Mama," he'd said when he picked up after a ring.

"Hey, son. How's it going?" Wren said.

"Uh, it's going pretty good. Having roommates after being an only child is a little weird, but I don't hate it, I guess," he said. "So how's your trip? How was the cooking class? It looked fun online."

Wren cut me a glance, and I lifted a brow. "It was a lot of fun, bub," she said with a smirk. "Dad's here, too." She adjusted the phone so he could see us both. "We want to talk to you about something."

Sam went completely still, his face changing and looking at us in a way that felt eerily like looking into a mirror. "Yeah?" said Sam. "Is everyone okay?"

"Everyone is good, son," I said.

His eyes darted between us. "Everyone is good?" he asked quietly, and his expression was so hopeful that my vocal cords felt raw when I replied.

"Yeah, son. Better than good."

He'd started nodding quickly, his lips closed tight on a smile.

"Dad and I want to get back together," said Wren. "Would you feel okay about that? If that's weird for you, it's okay to tell us."

"Yes, Mom. I'd . . ." He put his forefinger and his thumb into each eye, trying to jam back his tears. "Yeah, I would feel okay about that," he'd said.

Back at home, I pull Wren into me again and whisper in her ear, "Want me to get rid of them so we can go sleep in our bed?"

She hooks her arms around my middle and looks over everyone making themselves at home in ours. "No. We'll just slip away when we're ready." Her chin tips up against my chest, and our eyes catch. "We have whatever's left of forever, you and me."

CHAPTER 39

———

WREN

Ellis gives my ass an appreciative squeeze.

"Don't get distracted," I warn him under my breath.

"Too late. Shouldn't have worn these jeans," he murmurs.

"Ellis Orion Byrd. We have to stay focused here. They're coming any second now."

"Coulda been you, too, but you turned me down," he complains.

I try to give him a stern look, but it stutters when I see his heated smile in the moonlight. "I seem to recall saying a lot of yeses when I closed the bakery for lunch this afternoon." *Lunch* is in air quotes. "We're gonna get caught again." I let a groan slip free when I remember the exasperated look on my mother's face when she came in the back door and found Ellis and me scrambling to right ourselves one afternoon two weeks ago. "We pushed my mother into an early retirement."

"She was looking for an excuse."

He's not wrong. When we came back from our trip (a little over a month ago now), I found out that Mom had just straight up left the bakery closed for two of the days I'd been gone. She closed early on the others. Rather than let us throw her a party to celebrate her officially passing the whisk on to me, she and David jetted off to Hawaii on a whim.

Still. "Tonight isn't about you or me or my mom, Ellis. Keep your eyes on the water."

He rustles around in the sand next to me, rolling from his stomach onto his side and propping his head in his hand. "You look beautiful, Byrd. The moon makes your hair look silver." He reaches over and plays with a stray coil.

I melt a little, even as I shake my head at him. He's sharpened and honed his skills with compliments as of late. Sometimes he catches me so off guard that I don't know how to reply, which is when he gets the smuggest. "Speechless again, I see," he'd said yesterday morning when he met me at work and told me that watching me bake was like watching a conductor in an orchestra. "All passion and concentration for something with a bunch of moving parts that all need just the right amount of attention. All for something for everyone else to enjoy." I stood there a little dumbly, flour on my face and a half-empty piping bag in hand.

Later, he told me he'd figured out that the secret to compliments is just saying them the minute they're in his head, without trying to arrange them perfectly. It felt like he'd cracked an egg inside my chest, knowing that he's been trying to speak from his so purely.

I wriggle closer to him, heedless of the sand scraping along my torso.

"I can't wait to see her face," he says.

"Me, either," I say. Which is when a light catches my eye from down the small beach we're currently hiding on. Two little phone flashlights, I see, upon closer inspection.

"It's Micah and Silas," Ellis says, and I can just make out their faces now from where they're hiding behind another log, just like Ellis and me.

It's a perfect late July evening. One of those rare warm(ish) summer nights we get in Spunes. The moon is full and bright in a cloudless, starry sky.

"Hopefully, Indy gets here in time," I say.

"She will. She had to be at the house when they left so Sage wouldn't suspect anything."

Micah starts a crouched run over to us, kicking up tufts of sand and tripping over his own feet.

"What are you doing?! Get back to your hiding spot!" Ellis yell-whispers at him.

"Relax! I just need to ask Wren something real quick," Micah replies. I hear a car door shut in the distance and see Indy making her way down to the beach a moment later.

"Wren," Micah starts. "You know that little arched window above your kitchen sink? Do you happen to know where I could find a replacement?"

"*Micah*," I groan. "No, I don't. You are officially the worst tenant on the planet!" I've moved all my essentials back home with Ellis, as Micah has been making himself at home in my old place. It would be the ideal situation for all, if Micah didn't happen to accidentally put a hole in a wall while moving furniture, break the refrigerator, and now break what sounds like a second window all in the span of a few weeks.

"Hey!" Indy says, excitedly jogging over to us. "You have the camera ready?"

Ellis lays a quick kiss to my hairline, still chuckling warmly over Micah's cursed clumsiness.

"Yeah, I've got it here," I say.

Micah tries to plop his body between Ellis and me, which makes Ellis bodily remove him and shove him back toward where he came from.

"Fine, damn," he whispers. "Indy, come with me. The view is better, anyway."

When they've settled back into their hiding spots, I meet Ellis's stare. "How's the tattoo? Lying like this doesn't feel good."

He pats the spot high on his thigh, where, under his jeans, he's got a bandage covering a tattoo, twin to the one I've got on mine. We haven't planned when exactly we'll do a ceremony yet, but we wrote our own vows to one another in the meantime. His is in my handwriting, mine is in his.

"I kinda like the little bit of pain. Reminds me they're there," he says. But just past his head, I can make out a bright neon light on the water.

"Shhh, they're here. Duck down!"

We go as still as we can manage, lowering down behind the log until we can't see Fisher and Sage in their little glass-bottom kayak anymore, relying on sound to know when they've made it onto the shore.

"That was kind of a short ride," we hear Sage observe curiously. "What are your plans with me?" she asks, an implication in her voice like she hopes they're not innocent. We hear the unmistakable sounds of kissing. Ellis's mouth quirks down at the corners. I smother a laugh.

"I have so many plans, Sage," says Fisher. That devious man knows all three of her brothers are within earshot. I respect him for it. "But mostly, I just want the everyday stuff. I want to know what your hair looks like when you wake up in the morning when we're sixty. I want to see what robe you wear next week."

I can feel Sage's laugh in my solar plexus, like her happiness is my own. My eyes start to fill when I notice Ellis's already have.

"I meant here, as in, onshore," says Sage. "Did you pack a blanket or something this time? You know after last time, it took like a week to get all the sand out of your—"

"I know what you meant," he quickly says. "I'm talking about making plans for something else, sweetheart."

"Oh! Oh, okay," she says. "We can make plans for whatever you want."

"I was sorta hoping you'd say that," says Fisher.

We hear Sage gasp, and I imagine Fisher's gone down to one knee.

"Sage," Fisher starts, emotion roughening his words. "I didn't know what I was doing when Indy came to me. I didn't know what I was doing when I showed up here. You helped me see that it was okay not to know. You helped me take care of my moments, and time took over from there. I don't know what the future will look like with me. I don't know if I'll end up with my own place, and I don't know if I'll struggle for money. I don't know if I'll make a good husband." His swallow is audible. "I don't know if I'll make a good dad. But I sure as hell know I'll try. I just want—I want to keep trying life with *you*. I will do everything in my power to make every minute I get with you count. But. But would you please plan on forever with me? Would you be my wife and spend your life with me?"

Ellis leans over and kisses me, his smile glowing in the moon-light. His happy tears pelt the sand beneath us.

"*Yes*," Sage manages to say, and we all jump up from our spots. Neither Fisher or Sage even flinch in surprise. They're too busy reaching for one another and crying and laughing into each other's mouths. I start snapping photos just as Indy gets Sam on FaceTime, and the Byrd brothers all cheer, jogging over and huddling around into one great hug. Fisher's head manages to stick out above the blob, and he looks over to me and mouths, *Thank you*. I keep on taking pictures.

"Don't thank me yet!" I call over, just in time for Micah, Silas, and Ellis to each grab a part of Fisher, peel him away from Sage, and haul him into the frigid Pacific. Fisher bursts up from the water, sputtering and gasping and cursing up a storm, while Indy and all the Byrds laugh their asses off.

"It's like an initiation!" I yell to him, then screech when Ellis tosses me over his shoulder and starts to carry me up the beach back to our car.

"I love you, Sagey! Congrats!" I say.

"I love you, too! Thank you!" she calls back, gathering a shivering, wet Fisher into her arms.

Ellis and I race up the stairs when we get home, tossing our sandy-damp clothes in a heap when we practically skid into our room. I press him down onto our bed and kiss the still-healing vows on his thigh before I take him into my mouth and love him that way as long as he'll let me. It's just him and me here, and we're as loud as we want to be. We laugh when we get tangled in our sheets and topple onto the floor, where he puts me on my knees and elbows and makes love to me from behind, holding my hand on my shoulder the whole way through, like one extra piece of connection.

When we lie in bed together after, he holds one of my hands to his chest while we talk about mundane things. He goes back to work tomorrow after having a few days off. It'll be Silas's first week back to work after being off for eleven months, too. Two days ago, I got to meet Lennon Kirby on a FaceTime call. She's adorable and playfully harasses Ellis, and I love it. If she lived closer, I would be scheming to set her up with Micah.

We talk about what I'm planning to make this week at the bakery. I want to try a few things with pistachios, and he lets out a little whine and asks me to make sure I can make a few of them when he comes back, too. I'm not sure at what point he drifts off, but when his hand loosens over mine, I bring it down to trace over the words in his skin, just before I feel myself slipping away, too.

If you're lost, I'll find you.
I'll give you my body, my heart, and my soul.
I'll cherish every bit of yours in return.
I'll fight with you. I'll fight for you.
I'll love you for everything left of forever, in every lifetime we get.

PART 3

———

Forever

FOREVER

WREN

I'm laughing at myself in the full-length mirror, watching my re-flection contort and struggle to reach the top button on the back of my dress, when a soft knock comes on my bedroom door.

"Oh, thank god," I mutter. I hurry toward it, passing my favorite worn-in boots on the floor, tucked beneath the wall of windows looking out onto a drizzly day. My bouquet is sitting on a dressing table there, too. Sage designed something uniquely perfect, of course. Thorn-free stems of unripe marionberries ranging from green to pink to reddish purple sit between trailing eucalyptus, delicately spiky pieces of smoke bush (to represent Ellis, she'd said), coral nasturtiums, and dark cosmos . . . among a few others whose names I can't remember. Despite being me-ticulously curated, it looks like something collected at random. Little pieces of life—familiar and new and yet to reach full bloom.

I'm assuming it's Sage herself at the door now. Either her or my mom, who've both been wringing their hands ever since the forecast called for rain and all our plans for today had to shift.

"Perfect timing," I say, unlocking and opening the door.

"That's a first," says Ellis, leaning onto an arm on the doorframe.

I breathe out a surprised laugh and quickly try to tuck myself behind the doorframe. My entire face heats at the sight of him in expertly tailored dress pants and suspenders cutting over a crisp white shirt. An undone tie dangles loosely around his neck. "Haven't you heard it's bad luck to see the bride?" I ask playfully.

His mouth curves gently, and he shakes his head. "Nah. You and I make our own luck, Byrd." He pushes himself up straight. "Besides, I think our bad luck quota got met with the rain. Let me see you, baby."

I open the door wider to let him in, hear the sound of him shutting it over my heart thumping hard in my ears. I turn my back to him and lift my hair off my neck.

"Can you do up the last button?"

I feel him step closer. His swallow is audible before his knuckles brush my skin to draw the clasp closed.

"Perfect," he grits.

I smooth my hands down the dress. It's ivory and simple, fitted over most of my shape, loose enough on the bottom so I can move my legs to dance. No lace or embellishments on it, just gauzy, transparent sleeves that start off at the shoulder and end at my wrists. No jewelry other than my mom's teardrop pearls and my former ring, a little band of emeralds, because he really has always liked me in green. I left my hair down and wild and decided to skip the veil. We know exactly what we're getting into, and I don't want anything pulled over my eyes.

I turn to face him, and he puts a splayed hand to his chest. The bare emotion in his eyes is about to ruin my makeup.

"So perfect," he says again, a choked whisper.

I take him in and have to swallow twice. "I don't care what they say. I feel so lucky right now." I chuckle, tears pooling in my eyes with just how much I mean it. "Need me to help with your tie?"

He looks down like he just remembered it was there. "Oh, yeah. Not sure where everyone else went."

I knot his tie with shaky hands, the weight of his gaze chasing over me. He idly traces a fingertip down one of my sleeves. I press my palms into his firm chest and grin up at him, utterly punch-drunk in love. He tucks a piece of my hair behind an ear and goes on cataloging me with his eyes.

Just then, we hear a noise from outside and peek out of our bedroom window. Sage is down below, on the gravel walkway leading from our house to the stable. Fisher's holding a clear umbrella above her while she sprinkles petals all around the path. We watch them kiss after he plucks a stray petal from her hair. In the open doorway to the stable, we spot Silas pacing side to side, clearly reciting something to himself.

We hear a car door shutting and scurry across our room to look through the windows on the opposite side, out front. Micah is there, greeting Venus and Athena and handing them their own umbrellas. They visibly coo over him and kiss his cheeks.

Martha and Walter pull in next, followed by Lennon Kirby, Bea Marshall and her mom, then Serena Lindhagen and her fiancé, Peter. Turns out, Ellis had spotted me talking with Peter at the Starhopper grand opening the New Year's before last, and he'd assumed he was my date. These days, it's easy to laugh and get a kick out of the things that were badly timed in our lives.

Ellis threads his fingers through mine and leads me back

across our room, where we watch the people we're closest to all filter into our little stable.

"Thank god we kept it small, huh?" he says.

Another knock sounds on the door, and then Sam is opening it and stepping into our room. Ellis and I let out the same happy sigh at the sight of him.

When he came home for Christmas last winter, he'd been a little gaunt but seemed genuinely excited about school, inspired by everything he was learning so far. As far as we can tell, he's happy and handling himself well in California. I'm secretly pleased that he keeps coming home over his breaks, though.

"Hey, there you are," he says to Ellis with a smile. He passes him a navy jacket that matches his own, and I notice a few Band-Aids on his fingers. "Gram says you gotta get down there now. Almost time to start."

"What happened to your fingers?" I ask.

Sage flutters in through the open doorway. "There you are! You gotta get down there!" she scolds Ellis. "Go, go!" She starts making a sweeping motion with her arms, and I note a bandaged finger on her hand, too.

"What did everyone cut themselves on?" I ask to no avail.

"All right, all right, I'm going," Ellis says, laughing. "Give me ten seconds with my bride." He pulls my hand up to his lips before either of them have a chance to say anything more. "I'll save you a seat, Byrd."

I warm all over and watch him walk away.

"Think they expect you to stand," says Sam, frowning.

Sage dives for me and lays a quick peck to my cheek. "You look incredible." Her shoulders rise with glee. "I can't wait for you to see it. I mean, it's not outside like we planned, but . . . I think we managed."

"I love you, friend. Thank you." As long as these people are there and that man is waiting for me, I couldn't care less about the rest. We wanted to do this wedding to celebrate what we've already earned together. What we *know* we have, for however long we have left to keep it.

My son comes to stand beside me as we watch everyone else head into the stable. Ellis looks up from under his umbrella and blows a kiss our way.

"You ready?" Sam asks, offering me his arm. I loop mine through his and grab my bouquet.

"I am," I say. "I'm glad we get to have you be a part of it, too." I wouldn't have it any other way. He smiles at his feet before he gives me a wide-open look.

"You look beautiful, Mom. I'm so happy for you. I'm so happy for Dad."

"I'm happy for us, too, bub."

Sam walks me past his old room, over the stairs he once fell down and broke his wrist. Through the kitchen where I used to perch him on a stool beside me to bake. He touches the table we took back from my former house, where he told us about school and his first grown-up dream coming true.

I momentarily let go of his arm when we step out back so he can open up an umbrella. My mom's boyfriend, David, waits at the sliding stable door, music floating out from within. David nods to us both at the appropriate point in the song, then pulls the door away, taking the umbrella from Sam.

The aisle divides two narrow rows of seats, only two chairs wide by ten rows long. A pile of flower petals makes up the path that leads to the love of my life. The person I'd choose, every time. In every life. Our beautiful son guides me a few more steps, and everything else comes into focus.

Sage, waiting on my side of the aisle now, smiling while tears roll down her face. She's decorated the areas she could with more beautiful arrangements. There are wreaths on the stable doors. Bud pokes his head out of one now and snorts softly at me. Ellis and I debated whether or not we should even take him back after Sage had held on to him for so many years, but she insisted it was fine. Plus, after last fall turned out to be another bad fire season, more animals were displaced, and she wasted no time in taking in two new additions. Major and Kelpie's owners decided that they'd rather risk hurricanes than fires, and relocated to Florida. Given their age, they wanted their horses to find a home that could give them the love and attention they deserved. Sage and Fisher drove out to Colorado and fetched them the very same day I saw the post.

Not long after that (not having learned my lesson about re-maining in these groups, apparently), I saw a local shelter post about a single horse who'd lost her home and gone unclaimed. When I saw her name, I told Ellis through tears that I knew she was meant to be ours. Hope's dark head emerges from her stall now, and she whickers happily at Sam and me.

Strands of bulb lights are strung from the ceiling, but more than that, everywhere, dangling from different heights, all dif-ferent sizes and varying colors, are origami birds. I turn to Sam and find his eyes shining. I look down the aisle and search for Mi-cah's hands and, sure enough, see them decorated in Band-Aids, too. Silas appears to be unscathed, grinning broadly with tears falling freely down his handsome face. All my best friends. My family, my people. My Byrds.

"When did you guys manage this?" I ask, laughing wetly.

"Last night," Sam says, his first tear slipping away. "Dad said he'd keep you busy."

I look down the aisle and find him. I can't believe I ever

thought he wasn't romantic. And he did keep me busy. Took me on a one-night camping trip down on Founder's Point. Same old Coleman tent, with a new, upgraded air mattress.

Ellis isn't smiling at me. He looks like he's afraid to blink, like he wants this memory branded onto his soul. The three of us hug when Sam and I make it down the aisle, before Sam takes his place next to Micah at Ellis's side. Ellis takes my hands in his, a tear falling right from his eye and onto my ring finger.

"Hi, everyone," Silas begins. "We're all family here, so I won't waste time on introductions. Especially because the first time these two did this, I was robbed of the opportunity to give a speech. I've had years to build up to this, and I'll be damned if I'm gonna be robbed of my moment."

"*Silas*," Ellis groans.

"Robbed of my moment to tell you all about my heroes, Wren and Ellis Byrd," Silas adds.

We both look at him now, and his beaming grin turns downright smug.

"You see . . . my brother was always my hero. And you might think there's nothing special about that; every younger brother looks up to his sibling. I think sometimes that's a by-product of proximity and that person being older and cooler than you, but in my case, Ellis was never even remotely cooler, so . . ." The room chuckles. "Ellis taught me how to tie my shoes and how to shave, but above all else, he taught me what kind of man I should aspire to be. I know everyone thinks he's this calm and careful guy. Hell, he's the first one to say he thinks he's been too careful in his life. But I've always seen the truth." Ellis looks at me, his eyes blue from tears, and Silas presses on. "When Ellis fucks up, he owns it. Even if it takes him a little while. And when he does, he fixes it with singular determination. He is unfailingly there for anyone who needs him, even"—he clears his throat—"even when they have a hard time letting him. He's why I wanted to become a firefighter to begin with. I knew he'd stand against a wall of flame if it threatened someone else, so I thought maybe he should have someone watching out for him, too. My brother has saved my life in the literal sense, more than once, so when I fell off a mountain in a ball of fire, all that went through my head was holding on long enough for him to find me. It never once occurred to me that he wouldn't." I think I can hear Ellis's heart keening. "The reality is I've never known another human more unflinchingly brave than Ellis. Save for one.

"It was easy to admire Wren from the beginning, if only for the fact that she was the one person who could really shake Ellis. In all my memories, I realize that her mere presence in his life made him a more adventurous kid. He was braver about trying little things, and I think that probably trained him for the big things he'd end up taking on later, like when he had to take on raising all of us when he was only eighteen. And about that . . . he never truly did it alone. My siblings and I saw Wren courageously step into a role that included so many hats. Each of us called her to bail us out of trouble and to go around Ellis." Ellis levels a confused pout at me, and I sputter a laugh. "She danced between being a new mom, being a parental figure to us, to becoming our very best friend with more grace than anyone could ask. Wren thinks we absorbed her into our family, but she's the one who made us into hers.

"Watching you two lay the foundation for a life together and then go on to build a beautiful one was one of the most inspiring things I've experienced. Seeing you lose it for a while was . . ." He shakes his head, visibly struggling. "Seeing you lose it for a time was gutting. Some of us, who shall remain nameless, were too scared to hope you could figure it out again. Those unnamed people should have known better. Hoping with one another is how you two got so brave in the first place. After all, what is bravery if not hope in action?

"I love you. I'm honored to stand here with you today and help you both get this shit right." The whole room boils over with laughter.

We recite the vows we inked into our skin.

We eat food that Fisher makes, including cake. Ellis and I surprise attack Silas and shove it into his face.

We dance. Oh, we dance. Half in the stable, and half outside in the rain when it's faded to a mist.

Since it's such a small party, we get everything cleaned up and everyone headed out just as the sun starts to set. Sam tells us he'll be staying at Micah's for a few days. We make plans to go over to Sage's for a family dinner before his spring break is over.

And later, in our quiet and warm home, after we've made slow, rocking, gasping love once, and fast, clawing, loud love another time, I'll fall asleep the same way I'll fall asleep a million more times in this life. I'll run my fingertips over the vows on his skin and the birds on his back. A hummingbird for Sage, a crow for Micah, a red-tailed hawk for Silas, a swallow for Sam, and a wren for me. I asked him if he knew that wrens mated for life when he got it, to which he laughed and said no. I got a matching wren on my hip last Christmas, because if he can carry all of them, I can carry him.

At sunrise, we'll take Bud and Hope on a ride. We'll make plans and we'll tease. We'll flirt and we'll fight. One day, when we're very old and gray, one of us will open our eyes to a day that the other won't, but we'll smile knowing how full life has been, knowing how we spent forever. Everything left of it, together.

ACKNOWLEDGMENTS

As always, thank you for picking up this book in whatever format you have chosen and for reading it. You are one of the reasons I get to keep doing this! Especially those of you who fell in love and demanded this book from the moment Ellis said the words, "She's still a Byrd," in *Savor It*. Thank you.

I wonder if I'll ever be able to write a book that doesn't feel deeply personal, but, so far, no dice. This one was the most personal yet. I have never had a story feel so fully formed before I even began. Which might sound like a great thing . . . something that should have made the process easier, right?

Wrong.

Instead, this made it so I wasn't sure at *any* point along the way that the words I was typing were doing the story in my head any justice. Which made me a raw, fragile little monster to be around. Therefore, thank you to my family and friends for your constant reassurance and for your infallible belief in me.

Ty, the guy I fell in love with and had babies too young with: thank you for holding my hand extra tight during this one.

To my dogs and my cats, you're the real heroes carrying the weight of my mental health between your soft ears.

Thank you to my team at SDLA: Jen, "the financial patriarch"; my foreign and subrights agent Andrea Cavallaro; and my literary agent Jessica Watterson most especially. This has been a tumultuous year that you've helped me navigate, and my gratitude for you will never end.

Thank-yous to my team at St. Martin's Griffin: Brant Janeway and Anne Marie Tallberg; my editors Cassidy Graham and Alex Sehulster, as well as Ashley Quintana. Thank you to my publicists and marketers for getting my stories into more hands and for getting me and all my bad jokes in front of more faces (sorry for the flagrant F-word usage). Alyssa Gammello, Kejana Ayala, Althea Mignone, Sophia Lauriello, and Marissa Sangiacomo. Your hustle motivates me to work that much harder.

Thank you to Liza Rusalskaya and Olga Grlic for the most beautiful cover in the game.

Forevermore thank you to the librarians, booksellers, Bookstagrammers, and BookTokkers who go out of their way to yell about my books. I am always deeply awed and humbled by your support and love. Please never stop.

ABOUT THE AUTHOR

Jacob Carpenter / @jcarpenter_photos

Tarah DeWitt writes character-driven romances filled with laughter and Big Feelings. She loves stories centered around perfectly imperfect characters, especially those with just enough trauma to keep them funny, without ever being forcefully cavalier. She's the national bestselling author of *Savor It, The Co-op,* and *Funny Feelings,* with plenty more to come.